THE RINGS OF SATURN

PART ONE

BY APRIL ADAMS

For information address April Adams, 325 7th Ave. Suite 1708
San Diego, CA 92101

First Print Edition: August 2016

ISBN: 978-0-9844003-7-9

Cover design by Tracey Thompson

For Grandma,
The True Iron Dragon.
Vaya con Dios.

TABLE OF CONTENTS

PROLOGUE

Most people live their lives and then eventually end up as ghosts. I went in reverse. I started my life as a ghost and ended up living.

Not to say that I was dead. I had lived and grown for twenty-two listless years. I went to school like any average boy, but not to college. Hard learning was not for me, I wasn't so dense that I didn't know that. But I had no fear of hard work and learned my father's trade and started working with my hands when I was twelve. I started as an apprentice but I was a Journeyman by the time I was seventeen.

Though I made Journeyman before I was even legally an adult, my older brother was already in flight school to be a fighter pilot - so no one in my family really gave a shit. So I, ghost that I was, decided to further my career elsewhere. I could attain the next guild on another moon, preferably in another system.

Brad, my brother, was not so bad as far as brothers go. He could be an asshole, sure, but for the most part he was a decent guy. As far as my parents went, however, Jupiter rose and set on him. I could have found the cure for SM, but if Brad so much as looked at a girl in church the whole family would be dancing with hopeful anticipation.

"Brad finished his safety courses," my mother told me on the day that I left. I thought if her chest swelled anymore with pride she was liable to pop the buttons off her yellow-flowered jumper.

"Wow," I said, getting ready to be put in cryo and travel to another galaxy. "After a year in simulators they might let him fly an actual jet."

"I know, right?" my mother exclaimed, clasping her hands in joyous bliss and oblivious to my sarcasm.

The infamous Brad himself could not make it home from flight school to see me off, though it was less than an hour away from One Mile and he was on break from what passed for his studies.

My father, knowing my accomplishment of attaining a second guild at my age clapped me on the shoulder. "I know you don't need recognition, son, but I know you need something. I hope you find it."

He pulled me close and crushed me against his large frame. It almost made me feel real for a second. All I could do in return was clap him on the back and give him a sheepish smile when he finally released me.

"Work hard." my grandmother said in French. Though everyone on the moon spoke Anglicus and she had learned it herself back on Earth, she never spoke it. "And go with God."

"I will," I answered in French. "I promise."

She held something out to me, yellow and rectangular and bent at the corners. I took it and turned it over in my hands. It was a book. She had small collection of real books that she had gotten before she left Earth. I already had two of my own in the small duffle of belongings I was taking with me. I glanced at the title before I tucked it away and looked back at her. She gave me a satisfied nod and I kissed the wattle that served as her cheek.

I hefted up my bag and threw the strap over my shoulder. I kissed my mother high on her cheekbone and let my father clap me on the back once again, almost knocking me down. Then I left the eighty-story apartment building where I had spent most of my young life.

It never occurred to me that by the time I made it back home I would be the living, and they would be the ghosts.

ONE

The first attack came from his right, as he knew it would. It was his weaker side, so it was only natural for Yonif to target him there. No sooner had Hahn blocked the blow from Yonif's staff than the other attackers came at him. Not one at a time in the usual perfect synchronization, but all at once - which meant it had to be on orders from the Temple Abon himself – a mass collision in the blackness.

All manners of weapons came at him - swords, knives, nupa-sticks. Hahn blocked all attackers with such skill that, had there been any light to see, it would have looked easy. The dark, humid air of the temple was marked with a near silent rasping - the resonance of controlled breath from half a dozen monks, punctuated with grunts of surprise and the clatter of weapons as they were taken from the attackers and sent flying back into the directions from which they had come.

With or without their weapons, they came at Hahn again without pause and again were thrown back. Doubling their intensity, knowing that failure would mean shame, or worse - the monks came at Hahn for a third time, crashing against him like a livid wave upon a defiant rock. Again it was the rock that persevered.

Despite the mental and physical toll of fighting off numerous attacks, Hahn remained calm, diligent in the way he patiently took each assault and threw it back with shoulder-popping arm twists and gratuitous kicks to departing robe-covered hind-ends.

Suddenly, the lights came up in the Temple and a booming voice filled its timber-slated walls, reverberating off of the smooth wooden floor.

"Enough!"

The Temple Abon - enormous, round, and bald - descended the altar steps. Around his neck was a fine chain, holding a key that was tucked safely into the neck of his robes. The key was the old-fashioned type that would fit into and actually turn the tumbler mechanisms of a lock. A similar device was carried on a chain around the neck of every monk present.

The keys opened the door to the Temple, a great structure in the monastery where they trained and fought. The only difference in the keys were the type of metal from which they were forged, each type being a representation of the rank for each monk in his fighting ability.

The key carried by the Abon was hammered steel, made of iron from the Dragon Mountains, where the last living Dragons of the universe had lived before succumbing to the immortality that the humans had offered them. The steel had been so darkened by Dragonfire that it appeared to create a vacuum of light and color. Only the Abon carried such a key. It was sign and symbol of his status, his dedication, and his authority.

Today the monk Hahn had left his own key, one made of copper so long ago that it had a fine patina crust, on the altar in the north end of the Temple. Today he had fought to exchange it for one of cast-iron, a key that was second only to the Abon. He knelt at the approach of their leader, as did the other monks, on the smooth wooden planks of the Temple.

The great man drew near the spot where Hahn knelt on the floor with his head bowed in what he hoped was the picture of utter humility. The Abon was having none of it. Three hundred pounds of quivering justification approached the kneeling man in yellow robes that waited, perfectly still, for judgment.

The Abon, his hands tucked into the voluminous sleeves

of his own belted yellow robes, stopped before Hahn, his momentum creating waves in his flesh that eventually subsided to gentle ripples. The colossal human, with a cast-iron key dangling from a chain that spilled from between his great fingers, let out an immense sigh and Hahn could feel it like a gust of wind on his tan and golden pate.

"Hahn Chi," the Abon called out so that all present could hear, "it is with extreme displeasure that I give you this key."

Hahn, surprised out of his discipline, looked up in shock. He bowed his head again immediately, the normally golden color of his face turning red with shame. Never before had the Abon spoken in such a way when bestowing a key.

"I only award this to you because it is my duty. The test for a key is a test of fighting skill, which you have demonstrated here today. You are an excellent fighter, you always have been, and have been not only the best but also the youngest to master the forms required of you to earn this key. The problem, however, is that you know it."

Hahn, his head still bowed, felt his whole body turn as red as his face.

"You kneel there with your head bowed as a sign of humility," the Abon continued, his voice thick with undisguised contempt. "We kneel and we bow to show respect and to show our meekness before the universe, but you - you do not feel it. Pride will be your downfall." He sighed again, stowing his emotions in an effort to instruct. "Think of the water, Hahn Chi. Water has the utmost humility. It seeks the lowest place, it dives into the filth without question. Yet it will wear down rocks, move mountains, and give life only to renew itself again and again. My only hope is that, like with the water, time will be on your side."

The Abon leaned forward and put the new chain over Hahn's head, letting it settle down on his neck. The key hung below his throat, just above the place where the sides of his robes met. Hahn remained with his head bowed, his entire concentration focused on the iron against his skin. He committed the feel of it to his memory – the shape of the key, the weight of the iron, the cold texture of the metal. Then he lifted the chain from around his neck and placed it, along with the key, at the Abon's feet.

Hahn rose and bowed deeply to the man and then turned and left, passing through the circle of his friends. They watched with round faces, bright with shock. His footsteps made a quiet padding sound across the wooden floor before he opened the great door and closed it quietly behind him. Hahn never returned to the Temple.

TWO

Cronus walked across the grass, pushing a graying lock of hair away from a face that was narrow but hardly showed the truth of his years. Though a bit long in the front, the elf's hair was cut short in the back and was almost the same color of his eyes, like storm clouds in winter. He was tall for an elf since he was native to a planet with a lower than norm gravity, and somewhat lanky in the limbs, but walked with a comfortable grace and ease. Like his hair, his suit was gray and of the latest style. The vest fit snug across his chest and the top buttons of the white shirt underneath it were fashionably undone.

He passed through a gate in a white picket fence and I followed, keeping pace easily despite the elf's long stride, and staying a few steps behind since I knew he preferred the distance. I had been working for the man for almost a year and knew that he considered himself well above others. I considered him a pompous prick, but didn't care much. I was lucky to get the job, as fresh out of school that I was, and it paid twice what I could make on my home moon.

We walked up the stone pathway that led to a cottage on the rise of a grassy hill. Faith had told her grandfather that they were moving into the cottage for the quiet, so she could work in peace, but Cronus suspected it had been Gwen's idea. Faith would sleep in the lab if she were allowed to do so. As would he.

I saw his chest swell a bit with pride as we reached the front door and guessed he was having similar thoughts. The front door was made of fabricated wood and had been painted a farmhouse green. Not seeing a button for a doorbell or a holo for a com, he sighed and grasped the heavy brass knocker that had been fastened to the door, thumping it against the plate, feeling clumsy and vaguely ridiculous.

The door swung open almost immediately and eyes of brown and gold greeted him, beaming at him from a woman's face that was surrounded by hair the same tawny colors as her eyes. The young woman was average height and slim, and wore a short but stylish sundress and sandals with heels.

I knew that the woman had to be Faith de Rossi, his eldest granddaughter, or the dyer that he had made for her when she was five years old. I had never met either, so I had no idea which one it might be. And, for a fleeting moment, I had the feeling that that neither did he.

"Grandfather!" she exclaimed, stepping forward quickly to embrace him.

"My darling Gwendolyn!" he greeted as they exchanged a kiss on each cheek. She laughed girlishly and took him by the hand.

"Thank you so much for coming to visit. Faith has been wanting so badly to speak to you...I mean we," she added with another girlish laugh. "*We* have been wanting so badly to speak to you." Her bright eyes darted over his shoulder and widened in surprise as she spied me. "And who is this?" she asked.

Cronus turned, surprised himself, as if he had forgotten that I was with him. "Oh!" he exclaimed, glancing at me. "Mason," he said by way of introduction.

"Ms. de Rossi," I greeted, dipping my head.

"It's a pleasure to meet you," she returned, looking at me curiously before pushing the door all the way open.

I drew those looks often enough not to be bothered, quite the contrary. I considered myself fairly ordinary looking for a human, neither my blonde hair nor my blue eyes being very remarkable. But I had found that humans were scarce in the Flower Galaxy (outside the two main moon-planets) and a bit of a rarity on this particular moon, especially far away from the big cities.

I'm sure I was giving her the same look of curiosity, since I had heard that she was practically indistinguishable from Faith de Rossi. I knew that Cronus had made a twin for each of his granddaughters when they were children but until now I had not met any of them.

Cronus and I followed Gwendolyn down a short hallway, through a cheery kitchen, and into a dining room with large windows that looked out onto an enormous flower garden. At the farmhouse table sat a woman that looked identical to the one that had ushered us in, and I mean identical. Not related, not similar, not even the way close sisters sometimes look. If not for the fact that she wore a sleeveless suit rather than a dress and jewelry on her left hand, I would not have been able to tell one from the other.

The young woman looked up from the small computer in front of her when her grandfather entered and beamed at him, closing the computer quickly and rising to greet him with a hug and a kiss on each cheek.

"Would you like some coffee?" Gwen asked as Faith pulled out a chair for him to sit. "Or tea, perhaps?"

"Coffee would be wonderful," Cronus answered. "Thank you."

I was not introduced, and not surprised, yet Cronus motioned for me to take a seat at the table.

"Mason?" Gwen inquired politely, regarding me with brows raised over her eyes of brown and gold.

"Why, yes. Coffee for me as well. Thank you."

Gwen disappeared into the kitchen as we seated ourselves and Cronus exchanged the standard pleasantries with Faith.

The dyer was back shortly with a tray of ceramic mugs and a steaming pot. Cronus beamed proudly at Faith as Gwen poured sweetened coffee into the mugs and handed them around. Faith accepted a mug from her twin with a smile of gratitude and glanced at her grandfather, her smile turning suddenly sly as she anticipated his question.

"Were you offered the job?" he asked without any more fanfare.

"I was," she replied as Gwen sat down next to her and across from Cronus, the same smile on her own face. Faith continued before her grandfather could speak. "I turned them down." She took a sip of coffee and looked over the rim of her mug at her mother's father. The bewildered look on his face made him look suddenly very young and Faith laughed.

"You did what?" Cronus asked. He put his mug back on the table and his expression of surprise quickly became stern befuddlement. I took a drink of the coffee. It was overly sweet for my tastes but I was enjoying Cronus' vexation.

"I turned them down," she repeated.

"But why? It is the highest paying job in the industry! You are the youngest person that has ever been offered such a position, and the first woman!"

"I don't want the position," Faith said, her mind obviously made up. "And I don't want to work for anyone. I want to work for myself."

Her grandfather gaped at her, bewildered once again. "Doing what?" Cronus asked, sounding truly mystified.

"Well," Faith said, placing her own mug on the table while Gwen watched, smiling. "I want to learn the family trade."

"We don't have a..." There was a moment of silence as he realized what she was saying. Neatly trimmed gray eyebrows shot up over his sharp, gray eyes. "Dyer making?" Cronus demanded as if he had been struck. Faith nodded.

"But not dolls." She drew a breath and inclined her head towards Gwendolyn. "I want you to show me how to make people. Like you did. Well, almost like you did."

The aging elf looked as if he had sat on a tack but Faith as well as I knew that it was not the time to laugh. She kept her gaze fixed on him as his gray eyes darkened, becoming cold and hard.

"Mason," he ordered quietly, "leave us."

I looked around and saw that there was an archway that led to a room with an overstuffed, mustard-colored couch and a pair of reading chairs that matched. Gwen rose quickly and kindly refilled my mug and extended her arm in the direction of the chairs, inviting me to make myself comfortable in the next room. I left the dining room and took the chair farthest from the group at the table, moving a scarlet pillow with silver embroidery out of the way.

I thought it obvious that I could still hear them but they didn't seem to mind. Still, I picked up a heavy book of Grecian art off of the coffee table and opened it on my lap, just to be polite.

Gwen returned to her seat, clearly admiring Faith and her stoic determination, though I saw her fingers twisting together under the table. I kept my eyes averted from her wringing hands and it occurred to me that Cronus was most likely never cross with them but, when he was, he frightened her.

"Faith," he said, his voice low. "Girls," he corrected, looking at them in turn and shaking his head slowly. "I do not think that is a good idea. Not at all." He considered his words carefully before he continued. "I don't think you are considering the possible outcomes of such a dangerous expedition, nor the pitfalls that will waylay your path. Even if you are able to sidestep every law in the galaxy that prohibits cloning, there are people and groups that will be outraged by this. You could very well be putting your lives in danger."

He wanted to add that at times he had second-guessed his own decision to create the replicants, but it had made the girls so happy, and even he had grown quite fond of the dyers. Besides, he did not want to hurt Gwendolyn's feelings.

Faith put her mug down and reached across the table and grasped his hand. Cronus looked at her, surprised. She had not held his hand since she was a child and, like when she was a child, it diffused his outward demeanor and warmed his heart.

"Let me tell you a story," she said, her smile fading. "A story about a little girl. A little girl that was lonely beyond belief. What children lived near her, she was not allowed to play with. She was allowed few books and though she had some lovely toys, she had no one to share them with."

The graying elf sat frozen in his chair as he realized that Faith was telling her own story.

"And one day," Faith continued, "she was given a present - a present like no other. She was given a friend. Someone not just to play with, but to share her life with. All of her secrets and dreams, all of her joys and sorrows." Cronus saw Faith's gold and brown eyes fill with tears, something else he had not seen since she was very small. He glanced at Gwen and saw that she was blinking rapidly at her coffee. "My life was made full by being able to share it," Faith said quietly. "I feel so blessed to have been given this as a child, yet I know that so many people go their whole lives and do not know this joy." She squeezed his hand and the elf could feel tears threatening his own eyes. "This feeling should be made available to everyone."

"Cloning is illegal in every system," he said softly. "The crime is punishable by death. There are no exceptions."

"I don't want clones, and you didn't clone us. Not exactly."

"But I used your DNA, and the DNA of your sisters for their dyers. It would be considered cloning by many."

"Well, to begin with, I'm not going to make replicants."

"You're talking about splicing, then."

Faith shrugged. "To an extent."

"Not quite illegal, but you are still treading dangerous ground. From a legal standpoint you..."

"If a DNA splice is less than a meta," Faith interrupted, "it cannot be owned outright. More than a meta with no repeat that has no match can be written."

Cronus opened his mouth to object and then closed it softly as he considered her statement.

"I can write a completely original double helix," she continued. "And copyright it." Silence followed her words.

I was looking at pictures in the book and not really seeing them. Though I could not grasp what exactly it was that they were talking about, I grasped the meaning well enough.

The soft sound of a ticking clock came from the kitchen. Finally Cronus sighed, knowing that it would be as hard as it always had been to deny her what she wanted. Especially when she was so damned reasonable.

"You already know how?"

Faith's sly smile returned and she gave a nonchalant shrug. "You could teach me some things, but for the most part I know which road to take."

"And you need start-up costs?"

Faith shook her head. "Charity wants to be in on this with us," she said, glancing at Gwendolyn. "She has investors that can..."

"Bah!" Cronus interrupted. "I will cover the start-up costs," he told her. He didn't want to think about what his younger granddaughter might be doing to raise funds. Charity, and her dyer Llewellyn, already had a reputation of sorts. "But if you didn't ask me here to invest, what do you need me for?"

Faith squeezed his hand again. "Your blessing, your advice

on molecular construction. I'm sure I will have questions along the way. But, most of all, I would like you to be part of this." Cronus returned the squeeze and then released her slim hand so that he could sit back and stroke his long face.

"Very well, but just as an investor and an advisor. I'm not having a hand in anything else," he said, looking at each of them. Gwendolyn smiled broadly at her twin as their grandfather continued in a softer voice, as if he were thinking out loud. "You will need an entire compound," he mused. Faith nodded, trying to subdue her grin. "At least two g-labs, surgical, a hi-lamne studio, training center..." Cronus mumbled facts and figures as he calculated, then turned his sharp gray eyes on Faith. "I will set the minimum price for the prototypes," he told her, his voice firm. "And I will keep the pay for them, to cover my investment."

"Absolutely," Faith agreed.

Cronus shook his head as he regarded the girls fondly. "When do you want to start?" His sharp eyes saw that Faith's sly smile had returned and he sighed. "You've already started, haven't you?"

Faith laughed lightly. "Just on the DNA acquisition so I could start in on a little programming. I wanted your opinion before I went any further." She had a small smile tucked into one side of her cheek.

"My opinion?" Cronus huffed. "Like you would have waited long!" He took a sip of coffee and looked at Gwen and the similar smile she had tucked into the corner of her mouth. "And I suppose you will be doing the exterior design?" he asked. Gwen nodded, demure but proud.

"Certainly."

Cronus blew a puff of air through his cheeks. "I have the perfect place," he told them, "just a few kilometers from here, in Della Reina. I have been in the process of building a research center, which is why Mason is with me. He is overseeing construction."

I looked up from the book on my lap to see him jerk his head in my direction. The girls peered through the archway at me and Faith's tawny eyes locked with my own. I looked back down at the book.

"We were on our way there," he continued, "to go over the progress. At this point it can easily be converted into the compound you will need, though we will have to add to it." The girls nodded in unison, excited. Cronus drew a long-fingered hand down over his smooth face and sighed. "I am glad to give up the center for your endeavor, but I do not want to abandon my project." He tapped a finger on his lips, thinking.

"Can we work together?" Faith asked.

The handsome elf shook his head. "You will need all the room, and it will take up a good portion of my time to get you started," he held up a hand to prevent argument. "I know you are extremely capable, but you will need more help than you can imagine, even if it is just as an extra pair of eyes. Molecular biology is not a game."

Faith tucked away a smile as if she thought differently.

"What were you originally planning for the center?" Gwen asked.

"What do you know of ZPE?"

Gwen laughed. "Absolutely nothing," she admitted, looking at Faith. Faith's small smile widened.

"It stands for Zero Point Energy," she told her twin. "I know of it, but not much. It's a physics issue, not biology."

"Well," their grandfather informed them, "it will concern you soon enough."

Faith's brows went up as she sipped her coffee. "Someone is close to harnessing it?"

"There are a few groups that are rumored to be getting

close. I had a physicist lined up to head the research." Cronus smoothed down his gray vest as he sat back again in his chair. "Still," he murmured, "if I cannot conduct my own research, I am not above collaborating with others." Faith smirked.

"You mean to send your physicist in as a spy," she remarked.

Cronus feigned surprise, or offense, I was not sure which.

"Spy? I prefer the idea of guarded cooperation."

Faith grunted. "Well," she said. "We will do what we can to help as well." She held out her hand to her grandfather, not to hold, but to shake. Cronus grinned and shook her hand. Gwendolyn reached over the table and shook his proffered hand as well.

Cronus finished his coffee and glanced at the young women. "Have you heard?" he asked, placing his cup back onto the table. "The eggs from the Second Year Dragons are going to hatch."

"I thought they already had," Gwendolyn said, surprised.

"Aye," Cronus agreed, "the eggs from the Onyx Dragon did. Copper and Silver Hatchlings that will soon become Fledglings. I meant it would be the eggs from the Pearl Dragon that will be hatching this year."

Faith nodded and her chest swelled. "It is a good year for Dragons to be born," she said. "It is a year for legends to be born."

Her grandfather regarded her with a grin that was proud and yet cautious. "If you succeed," he warned, "you will make history." Faith gave him her sly smile.

"If?"

"The course of the universe will be changed," Gwen said with a small smile of her own. "All you need is Faith."

Cronus stood to leave as the two women at the table laughed, sounding like the girls they once were not so long ago.

They both rose to escort him to the door as he called out for me to join him.

THREE

Elaeric ambled through the garden, feeling the bright sunshine warm his bald head. He walked with his hands tucked into the sleeves of his belted yellow robes, relishing the feel of the silk against his skin and the silken warmth of the sun against his face. He loved life at the monastery. He loved being a monk. It was a life he had always dreamed of for himself. Not so with his parents.

His father was a member of the Yakuza Elite on the Indasian moon of Jupiter. His mother was a cutthroat businesswoman, literally. Liu Mau had no qualms about spilling the lifeblood out of someone who threatened a deal or position, usually by way of the razornails on her left hand. It was one of the few reasons she did not have carpet in her office. When Elaeric had announced to them his intentions to become a monk, he thought that his own lifeblood might be staining the rug of their family zurat.

"Anything!" his father had shouted. "Anything, but that!"

"The Zenarchist monks are the best fighters in all of the galaxies," Elaeric said in an attempt to assuage his father, but Yon Mau had made a face of disgust.

"Do not lie to me! You have no intention of learning to fight! You will spend your time among flowers and birds and bugs! It is disgraceful!"

Elaeric had bowed his head in shame. His father was right, though he did not know why his father found it so appalling. At the sight of his son, laid low before him, Yon Mau relented for a second.

"Not all members of Yakuza are samurai," he told his son in consoling tones. "You could find a place as a page, or as a PA." Elaeric swallowed against the dry ache in his throat and looked away, unable to meet his father's eyes. "Bah!" His father shouted before storming from the room.

Elaeric looked hopefully at his mother, her black hair cropped close to her round head and pale face. The normal line between her dark brows that always stood out like an exclamation point on her face was gone. And, for the first time in his life, Elaeric saw tears in her almond-shaped eyes. He looked away, brimming with shame, yet his mother embraced him.

"I do not approve of the choice you are making," she whispered hoarsely into his ear. "But you have the courage to do the one thing I could not - stand against *my* own father." She kissed his cheek and left quickly in the same manner his own father had done. It was the last time he had seen either one of them.

The memory did not trouble Elaeric, not now. He looked at it quite fondly, finding the good in it, as he did with most things. He had no idea why it was on his mind on such a fine morning, but he gave it the same attention as he did the breeze - as something intangible that was simply passing by.

Elaeric himself passed by a series of seven waterfalls before entering the stone garden. A jumble of rocks - some as large as huts, others only pebbles - had been artfully placed across a sunny hillside in the garden amidst the stunted pine trees that grew there. The cheery monk wove his way down the side of the hill away from the monastery. He passed between a series of river boulders taller than himself until he came upon one that was large and quite flat.

Upon it sat his best friend, cross-legged and with his eyes closed. It had only been a single lunar cycle since Hahn had left the Temple, and still he struggled with quiet meditation. Though some might want to politely clear their throat to announce their presence, Elaeric stood quietly, listening to an insect buzz - not wanting to disturb his friend.

"Why bother?" Hahn asked irritably, opening his eyes. "I am already disturbed!"

Elaeric laughed as he climbed onto the rock to sit next to his friend. He knew from experience that Hahn could hear the approach of a flea in the grass. Together they looked across the valley. From where they sat in the rock garden, the monastery grounds fell into steppes used for agriculture – mostly by way of rice paddies.

"You are lucky, Elaeric," Hahn told his friend, "to have never been seduced by the Temple."

"I am a lover, not a fighter," Elaeric informed him with a mischievous grin.

Hahn sighed. "So am I. But, unfortunately for myself, I love to fight."

Elaeric patted his friend's knee and turned his face towards the blue sky, feeling the sun warm the golden skin on his face. It had taken him years to become accustomed to the color of the sky. The atmosphere of the moon on which he had been born and grown to adulthood was tinged a deep red. It was a color his people believed represented passion, luck, and power. Elaeric found that blue suited him better.

"I can close my eyes," Hahn said, "but not my mind. Instead, I listen for the approach of an attacker. When I hear nothing but the wind and the ladybugs, my mind drifts to focusing my strength in a strike, or schematics on defensive positions. It is never still!"

"Shhh," Elaeric soothed. "Be patient with yourself. Be gentle with yourself. Each time, return your attention to your breath, and listen."

“What could I possibly hear?” Hahn demanded. “My own snores as a I am bored to sleep? Bored to death? What am I listening for? What?”

Elaeric fixed his dark eyes upon Hahn, his usually merry expression quite somber as he placed slender fingers over his friend’s robe-covered knee.

“For your soul to come home.”

*

Faith shook her brown and golden hair and looked at Gwendolyn. Other than their clothes, since Gwen wore a sleeveless dress and Faith had a white lab coat over her taupe-colored skirt suit, it was like looking into a mirror. She never tired of it. Gwendolyn gazed back at her twin.

“Are you sure you want to do this?” Faith asked, a tiny smile hiding in the corner of her mouth.

They sat together in Gwendolyn’s studio in the semi-darkness as the sun set outside the glass walls of the building in a blaze of color. Their part of the compound had only been up and running for seven days but already Gwen’s studio looked as if she had occupied it for at least a year.

The biodentical returned the same coy expression that Faith wore and nodded.

“Absolutely,” she answered. “How about you? Second thoughts? Cold feet?”

“Absolutely not,” Faith answered.

Gwendolyn shrugged. “Then we might as well get on with it.” Her breath evolved into a soft sigh, but the coy smile stayed on her lips.

“Very well.” Faith smiled, more to herself than to her manufactured twin, as she stepped down from the stool and began gathering her things from the glass countertop. Gwendolyn reached over and caught Faith's clean hand in her own, a hand that was crusty along the knuckles with drying clay.

"Thank you."

Faith looked at her, startled. "What for?"

Gwen beamed at her, her face seeming to glow with anticipation and joy, brown and gold eyes catching the diminishing light like polished stone. "For the lives you have given us. For the lives you are about to change."

The smile returned to Faith's lips as she squeezed Gwendolyn's hand before removing her own. She brushed off the crackles of clay that had been left on it with quick efficiency, having done it so many times before, and tucked her credentials card into her lab coat. She picked up her portable computer and held it in the crook of her elbow. "We," she corrected. "For the lives *we* are about to change."

She gave Gwendolyn a peck on the cheek, a cheek just like her own, and stepped delicately over the mess on the ground. Wet chunks of clay littered the plastic covered floor around Gwendolyn's sculpting table like a minefield. Faith navigated her way out in a pair of shining black pumps, avoiding the clumps that waited with evil purpose to ruin yet another pair of her shoes.

Her lab was in the room next to Gwen's studio and, though the girls were virtually identical, their workspaces were not. Faith's lab was immaculate to the point of sterility. Glass and steel gleamed under thermo burners and viro dishes. Oversized acrylic screens were mounted on three walls so Faith could see all of the information she needed at a glance, and could move equations from one side of the room to the other with a flick of a manicured finger.

Gwendolyn's studio, on the other hand, looked like an ancient temple that had been sacked by technology. Resin pillars lined the walls, topped with holo pads projecting sculptures of ancient statues. Most were missing the arms and a few were missing heads. The walls themselves were adorned with lithographs of antiquated art.

Paintings on board-stretched canvas were stacked in seemingly random piles. Clammy bricks of plastic-wrapped clay hunkered on the sculpting table and on the floor. A computer with a large acrylic compute screen, smudged with fingerprints and flakes of dried clay, shared the same table with a myriad of muck-covered sculpting tools.

Gwendolyn turned to the large, if outdated, compute panel on her left. She waved a hand at the bottom right corner and the panel flared to life, reopening the two programs that had been running when it had gone to sleep. The old processor and panel were two of her favorite pieces of technology, since she could run the device without touching it, a godsend since her hands were almost always dirty.

Her eyes moved from left to right along the top of the display, expanding the music program. Still using only her eyes, she scrolled through her music, looking for something classic yet romantic. Though setting the mood was not a crucial factor when she sculpted, it was a luxury that she enjoyed. Her brown and gold eyes stopped, highlighting her selection as a smile spread across her face. It was a piece by Turner and Bernstein, one of her favorites. It was one of their first pieces, she knew, before they had begun to compose on a professional level. It was a bit lonely, almost mournful, yet the notes of the piano seemed to carry an aching melody of hope. It was perfect.

With a sharp glance upward, she started the piece and raised the volume a touch as the sounds of the piano began to emanate from the corners of her studio. Satisfied, Gwendolyn turned to one of her least favorite pieces of technology - the HoloSculpt. At the sight of it, the corners of her mouth pulled down like a child that had been forced to take some bad-tasting medicine.

It had been a gift from Grandfather. It was extremely expensive, exceptionally high-tech, and unquestionably the most progressive piece of equipment in the art industry. Gwen detested it.

On the very first day they had opened the compound, the only completed parts of the building had been the three labs, Faith's office, and Gwendolyn's studio. Cronus had held Gwen by the hand and led them both into the new studio. With a huge grin and an exaggerated flourish he presented the machine, still in the box and bedecked with a large red velvet bow.

"It's a HoloSculpt!" he had announced proudly, as if she couldn't read the blue holographic print that ran around the outside of the box along with the instructions for unpacking the thing. Gwen swallowed hard, her brown and gold eyes wide.

"Grandfather!" she exclaimed, rendered otherwise speechless for the moment. She embraced him, holding him tight while she overcame the shock of seeing it. "What a marvelous gift!" she finally gushed. From the corner of her eye she caught Faith biting her bottom lip in an effort not to laugh, knowing full well that Gwendolyn would have been just as happy, or happier perhaps, with twenty pounds of raw terra-clay rather than a fifty-million dollar machine.

"I'm going to instruct Mason to have the compound tech link it directly to Faith's system in the next room," their grandfather continued with the enthusiasm of an enraptured child, "but the best part is that it will transmit your work directly to the mainframe! Faith can use your finished product to wrap each construct without having to overlap the bio-feeds! The time it will save!"

Gwendolyn embraced him again and kissed his cheek. "Ingenious!" she declared. "And so thoughtful! You are too generous!"

"Pshaw!" Grandfather admonished. "It will do away with having to do a screen wrap of a model and translate it onto the graphical interface - you won't even have to touch a block of clay!"

Faith turned away, coughing delicately into her hand. Gwen, a smile frozen to her face, wanted to kick her. "Much too generous," she said.

Grandfather laughed. "Don't you worry," he assured, giving her a nudge in the ribs with his elbow. "I'll recoup my investment a hundred times fold." His gray eyes had danced about the studio, taking everything in without focusing on any particular object. "You two are going to make magic!"

The skin on Gwendolyn's arms prickled into gooseflesh at the memory, or perhaps it was the music. She let out a deep breath and activated the HoloSculpt. Broken down to the most basic components, it was a perspex box a meter square with a metal frame, open at the front and filled with a three-dimensional grid laid out in blue laser light. The box could expand to ten times its normal size, as needed.

Gwen put her hands inside the box and began to form the most basic element, a sphere. The beams of blue light moved with her hands and, when released, the shape stayed firm as if made of putty. The crafty device would also record the coordinates into her computer. It made it a million times easier to correct a change if she didn't care for the way a sculpt was going, since it was just a matter of touching a button that would undo her last modification, though she would never admit any fondness for it.

Once the sphere was made, Gwen began to pull it down, making it ovoid. From there, creating a face was easy. Too easy. It was the main reason why she disliked the HoloSculpt. She felt like she was cheating. Stone, grhnam composite, clay... those were work. The machine, however, brought to mind a term that she had heard Hope use from time to time - fairytale tech.

Gwendolyn bore it with a patient exasperation, knowing that it was necessary. Faith certainly couldn't take a biological being and cram it into an inanimate carving, and making a mold and a wrap would take too long. So Gwen used the machine, ignoring the distaste she felt. Even so, after only a few minutes, she was lost in her work - shaping ears and molding cheeks.

Faith had work piled up both literally, on her desk, and figuratively, on her mental to-do list. Even so, she uncorked a bottle of champagne as discreetly as she could, poured herself a generous amount into a tall flute, and watched Gwen through the pane of glass that separated her lab from her dyer's studio.

The eldest de Rossi sister was well aware that there were many in her field who thought that the work she did in molecular biology was cutting edge - phenomenal she heard a man say once. Though she knew it to be true, and what developments she made on her own always delighted her, they did not impress her much. In her heart, she believed that it was what Gwen did that was truly phenomenal.

Faith knew that she rode on the backs of others, as was the case for nearly every scientist making universal advancements - taking the knowledge and discoveries that had come before and learning more, taking it farther, making it better. All things considered, she thought herself an excellent editor, at best. But what Gwen did, she believed, was true creation.

It had come as a complete surprise to her, almost at the end of their college days, to find that Gwendolyn was truly talented in an artistic realm that was all her own. For years Faith, and she knew that it was her own vanity that drove the idea, had simply assumed that Gwen was pursuing a hobby – something to take up her time while she was waiting for Faith to come home.

On a picturesque day before the onset of mid-term exams, Faith had been quarantined by a common cold to the flat she shared with her twin. Though she knew it was necessary, she openly sulked at being banished from the lab for a full forty-eight hours. When she did all that she could from her virtual terminal, she wandered about their place, sullenly blowing her nose and looking at the sculptures that adorned their living room.

Faith had stopped in front of a carved bust of a young man with wild eyes and curly hair. He was impressive in face, form, and features. As she looked around, grateful for the hundredth time that Gwen liked to decorate (if left to herself the place would have been barren save for lab equipment), she noticed that most of the pieces had a striking similarity. The detail put into each figure was painstaking, almost mathematical in the breakdown.

"Where did you get these?" she had asked.

Gwendolyn had handed her a steaming mug full of hot, fragrant tea and shrugged. "I brought them home with me. From school."

It took Faith a moment to comprehend what she was saying and, when she finally did, she turned to her twin, gawking at her.

"You made this?" Faith asked, pointing to a delicate carving of a woman dancing, wearing nothing but a loose scarf around her hips.

"Of course!"

"What from?"

A shrug. "That one was carved from sleta." Then Gwen had looked around, turned and pointed. "That one was sculpted with terra. That one, from cast clay. The one over there is from a dup-mold that I carved..."

"You made *all* of these?"

Gwen had nodded, a small smile tucked into her round cheek. Faith did not know if the smile was from embarrassment, a sense of pride and accomplishment, or from the fact that her twin had been too dull to ever notice what had been in front of her face for weeks. Or months. Or years.

Faith had taken a drink of the tea without really noticing the sensation that it caused as it scalded her tongue and burned its way down her throat. She had taken another drink and another, her mind far away and racing faster than her heart. She had practically gulped down the whole mug while Gwen had watched her, bemused.

It wasn't until that moment, when Faith realized what Gwen was capable of doing, that she realized what she herself might be capable of accomplishing, and what they could do together.

Now Faith, only a few years later but already a good deal wiser, leaned back against her new desk in her new lab and took a sip of champagne, watching Gwendolyn work. Watching her create.

It was just the base, of course. The details would come later after they had met with Charity and Llewellyn. Their younger sisters had eagerly offered to take care of buyer predilection and researching prospects. What Gwen was working on now was merely the physical foundation of the first person she and her twin, and all of her sisters really, would make.

Faith had already completed her part for the base of the first construct. She had gone through just over an entire Anglicus alphabet of structural compikes and a full twenty-eight genetic splices. It had taken nearly an entire standard year and three different labs to build the biologistics of the base for their first construct. Details would be added later to meet the wants of their buyers.

Though her work in technological science was meticulous down to a sub-molecular level, it was with bated breath that she watched while Gwendolyn made the physical foundation for their first construct. It was a process so detailed and so precise - yet it would take her twin less than two days. Like

Faith, she would have to add the details later according to the specific desires of the buyer. But to the eldest de Rossi sister, even though what Gwendolyn did would take much less time, it was no less magic.

She watched her twin through the glass - watching her work, watching her get lost in her work. Watching her create.

Faith took a long drink of champagne and was only vaguely aware of the sensation it left as it bubbled its way down her throat. All she knew was that, for once, her heart was racing faster than her mind.

I was working at the compound that night, finishing the install of the com system. Though I had put in a lot of long nights over the past year, anything techy made my days even longer. I could run electrical wire and magnetic contacts with ease, pretty much anything that I could get my hands on and touch. But when it came to programming something... well, I was no de Rossi.

I had a guy under me that was an actual expert in tech, but he was already gone for the day. The one thing I found that Faith de Rossi and I had in common was being a stickler for deadlines. Unless I thought I might genuinely electrocute myself, I was determined to finish before I called it a night. There was only one more line to hook up and I did not want to start the next day backlogged. I knew as much as she that one late start led to another. And another.

Faith's lab/office was the last room I got running. I think all of her equipment was causing a bitch of a problem by interfering with the relays but I was not an expert on tech so it was always my first suspect. I could see her through the glass that separated her workroom from the hallway, drinking champagne and watching her twin. A gadget was in my ear that looked to me like a blue jellybean but all I could hear on it was static. I looked at the open panel of wires and frowned at the device in my hand.

"God hates a coward," I muttered and punched a few buttons that I thought would bypass the central circuit. I actually cringed a bit, afraid that an explosion of some sort might follow. Instead of a disaster, I was met with a success. Of sorts.

"We are now the parents of a brave, new universe," Faith whispered and her words were as clear as a bell via the jellybean in my ear. I closed the panel in the wall outside her lab as a shiver ran down my spine and then chased its trail back up, making the blonde hairs on the back of my neck stand on end.

FOUR

Cronus left his driver in the aircar and walked up the gentle slope to the cottage. It was an immaculate day. The grass all around him was a deep and vivid green and the sky was a brilliant and sparkling blue. The warming air was crisp and clean with just a touch of a breeze. A freshly laid path of crushed stones crunched under his polished shoes as it meandered through the gate in the picket fence and led the way to the house. An extensive flower garden ran along both the outside of the house and the inside of the fence, swaddling the grassy yard with waves of carefully tamed explosions of flora in all sizes and colors. It was obvious to him that Gwendolyn had been as busy here as she had been at the compound and he idly wondered where she found the time.

The tall elf let himself in through the gate and immediately spied a young woman lying on her back in the sea of grass between the flowerbeds. She had wild, copper-colored hair and her large green eyes stared upward as she watched the fluttering dance of the garden's resident butterflies. She wore a simple dress printed with tiny flowers and short, puffed sleeves that covered her white shoulders. Her feet were bare.

"Hello, Madeline," Cronus called to the young woman, pushing a gray lock of hair away from his narrow face.

"Hello, Grandfather," she replied dreamily without so much as a glance in his direction. "Hope is inside."

Cronus nodded as he continued to the cottage. He had been delighted when Hope had finished her secondary schooling, called "high school" by humans – a term that always made him laugh, and had come to stay with Faith and Gwendolyn. She had a month off before she started up again at the local university and he wanted to see her as much as possible. No amount of time could be enough for his youngest granddaughter. If Faith was his pride, Hope was his jewel.

He reached the door and paused for a second before opening it a crack without bothering to use the silly knocker.

"Hello?" he called, pushing the door open farther. "Hope?"

"I'm in here!" a voice called from the direction of the dining room.

Cronus walked through the kitchen to the dining room where a young woman sat with a cold plate of food in front of her that appeared to be untouched. She looked identical to the young woman that he had passed lying in the grass on his way to the house.

"Grandfather!" she exclaimed, bounding up to embrace him as he came around the table to give her a hug.

He kissed her on the crown of reddish-orange curls that spiraled down around her pale face and held her at arms length so he could look at her. Her green eyes were bright, but he could see a touch of sadness lurking in their depths.

"What's wrong?" he asked.

"Oh, nothing," she told him, as her excitement at his arrival faded away and she returned to her previous mood. "I'm just bored. Faith and Gwen spend all their time at the compound now. Charity and Llewellyn too."

"Why don't you..."

play with Madeline, he was about to say, but realized that the phrase would displease her. Though she was still considered a girl by elfin standards, her human blood made her a young woman.

"...and Madeline do something together?"

Hope sighed. "What?" she asked, pouting. "Pick flowers? Braid our hair?" she sighed again. "The other girls are doing things. *Important* things." She plopped back down in her chair and pushed the plate of food away.

"You are just as important," her Grandfather told her quickly, sitting down next to her and gathering both of her delicate hands into his own.

"But not the same," Hope said.

"Nobody is the same," he told her. "Look at how different Faith and Charity are! Look at how different you girls are even from your dyers, despite the fact that you have identical genetic codes!"

Especially you and Madeline, he thought, but did not say.

"But Faith is a scientist," Hope argued, "and Gwendolyn is an artist. Charity is a financial genius!"

"Genius?" Cronus exclaimed, his gray brows arched high over his gray eyes as he smiled broadly.

Hope shrugged. "That's what Llewellyn says, and she must be right since Faith put Charity in charge of so much of that stuff." Hope's shoulders sagged and she gently pulled one of her hands from her grandfather's. "I just don't know what to do. I don't know what makes me special."

"Faith said you aced your exit exams," he consoled. "She told me you scored the highest in physics!"

"Physics is nothing," she said. "It doesn't make me special." She planted an elbow on the table and put her chin in her hand.

"Ah!" Cronus said, letting go of her other hand to drum his long fingers on the wooden tabletop, admiring the wild mane of hair that he knew she detested. The still handsome elf brightened suddenly. "Well, I will tell you what. There is a galaxy fair in the orbit. Why don't you let me take you?"

Hope's shoulders dropped even farther in exasperation. "A fair? Grandfather, I'm trying to tell you that I'm not..."

"Ah, ah, ah!" Cronus interrupted. "I'm not talking about taking you on rides like a baby." He leaned back in his chair, his fingers still upon the table and his tongue in his cheek. "What if I took you to do something your mother would never let you do?"

Hope sat forward, instantly piqued. "Like what?"

Cronus laid a finger along the side of his jaw, the tip touching the lobe of his pointed ear. "How about if we went to see a black elf?"

Green eyes went wide and round. "A fortune-teller?" Hope breathed. "Really?" Her grandfather nodded. She clasped her hands together. "I think that sounds wonderful! Today? Can we go today?"

Cronus smiled. "We can go right now if you like."

"Yes!" she exclaimed, jumping from her seat and giving him a hug that was powerful for one so small. "Just let me get my com-cuff," she said, bounding out of the room only to return a few seconds later, fastening a gold bracelet around her right wrist. "Okay, I'm ready!" She scooped up her plate and left it on the kitchen counter as she headed for the front door, the elf following her with a grin.

They came out to find Madeline still on the lawn, though she had rolled over onto her belly and lay with her face cradled in hands atop elbows planted in the grass, watching bumble bees dance lazily over the flowers.

"Madeline!" Hope called. "We're going to the fair! A galaxy fair! Would you like to go?"

Madeline cocked her head, either watching the bees or thinking of an answer - Cronus could not tell which.

"That's okay," she replied after a moment, her indication that the idea did not interest her enough to move from her spot in the garden.

"Alright," Hope said, "but go inside when it gets dark. I left a plate of berries and biscuits in the kitchen."

"Is there any honey?"

"Yes, in the cupboard over the stove."

"Okay."

Hope slipped her hand through her grandfather's arm but held back as if undecided. "Are you sure you don't want to come?" she asked her manufactured twin.

"I'm sure. But..." she continued, looking up for the first time, "will you bring me a balloon?"

Hope smiled. "Of course. But go inside when it gets dark."

"Okay," Madeline agreed pleasantly, turning her attention back to the bees.

"Let's go," Hope said, beaming at her grandfather.

"Very well," he agreed, patting her arm. He glanced back at the dyer in the grass, a happy smile on her face as she watched a flower bob under the weight of a bee.

Too soon, he thought as they went through the gate and down the hill to where his driver waited with the car. *Too soon.*

*

The young de Rossi woman rode with her grandfather in his private car to the spaceport where they were escorted to a private terminal and boarded a private spacecraft. Hope had only been on it once before when she had been much younger and had thought it to be magical. Now, looking through older eyes, she could see that it was extravagantly state-of-the-art, yet tastefully appointed.

A human steward waited on her while Cronus took a few holo calls and answered some messages that were waiting for him. Once they had left the atmosphere of the small planet-moon, a waiter set a table for her with white linens and tiered trays of cold appetizers.

"Champagne?" he asked. Hope looked eagerly at her grandfather, who frowned.

"Absolutely not. But," he acquiesced, seeing her expression fall, "you may have a cordial."

Hope brightened. "Cherry please," she told the waiter. The man smiled, bowed, and hurried to fill a delicate crystal glass with the sweet drink. Half an hour later, Cronus had finished his work and joined his youngest granddaughter at the table as another steward brought out small plates laden with hot hors d' oeuvres.

Hope bit into a cheese and mushroom pastry, her nose wrinkling as she smelled the splash of absinthe in her grandfather's water.

"Do you really think a black elf will be able to tell me what makes me special?"

Cronus smiled at her. "Only if he has days and days, for there are a million things that make you special."

Hope, though she usually disliked these types of compliments, returned his smile and dabbed her lips with a napkin. "I don't care about the little things," she said. "I want to know what is going to set me apart. Make me important - like Faith and Gwen, Charity and Llewellyn."

"Comparisons are odious," Cronus told her, though there was a glimmer of amusement in his stone-gray eyes.

"Grandfather," she scolded, "you know what I mean!" Cronus hid a smile behind his fingers as Hope shook her mass of copper-colored curls in mock exasperation. "I want to know if you believe that black elves can honestly tell fortunes! Can they really see your future?"

"Ah!" Cronus uncrossed his legs and sat forward, helping

himself to a meat tart and popping it into his mouth. He sat back, chewing thoughtfully and then swallowing. "The black elves, it is said, were the first race of the universe. In fact, the stories say that they are a representation of the universe itself - their dark skin made to mimic the darkness of space and their bright eyes to represent the stars. They are still called The Children of the One Song, though there are no known Zealots among them."

"But how is it that they can tell the future?" Hope asked. "How can they know a person's fate?"

Cronus smiled and his aging face looked youthful once again. "Because," he explained, "even now, they are still the closest ones to the universe itself. They still see the web of the song, and everyone's note and chorus."

Hope arched a copper-colored eyebrow at him. "Mother says they are all lecherous heathens and charlatans."

Cronus laughed. "Of course she would."

"Are you religious Grandfather?"

"Me?"

"Mmhmm. I never asked you - what religion do you believe in?"

"All of them, and none," he answered. Cronus leaned forward and held his chin in his thumb and laid one finger over his lips and another along the side of his face. Hope opened her mouth to chide him but something caught her eye and she turned her head so she could see out of the window.

At first she thought what had caught her attention was a star, or another spacecraft, but as the light grew closer she saw that it was perfectly round, a pink bubble in the black of space.

"Is that it?" she asked.

"That's it," the elf replied with a smile. He loved to see her so excited; she had been so despondent of late, which had been the reason behind his visit in the first place. It had been Gwendolyn, though, that had brought it to his attention. Like Faith, he was (more often than not) so involved with work that other people, even those dear to him, did not draw his attention the way they should.

Hope watched, breathless, as the little bubble grew to the size of a small moon. It really did look like a bubble, distorting the images within it so much that she could not decipher exactly what it contained. The steward returned to clear the table and prepare them for entry into the bauble satellite.

"It is always pink?" Hope asked her grandfather. She had never been to a galaxy fair before.

"No," Cronus answered. "If I remember correctly, the sky goes from blue to pink to lavender, then back to pink and then blue and all over again."

Hope clapped her hands, making her look much younger than her sixteen years. She watched through the window as everything in the cabin went bright pink, then dark, and then pink again as they passed through the five-meter thick walls of the bubble and into the artificial atmosphere of the fair.

Her ears felt as if they were filling with cotton and she opened her mouth wide, releasing the pressure on her eardrums with a small pop. Hope pressed her face to the glass, eagerly trying to see everything at once.

She could see a great stretch of land, divided into many parts. One of the largest parts of the landmass was covered with grass and people were racing on it – riding ostriches and creatures that looked like giant seahorses. Another part was covered with machines, some moving slow but others moving very fast, carrying people that screamed in both terror and delight. The last thing she saw as their craft turned, was a hundred tents in a myriad of colors along the edge of a body of water.

Then the ground was rushing to meet them as the craft

dropped quickly, plunging into the private spaceport and landing gently on the tarmac.

Hope undid her safety webbing but waited as patiently as she could for the captain to give them clearance and for the steward to usher them out of the craft. Once outside and down on the ground, Hope politely slipped her hand inside her grandfather's arm, letting him lead her away. Her head, alive with her wild, copper curls, turned constantly from left to right and back again.

As they walked from the port she could see the body of water she had spied from above. It was a lake of sorts, with small waves that lapped at a long beach of golden sand. There were people splashing and playing in the shallows and more people out on the water in rowboats and large paddleboats shaped like swans. Others lounged on blankets laid over the sand – taking in the warm, slightly sultry air under the soft pink sky.

Hope and her grandfather walked next to the beach on a pathway made of wooden beams. Vendors tending carts dominated the walkway, selling treats and sweets, many that Hope had never seen before.

"Would you like anything?" Cronus asked. He knew that the food on his personal spacecraft was far superior to anything they would find at the fair, and looked suspiciously at the carts displaying fragrant meat being roasted on sticks, but was ready to indulge his granddaughter with anything she might want. Thankfully, Hope shook her curls.

"Oh, no! I'm much too full. And much too excited!" she gushed, giving his arm a squeeze. "Where are the fortune-tellers?"

Cronus laughed and patted her hand. "On the other side of the midway," he said pointing.

Hope looked ahead and saw that the path of wooden beams ended, the beach curving away to their left. Ahead were rows and rows of large, brightly colored tents. Inside, hawkers were selling games of skill and strength and chance. They called out as she and her grandfather exchanged one path for another, shouting over the din of the crowd and the jangle of music that seemed to come from everywhere, inviting him and then her to try their luck.

Hope shook her head and clung to her grandfather, stepping carefully on the ground that was oddly uneven beneath her shoes.

"What is this?" she asked, looking down. "It's not dirt."

"No, it's sawdust."

"What is that?"

"Wood shavings."

"Oh."

Now that he had told her, she could certainly identify the sharp scent of freshly cut wood along with all of the other smells that were assaulting her nostrils. The most dominating scent was the dusty fabric of the stuffed animal prizes (hung on the nets that separated the games) and the tang of warm, unwashed bodies. Distantly, in one direction she could smell roasting meat and vegetables, in the other direction only sugar. The entire combination made her lightheaded.

Her hand still clinging to her grandfather's arm, Hope was pulled to a halt as Cronus stopped to flag down a passing S-pher. The droid was silver and round and the size of a child's rubber ball. It hovered patiently, chest-high, bobbing slightly in the dusty, fragrant air.

Hope released her grandfather's arm so he could produce his credentials card, which he slid down through a thin slot in the side of the droid. The bottom of the sphere opened, extruding a ledge that was covered with a ghosted keypad. Cronus typed in a numerical sequence and, after a short pause, the ledge extended. Cronus placed the palm of his hand on the shelf and it lit up with a green light before retracting and displaying the keypad once more.

The elf glanced about, taking in the costs displayed throughout the midway for games and food, and made a quick estimate of what he might need for the day. He never carried paper money, most people never did. It was obsolete on most planets and, where it was still used, the different currencies were a headache to remember. Though it had been at least a century since he had last visited a fair, Cronus knew that carnies (and that included the fortune tellers) did not accept credential cards.

After he had typed in his desired amount, the sphere rose up towards his face and took an eye scan. Hope looked at her grandfather, surprised.

"I've never seen a S-pher Droid do a retina scan!" she exclaimed.

Cronus smiled and accepted the paper bills as they were dispensed from the droid with an efficient clicking sound. "It is a requirement to access any of my accounts. The more you have," he instructed his granddaughter with a wink, "the better you protect it."

Hope nodded, tucking away the advice as she always did, while the droid sank back down again. Her grandfather motioned at the droid with a finger and the ledge extended out once again as a small hole opened above it, spraying out a mist that would dissolve any fingerprints left behind. Cronus gave the pad a quick wipe with a handkerchief just for good measure and they were on their way again, Hope's excitement bubbling once more.

Finally - after rows of laser circle and ball toss, tent after tent of ring the bell and win a prize, and one hawker after another that wanted to guess her name, age, or weight - the wide tents opened up to a different part of the fair. They were back out into the open air, spewed from the large, connected cloth pavilions.

On the left were rows of carts with billowing smoke, roasting and frying everything in the galaxies and selling them rolled in paper cones or skewered on sticks. To their right was a lane lined with high and narrow tents covered in striped silk. Cronus gave a nod towards the tents and Hope squealed with delight.

"How do we know which one to choose?" she asked, practically dancing on her toes as she held tight to her grandfather's arm.

"Well," her grandfather said, "if their curtains are closed it means they are with someone. Other than that, see which one calls to you the most."

"Calls to me internally or externally?" Hope asked.

Cronus laughed. "Whichever you prefer."

They walked down the lane and all of the elves that were not inside with customers called out to the pair, beseeching them for their business. Hope stared in wonder at the elves in their brightly colored robes and at their high, pointed ears. Her own ears had been rounded surgically when she was an infant, as had her sisters' ears. The fortunetellers had ears like her grandfather, but their skin was as dark as the night sky with no moon.

Hope walked along, clinging to her grandfather as the black elves called to her, their voices a soothing melody on the warm air. They tried to entice her with promises of love and fortune and adventure. As she passed one she stopped, curious. Unlike most of the dark-skinned elves that stood in front of their tents, trying to entice her, this one sat on a short stool and seemed unconcerned about procuring any business. His skin was more chocolate than ebony, she noticed, and he was smoking what appeared to be a large, hand-rolled cigarette.

"Pretty girl!" he called when she stopped. "You want your

fortune told?"

Hope nodded, her green eyes wide and eager. The elf stood and beckoned with the hand that held his cigarette.

"Come in, come in! I know what you are looking for. I will tell you what you want to know. What you *need* to know."

"Him," Hope said, inclining her head towards the black elf in front of the blue and white striped silk tent.

"I'm not sure," Cronus said, frowning at the man and the plume of white smoke that was wafting from the end of the blunt. "Maybe you should keep looking."

"No. Him."

Cronus eyed the man suspiciously from under his gray, drawn brows and sighed. "Very well."

Hope bounced up and down in excitement as her grandfather escorted her to the tent and the dark-skinned elf led them inside. Cronus waved at the smoke, aggravated. The elf laughed deeply and extinguished his sweet-smelling cigarette and invited them to sit in the two small chairs that faced a tiny table covered with crystals. Hope took her seat, admiring the different colored pieces of quartz and onyx and copper tuns.

"This is my granddaughter," Cronus said, taking his seat. "She wants to know what makes her special."

"Grandfather!" Hope admonished. "You are not supposed to tell them anything! That is how charlatans work, by guessing on what you have already given up!"

Cronus gave her a conciliatory smile as the teller's booming laugh filled the tent.

"Do not worry, little lady!" he assured her. "I am da real ting!" Hope eyed him doubtfully as he took his seat across from them and took up her small hand. "Oooh!" he exclaimed theatrically. "You don't want to know what makes you special, you want to know what makes you different!"

Hope leaned towards him over the table, her copper curls making long, wavy curtains of hair on either side of her face.

"Different from what?" she asked.

"Not different from what, different from whom!" the elf boomed. "Different from your sisters!"

There was a sharp intake of breath and Hope looked at her grandfather. "Did you tell him?" she asked.

"Of course not!" Cronus exclaimed, surprised himself. He had merely taken Hope to the fair on a whim in an effort to cheer her up. He certainly did not believe that the black elves would have anything substantial to offer. Though he did not believe them to be heathens, as his daughter Christa did, he certainly thought they were charlatans. After all, he was a man of science.

"Yes!" the back elf continued. "Your sisters! You tink that they important and that you – eh, not so much." Hope nodded, her face drawn and intense. The elf gave her a knowing smile. "They have much to offer the universe," he admitted, "that much true. But so of you."

Hope looked at him, her face brightening, expectant. "I do?"

"Indeed. It will be up to you to find key."

"The key?"

"Yes. It is up to you to find key. Your mission much more important than the work of your sisters. Key will bring all you desire. Key is everything you need."

"Key to what?"

The elf's deep voice dropped to a whisper. "Key to save the world."

At this point Cronus blew a derisive puff of air through his nose and received a reprimanding look from his granddaughter before her full attention was back on the narrow face of the fortuneteller.

"Where will I find this key?" she asked.

The teller straightened, taking on an air of commanding importance.

"First, in your dreams," he said. He reached across the table and grasped her small hand again. "Remember your dreams, write them down. Then you will find key. Key will bring you all you desire, and help you save all that you love. With key, you will change the course of the universe."

There was a loud snort from the graying elf that Hope pointedly ignored. She stared at the dark-skinned man, her green eyes blazing.

"I will do everything I can to find this key," she assured him solemnly. The elf nodded in agreement, just as solemn.

"I know you will. You are Hope."

The half-elf girl squeezed his hand in appreciation before she let go and rose from her seat in the small chair. With her mind already far away, she turned and slowly left the tent as her grandfather stayed to pay for the service.

"Laid it on a little thick at the end there, don't you think?" Cronus asked as he laid paper money into the palm of the dark-skinned elf.

"I walk in da truth," the fortuneteller assured him. Looking down, he saw the amount that he had been paid and gave a low whistle. "Very generous of you," he commended as he made the money disappear.

The teller held out a hand and, instinctively after years of doing business, Cronus reached out and shook it.

"Something for you then?" the fortuneteller offered, still holding onto the older elf's hand as Cronus belatedly realized his mistake. He shook his gray head, about to decline when the teller continued. "You wish to know if there will be more, no?"

The older elf froze, every muscle in his body suddenly taut. It was, indeed, what had been on his mind for some time - though it had begun to fade away as of late. The teller took his surprised silence for acquiescence and he nodded, his face as solemn as Hope's had been.

"Yes," the black elf confirmed. "Three more will follow."

Cronus felt his mouth open and his shoulders dropped in a similar matter, making the other elf laugh heartily as he released his hand.

"Do not worry my friend! It will not be for quite a while. You have plenty of time to get ready!"

Cronus gave him a look that expressed serious doubt, but only to his assurance, not in doubt of his premonition. He gave a quick dip of his head in acknowledgement to the teller, who bowed deeply in return, before he composed himself and followed his granddaughter out into the bright light.

"Did you get what you were after?" he asked when he joined her on the sawdust lane between the tents.

"I think so," she said, smiling at him. "But I am suddenly exhausted. And starving!"

Cronus himself felt as if he had been punched in the gut, but he would do anything to please his youngest granddaughter.

"Well," Cronus he remarked lightly, folding her small hand into the crook of his arm, "we can certainly take care of that."

They shared something called an artichoke on the midway, and a number of fried roots. Then he bought her saltwater taffy before they found a balloon for Madeline.

The pair walked down a lane where gypsies sold handcrafted items and, upon spying something in particular, the girl's Grandfather had her wait while he ducked into a tent by himself. Minutes later, he emerged with a flat package wrapped in a heavy, brown paper and tied with a rough type of string. Hope clasped her hands to her chest and then held them out, expecting the present was for her, but Cronus held it back, smiling.

"Not until the morning," he told her. Hope tried to feign a frown but was only able to produce a smirk, an expression that was queerly like Faith's, but did not protest.

Later, when the sky was turning lavender for the second time, Cronus tucked her into the guest bed on his aircraft with a kiss on her freckled cheek before retreating to the only office on the craft. He seldom slept, but when he did, it was usually in the chair behind his desk.

When Hope awoke, they were at the spaceport closest to Faith and Gwen's cottage and the package was waiting on the nightstand next to the bed. She pulled off the string and tore open the paper to reveal an old-fashioned book. It was large and bound with patched leather in an assortment of colors. The pages inside were real paper, and blank.

The only printing was on the cover where, embossed in a flowing flowery script, there were only two words.

Dream Journal

Hope held the book to her chest, delighted. Also tucked into the paper was a pen filled with purple ink. She placed the pen and the book on the night table and dressed hurriedly. She could hear her grandfather's staff moving about outside of the guest room and knew they were probably waiting for her.

Tomorrow, she thought, pulling on her shoes, feeling she might burst with excitement. *I'll start tomorrow with the dream I have tonight. I'll find the key.*

FIVE

Faith crossed her legs under the great, glass conference table and smiled at her two biological sisters and the three biodentical dyers that sat with them. The administrative section of the compound, the second part of the compound to be built after the labs, was practically complete and included a reception area and the conference room where the de Rossi sisters now held their first official meeting.

I was there, hanging large acrylic panels on three of the four walls. It was usually something my lift team would be doing, but I had two guys out sick and I was already a week behind schedule, though Faith had been surprisingly indifferent to an expeditious completion of the administrative division. I think I had stacked up some points by having her lab done to her approval and a day earlier than planned.

Once the finishing touches were put on the managerial section, I would be off to oversee the work already in progress for the classrooms and dormitories. I checked the first panel with a laser level and, satisfied that it was straight, stepped down from the air-stump. I gave the stump a shove with one foot, sending it coasting towards the next wall while I guided the panel with a simple field manipulator.

Cronus was there as well, though he chose not to sit. The older elf felt better watching the proceedings with his tall form leaning against a wall, his gray hair swept back from his narrow face and his gray eyes alert. He wore a mauve-colored shirt with a high collar and large, starched cuffs. Over it, he wore a pinstriped vest, but no coat.

I had gotten to know the girls and could tell them apart easily enough, though it took quite a bit of time since each pair was identical. I did not see Hope often, since she rarely came to the compound, and Madeline even less. Madeline, however, was easy to distinguish by the constant look of dreaminess that she wore. When I first met her I suspected some sort of drug use, then I learned that was simply how she was. Quite the opposite of her twin, her green eyes always sharp with stout determination.

"We are all here together," Faith announced, "because we are all in this together, or so I would like. Is there anyone here that does not wish to be part of this?" The young women looked at each other, unable to constrain neither their smiles nor their excitement. Faith let her eyes fall last on Madeline, unsure of how the youngest dyer might respond, but the girl simply looked around in the same happily curious manner as the others did - winding a long, copper-colored curl around one of her slender fingers.

"Very well," Faith continued, "then there are some decisions that I think we all should make together. The first, I think and to be typically superficial, is how we want the constructs to look. I'm almost done with Basic-28. Gwendolyn has already finished the foundation of his form, but we are going to need details, opinions, and the like."

"Well," Hope interjected, "they all should be gorgeous."

"Of course," Faith agreed, "that's a given. But we need to decide on some specifics. From everything as broad as what race and what color, down to the details of toenails and eyelashes if need be."

"They should definitely have eyelashes," Madeline announced.

"And they should be human," Cronus announced from his place against the wall. "They should definitely be human. All of them."

Faith gave him a dark look and cleared her throat. "I think backwards planning might suit us best for this. You all know," she announced, "Charity has been put in charge of all the finances. But Llewellyn, along with assisting Charity, has also been compiling a list of possible buyers, those that will be given the first chance at purchasing one of the first six constructs."

Llewellyn, the exact image of Charity (who Cronus thought was a spitting image of her mother), smiled at everyone and turned on the portable compute that lay on the table in front of her. Her eyes were bright blue and her hair was white blonde, though she preferred to wear her hair up in a frilly twist while Charity mostly wore her own locks curled or waved and down over her shoulders.

"Are you still planning on making the males first?" Llewellyn asked Faith, who answered with a nod. The dyer nodded as well as if to confirm her suspicions and continued. "I have compiled a list of our ten most likely buyers. The first is Ivana Uri-Van Zandt." Llewellyn paused and looked up. "Mason?" she called out, "are any of those working yet?"

"Ayuh," I answered, almost without thinking.

I stuck my hemler in my back pocket, stepped down off the air-stump and reached over to thumb the tiny circle on the bottom right of the panel I had just hung. Two meters high and three meters wide, the glass flared to life. Her blue eyes sparkled at me for a second and I returned to my work.

"Thank you." Llewellyn touched the compute in front of her and the image of a woman, barely clothed and stepping out of a Mys-jet, appeared on the device and was replicated on the wall panel. "Ivana is notorious for her lascivious lifestyle as much as for her ungodly amount of money. She is as impetuous as she is lonely and wanton, and I am quite sure that she will be our first buyer."

"What do you suggest?" Gwendolyn asked.

"Besides human and male?" Llewellyn asked with a devious

grin. "Tall and blonde. Muscular, but not bulky. Check records for images of humans from earth that are of Russian descent - it is Russian, isn't it?" she asked, looking at Charity.

Charity shrugged. "I think so. Russian or Prussian. I get human ethnicities mixed up. So start with those, but cross-reference Ukrainian and Lithuanian. Also check Olympians, or Olympiads, something like that."

Llewellyn nodded and Gwen made notes on her own small portable compute.

"Next," Llewellyn continued as the image of an elfin woman with hip-length snow-white hair replaced the human on the wall panel, "prospect number two. Ynestra Malin. I've actually got this one on a line like a fish. She wants an elf..." she paused and shot a quick glance at their grandfather before she looked at her twin who grinned like a shark and continued for her...

«...one that looks like her father!" Charity gushed. There was a moment of silence followed by exaggerated groans of repulsion as those seated at the table exchanged looks of disgust and rolled their eyes. Charity whispered to Llewellyn, sending the two off into identical gales of laughter.

Cronus looked annoyed, though he had to admit that he was relieved that all of his granddaughters felt the same way he did when it came to their father, which was a general feeling of revulsion. Nevertheless, he felt the situation was going from a filthy comedy to a bad reality.

"I don't like it," he said firmly. "I don't want you selling elves."

Faith looked over her shoulder but did not raise her face to meet his eyes. "It's just this one," she said quietly. "And we need to show what we are capable of."

Cronus grunted and, after a good long moment of thought, gave an angry hiss through his teeth and motioned for Llewellyn to go on.

"Number three," Llewellyn continued as the whispered remarks and quiet laughter picked up again as the screen was filled with one image after another of various women, "can be any number of these women, possibly a male or two. We aren't sure yet." She looked across the table at Faith and Gwendolyn. "Can changes be made afterwards?"

"Absolutely," Faith answered.

Llewellyn nodded and looked at Gwen. "Just make him generically handsome, for now. We can fine tune him later."

"I think the term you are looking for is 'classical,'" Gwen informed her.

Llewellyn shrugged. "Whatever. Next, regarding the females we will sell." She showed the group around the table pictures of the men that she and Charity had picked out for their most likely prospects, giving everyone a brief bio on each one. She shared what types of women, along with what type of construct they thought the men would be most likely to purchase. Charity pecked out a few notes onto the compute she shared with her dyer twin as the discussion came to a close.

"Thank you," Gwen said, her fingers moving wildly over her own compute pad. "This helps a lot."

"The next order of business," Faith announced, "is to determine a plan for their education, what they are going to learn and what extras should be added to increase their value."

"What do you mean, extras?" Madeline asked.

"For instance," Faith said as she motioned to the last image on the wall panel, a still pic of a compact man with black hair and almond-shaped eyes, "the one we make for Mr. Harasuka should know how to speak Japonesa. But I don't think they will all need to know Japonesa."

"Ah!" Madeline exclaimed, nodding thoughtfully.

"The one for Ivana should speak Russish," Gwen said.

"They should all speak at least two human dialects, and two elfin," Hope said. "Any cultured person today certainly does."

"Very good," Cronus approved from where he leaned against the wall. Hope beamed at his praise and Faith made notes on her personal mini-compute by speaking softly into the pinhole microphone.

"Anglicus is obvious for the first choice," Charity said. "What other human language?"

"Latin," Gwen said quickly.

Charity made a face. "Only the uber-religious ones speak Latin," she said. "Maybe not even all of them."

"But many of the Anglicus languages are based upon it," Gwen argued.

"You just like it because so much of it surrounds their art," Llewellyn said. Gwen opened her mouth to argue but Faith cut her off before she could begin.

"Charity is right," she interjected. "Most humans don't speak it. I propose either Spanish or Mandarin."

Words rapidly became indistinguishable as all of the girls began to talk at once. The arguments went round and round as I finished the install of the second panel. I kicked the stump over to the next wall and guided the last screen into place. Finally, the girls all decided that French would be the second human language, since it was spoken on so many of the satellites colonized by human earthlings, and other languages could be added as necessary.

Gwen acquiesced but appeared to be less than pleased. Hope did not want to argue, but wanted to be part of a discussion that seemed so important. Madeline did not seem to care at all.

"Neither French nor elfin can be taught by a program," Cronus interjected. I grunted in agreement as I pushed the panel against the wall. "The basics, maybe," the elf told them.

"But the constructs will need to speak daily during training with someone already fluent, preferably of direct descent, or else it will be a waste." He shrugged at the looks given to him by those at the table. "I'm sorry," he apologized, "but that's how it needs to be if you want a good product."

Faith sighed angrily at the inconvenience and Gwen put a hand on her arm to console her. "Any of us can teach elfin," she said. "Or at least speak it on a daily basis with the constructs so they can be fluent."

"And French?" Faith asked. "Where are we going to find..."

"I speak native French," a voice said. It took me a moment to realize that the voice was my own and I looked up, as startled as the rest of them.

All heads turned to me as if they had forgotten I was there. I returned to my work, my cheeks hot. I felt the way I had one time when I had been standing with some other boys in my Physical Fitness class in High School and the coach had asked for a volunteer. Some asshole had pushed me and there I stood, the only idiot ready to don a space helmet and drop into the pool.

The other seven people in the room waited to see if I was going say anything else, but I would be damned if was going to open my mouth again. This time, I had somehow betrayed myself. This time, *I* was the asshole. What had squeezed those words from my throat I will never know. And never regret.

"How do you know native French?" Cronus asked. "I though you were from Io."

I held a laser level on the bottom of the panel, shooting a beam of red light against the wall, my tongue poking my cheek. I wasn't sure how much I should actually share. "I am," I finally confirmed. "But my grandmother is French, and not from Europa, but from actual Europe, on Earth. I learned from her."

I watched from the corner of my eye as the girls looked

at each other in surprise and amusement. Faith and Gwen leaned towards each other, conferring in hushed tones. Cronus regarded me with a look of mild suspicion, though that might have been my imagination.

"Mason," Faith called, "how would you like to oversee the French lessons of the constructs?"

I tucked a v-tool into the belt around my waist and turned to the group and shrugged, making the air-stump bob under my moving weight.

"I don't know," I admitted. I looked up and I could see the blonde fringe of hair that had fallen forward over my brow. Time for a haircut. "The compound will be finished soon," I told her, "once the dormitories and the classrooms are finished. I know you wanted me to start a new wing. But we haven't discussed any details yet."

She waved a hand, diminishing the importance of the new wing for the magnitude of construct training. I knew that Cronus could use me, but I also thought that Cronus was a prick. A nice old guy for the most part, but - for the rest - he was a sanctimonious prick. I had been almost joyously relieved when Faith had taken over the building details of the compound and I had been remanded into her jurisdiction.

"And," I continued, "just because I can speak it, doesn't mean I can teach it. I wouldn't know where to start."

Cronus dismissed my argument with a wave of his hand. "You won't have to teach it," he assured me. "They will learn the language itself from a program, just as they will elfish. What they will need to learn from you is an accent, syntax. You'll just have to talk to them for an appropriate amount of time on a daily basis. You will still have plenty of time for your regular work."

The eldest of the young de Rossi ladies tucked a smile into the corner of her mouth. "Your wages would be increased, of course," she told me. "You would even be provided with living quarters at the center, should you desire."

I flashed her a smile and gave my blonde head a shake. "That won't be necessary, Ms. de Rossi," I said and then turned away to lower the stump. I really wasn't all that keen on where I lived but I was even less keen on everyone looking at me. She gave me a nod and I began to vac up the crete-dust that had accumulated at the bottom of the walls from my drilling and hanging.

"What else besides languages might help them?" Faith asked the others once they had turned their attention back to their meeting.

"Ivana Uri is notorious for having affairs with her chauffeurs," Charity mused.

"And a couple of her pilots," Llewellyn added. Charity nodded in agreement.

"She likes men who can take her places?" Hope asked timidly.

Faith nodded as she took notes on her compute. "Generally speaking, yes."

"More specifically," Gwen added, "she likes men who are in control, showing strength, though she has authority over them."

Charity laughed. "I know how she feels."

Cronus winced as the girls at the table tittered laughter.

Charity looked at her eldest sister with a grin. "Make sure he can drive or fly anything. Gwen can take care of his looks and I'll take care of the rest."

The laughter that followed this time was lower and knowing, making Cronus wince once again.

"Ynestra Malin has affairs with her bodyguards," Madeline said softly. All eyes turned to her in surprise.

"And how do you know that?" Faith asked.

"I read the tabloid zines sometimes," Madeline admitted with a shy smile.

"We all bring something to the table," Gwen affirmed, smiling broadly at Hope's dyer.

Faith nodded. "Ynestra likes men who can protect her," she said. "Part of her underlying issues with her father, no doubt."

"So imbed him with the bodyguard protocol," Charity said, "and, again, I'll teach him all the rest."

"Save some for me!" Llewellyn complained amiably.

"You're not partial to elves!" Charity exclaimed.

"I can always make an exception," Llewellyn commented in an uncharacteristically prim manner. The girls all laughed and Cronus finally stepped forward.

"Alright, that's enough!" he scolded. "You can finish your slumber party later." He looked meaningfully at Faith, who composed herself and nodded.

"Of course," she said to him and turned her head to address the others at the table. "Grandfather has something he wants to tell us," she announced. Faith looked back at the lean elf with graying hair, her face like a light beaming through the fog as she invited him to share his thoughts with them.

"Well," Cronus said, clearing his throat as he pushed his sparse form away from the wall and stood straight, tugging down on his vest. "As you girls may, or may not, know - there is a lot going on in the world of physics right now. There are a few groups that are on the brink of breaching the Zero-Point Energy dilemma." He looked around at the girls to see if there was a spark of recognition on any face but, other than a knowing smile from Faith, there was none. Cronus sighed. "Anyway, I have a brilliant young doctor in my employ in one of the labs that is very close to success. There is another very well-to-do lab that is close to success, though we are not sure..."

A silence filled the room as the elf trailed off meaningfully and yet vague.

"Are you asking if any of us knows someone who works in the lab?" Hope asked in an eager effort to be helpful.

"Well," Cronus said, clearing his throat, "actually, I was wondering if any of you knew...since you all have friends in the industry so to speak... any friends who... who might be interested in making a little extra money..." He cleared his throat again, unsure of how to continue.

"Are you asking," Faith interrupted, "if we know anyone who will spy for you in a restricted physics lab?"

Cronus shifted on his feet as he looked away, uncomfortable, and then nodded at her. "Yes."

Faith grinned at his discomfort with her tongue in her cheek. She was not used to seeing her grandfather disconcerted by anything. She glanced around the table. "Actually," she said as Charity and Llewellyn whispered to each other, "as I have said before, Hope is a very apt student at physics, and more than qualified to assist in a lab."

Hope looked at them both, her face crowned with her glorious copper mane and her green eyes bright. Cronus' gray eyes darkened at Faith.

"That is not what I was asking," he stated, his voice cold.

"Isn't it?" Faith asked, feigning surprise. "You had mentioned to me that you were looking for someone who would fit in, that would be completely unable to arouse suspicion, and that we could trust implicitly. Can you think of anyone else who fits that bill more than Hope?"

Hope looked at their grandfather, beaming with Faith's praise. He glanced at her bright face for a split second reaffixing his gaze on her oldest sister.

"No," he told her in Granalf, an elfin dialect he was sure that Hope did not know. "It could be dangerous."

"You did not mention that," Faith replied in the same dialect, "when you were asking if I knew of a colleague that might be of assistance."

"Well..." Cronus grumbled, "danger is not probable, but possible. And this is a touchy subject, as are all subjects on the brink of their revolution, which puts danger into a reasonable range of acceptance. But if there is even the slightest chance of danger, there is no reasonable range of acceptance where Hope is concerned. I do not want her involved in this!"

Faith looked at him, her lips pressed tight in disagreement as she shook her head minutely from side to side. "She is one of us," she told her grandfather. "And she is part of this. She needs to feel needed. Besides, you should know that I would have her back long before reaching a point where her safety may be compromised."

Cronus scowled at her and glanced at Hope, who still stared at him with the most joyous expression he had ever seen. Faith was right, Hope wanted so badly to be included in any way. How could he deny her what she wanted so badly? How could he deny her anything? It was then that he realized Faith had carefully cornered him. Cronus felt the blood rush to his face, but he could no more be angry at Faith than he could refute anything that would make Hope happy.

The old elf sighed. "Of course," he said in elfin so that they all could understand, "if Hope is willing to work in the lab and keep me up to date regarding the progress being made there, and if she promises to be careful..."

"Oh I will!"

"...then I will make arrangements for her employment, as well as a place for her and Madeline to live."

At the mention of her name, Madeline turned her attention back to the group. "Hmmm?"

"We're moving!" Hope told her, thrilled. "To..." she trailed off, looking towards her grandfather.

"Kerin," he said.

"Another planet!" Hope breathed.

Cronus had the satisfaction of seeing Faith flinch. "Still okay with everything?" he asked, leaning down towards her surgically rounded ear.

"When you said far," Faith replied, her voice icy, "you did not say it would be that far. But, yes. I know Hope is eager to help. She wants to contribute."

"I will," Hope affirmed.

"And I'll help take care of her, Grandfather," Madeline assured. "If we can get a little house, I will keep it. I can cook and clean - and help Hope."

"She will be working a lot," Grandfather told the youngest dyer. "I'm afraid you might be lonely."

"I'll be fine," Madeline said, her voice drawn out as if thinking deeply. "Perhaps we can have a small garden, like the one Gwendolyn has?"

"Perhaps."

"I can grow flowers for the butterflies, and maybe some vegetables for us." Charity and Llewellyn whispered and giggled at each other.

"I think that would be splendid," Grandfather told her. Madeline gave him a dreamy smile and Hope beamed as Faith turned to him.

"Give me a rundown on the laboratory, and what exactly it is that you are after, though I think I already know. I am quite sure I can get her into the lab under false yet welcome pretenses. Secure their lodgings, and I will have the two of them ready by the end of the week."

"Excellent," he replied, a smirk on a face that drew lines only at the corners of his eyes and mouth. "Will you be going with them, to get them settled?"

Faith's left hand clenched into a fist, but Gwendolyn was the only one who noticed. A lot was going on; the compound was in the last stages of being completed and they were about to start merging the prototypes, but Faith was not about to let Hope go that far from home by herself. Not without having a look first. She made a mental note that it was time to start thinking about hiring some sort of security detail.

"Is the lab already up and running?"

Grandfather's gray eyes looked away as he considered. "Not for another three weeks," he said. "They have a new wing under construction at the university that is being built especially for this project." Faith nodded and her hand relaxed on her lap. That would give her some time, even just a little, as well as an easy way inside.

"I will be there in three weeks, then," she said. "The girls will have time to get settled and unpacked - but I want to be there when Hope starts, the very first day even. I want to meet whoever is in charge of the lab."

Cronus looked doubtful. "It is of the utmost importance that they do not know what we are about," he advised.

"Don't worry about that. I'll give the college a false name with a real donation and they won't care in the least. I'll tell them that Hope won some scholarship to intern at the new wing or lab or whatever we decide to fund for them."

The elf moved to argue but Faith cut him off before he could speak. "If it pleases you, we can discuss the details later, Grandfather."

Cronus held very still, then nodded, giving in. "Very well," he acquiesced. Then he turned, giving the other girls at the table a stern glare from his gray eyes. "But," added emphatically, his voice suddenly becoming as hard and blunt as his eyes, "to return to the discussion of the dyer business – I have something that I wish to add before we are done here. You are to make only human constructs. Unless you get a direct request and a very large sum of money, like you expect from the Malin woman, you are not to make elfin constructs. Is that understood?"

Each girl nodded solemnly, understanding what Grandfather was asking of them, though not all of them understood why. He looked around the table at his granddaughters and their dyers and finally a smile broke over his still-handsome face. "You girls are going to do amazing things," he told them. Faith grinned.

"Let's get started then."

They rose to leave, chattering excitedly as their eagerness grew more and more. Hope brought up the rear and, as I moved the last panel into place, I saw her catch Llewellyn by the arm, gently holding her back.

"What did Grandfather mean by that?" she asked quietly. "That we shouldn't make elfin constructs?"

Llewellyn's blue eyes opened wide. "You don't know?" she asked, her voice low.

"Know what?"

The dyer's eyes darted around the room, seeking safety, then her expression melted into one of embarrassed patience and she lowered her voice even further and leaned close to Hope's copper curls. "Grandfather is a terrible racist."

Hope drew back, shocked.

She almost argued but she knew at once that Llewellyn was right. The only colleagues he considered equal were elves. And the entire extent of her grandfather's staff, meaning all of his servants really, was human. Llewellyn nodded as she saw the understanding break across Hope's face.

"He doesn't ever want elves to serve humans," the dyer told the youngest de Rossi. "He thinks they are beneath us."

I could have told her that.

"And he considers *us* elves?" Hope whispered as they left the room together behind the others.

"He considers us miracles," Llewellyn told her. "I think that it was entirely due to all of his genetic studying on how mother and father were able to procreate, that he stumbled upon how to create us, me and Madeline and Gwen, I mean."

"Oh."

Hope followed her sisters out of the room, her mind already forgetting about her grandfather's antiquated and embarrassing beliefs, as she was filled with excitement about the new enterprise before her.

The key, she thought, her heart starting to flutter. *It is up to me to find the key. Here is where it all begins.*

SIX

The monastery was a great, sprawling place of gardens and rivers and trees. There were no houses. The monks slept in long wattle and daub lodges with sod roofs that blended perfectly with the hillside. There was the voriste, a courtyard enclosed by a small building that held an office for the Abon and a long building that held the kitchen and the dining facility for the monks. There were places for chanting, places for prayer, and many *many* places for meditation.

The only large structure on the abbey grounds was the Temple, where the monks trained to fight. It was there that they learned self-control, strength and discipline. They were taught hand-to-hand combat as well as a multitude of martial arts that included training with weaponry from every known galaxy.

Behind the Temple itself were pillars that held up nothing, walls without roofs, and caves bored into the mountainside. Every piece and part was an area for self-discovery and self-discipline. And more training.

Hahn, self-cast from the Temple, spent another year in quiet meditation. Then another, and another. Each day he could sit longer, each year he became more still. Soon it became a decade. Though he did not hear anything that sounded like it might be his soul, he did become aware of the sound of his heart.

He could hear it beat within his chest, and he could move away from the sound to hear the heartbeats of the creatures around him - the squirrel in the tree, the hawk in the sky. Sound to him finally became not the alert of an attacker, but the pulse of the world. He found a power in the stillness, something that grew and grew within him and yet it still seemed untapped.

When he shared this view with Elaeric, the other monk had laughed as if Hahn had told him with surprise that the sky above them was blue. Elaeric confided that what invaded his meditations the most were smells.

"I cannot help but be interrupted by the aroma of the grass," he admitted to his friend. "Even the scent of our rock, so metallic! I believe sometimes that I even smell the sap of trees, though they are so far!"

The two enjoyed meditating together and did so quite often. Every day, sometimes twice a day, they would sit in quiet stillness on the flat warm stones of the rock garden to the west of the Temple. One of them would always bring their afternoon tea, and then afterwards they would discuss their meditations. Some discussions took them well into the night. It did not take them long to realize that they meditated on many of the same ideas: from extreme focus to complete surrender, along with the uniqueness of one's place in the cosmos versus the necessity of each individual to complete the pattern of the universal web.

Still, Elaeric would sometimes notice his friend look longingly at the large structure to the east of the rock garden. Beyond the high, stone wall rose a ziggurat of weathered wooden beams. From there one could hear the echo of an occasional grunt or cry that might make Elaeric cringe or Hahn sigh with nostalgia.

After he left the Temple, Hahn had thrown himself into his new study with vigor, as he had done his entire life with every challenge. As of yet, it was not as gratifying as he had hoped. He was not surprised. He enjoyed the clarity that meditation brought, but nothing had ever given him the satisfaction of fighting.

It was never that he wanted to harm another - the very idea of it was far from his thoughts. It was always and ever the fulfillment and the exultation he felt when accomplishing the next level of his own expectations. For as long as he could remember, Hahn Chi had worked to be the best of the best.

Elaeric, on the other hand, knew and was quite comfortable with the fact that there was no stick to measure accomplishment where meditation was concerned. He ached for his friend, hoping that the older monk would find peace, and offered both the escape and fulfillment that he hoped would help.

Today, Hahn walked through the garden, making his way past stunted trees and glacier-sized boulders, a teak tray cradled between his hands. In the pot they always favored, was boiling hot tea, though they would not drink it until done with meditating.

Setting the pot on the same warm stones upon which they sat their bottoms would usually keep the tea agreeably warm as well, if not hot, which was tolerable to Hahn as long as it did not get completely cold. He did not like cold tea.

This time Hahn joined Elaeric, already on their favorite rock with his eyes closed. Hahn placed the pot upon the warm rock along with the matching porcelain cups. Then he settled his own sit-bones onto its sun-heated surface. He closed his eyes and within ten minutes he was deep into meditation.

The fighter monk was not aware of how much time had passed before he became vaguely aware of the world outside, meaning the world outside of his body. He could sense that the sun had set and, with what he thought of as his outside awareness, turned an eye to the fact that his tea was cooling along with the air and it would soon be cold.

Hahn pointedly turned his attention inward and tried to

gather and draw in his thoughts, the way a fisherman would gather and draw in a net. It was a concentration exercise that Elaeric had taught him, one that had always worked in the past. This time, however, he felt that his net had hitched to a stop. As if it had been caught fast upon something.

Hahn drew a deep breath far down into his lungs, expanding into his belly, and let his whole body relax. He pulled the net of his mind across the cosmos. Unity with everything that there ever was and ever could be was the catch of the day, and had been the focus of all his mediations of late.

A fisherman's net could become snagged on many things in the sea: rock or coral, a drift of wood, even a piece of garbage or the hook of another fisherman. Sometimes the snag could be pulled free, sometimes the net had to be cut.

The mind and being of the monk were filled with the idea of oneness and harmony, but his net was catching on something. Gently, he tugged, trying to return his attention to everything the universe had lain before him, but his mind was stubbornly caught on something.

Forcing patience, he turned his attention to what had snagged his net.

It was a teapot, beautiful and delicate, filled with tea that had been brewed from jasmine blossoms and cardamom pods, and had been piping hot when he had first brought it out. At some point it began to cool, though stayed warm enough for quite some time, and was now growing colder by the second. It was not made better by the fact that Hahn had also become aware of how thirsty he was, and not for cold tea.

Hahn affected a mental sigh, and tried to turn from the teapot that had been painted by hand with dove twigs and cherry blossoms with an elegant pair of cups to match - but the teapot held fast, like a fishhook. Inwardly, the monk looked longingly at the mysteries of the universe, the hushed and comforting bedtime stories of the great mother, and still the part of him snagged, nagged at him about how thirsty he was and how much he hated cold tea.

Hahn fought his inward battle for long minutes until his patience finally found its end. In his mind he saw himself wind his hands deep into his mental net and yank with all his might. He had a momentary feeling of satisfaction as he felt the sensation of the net being released and entirely back into his control before he was nearly scared out of his skin by an explosion directly in front of him.

Hahn's eyes flew open to see Elaeric shielding his own face with his hands from the shards of the teapot as they burst through the air, an aerial attack of missiles shrunk to the size of needles. A particularly large piece tore through the air next to Hahn's face, taking a tiny memento of his cheek while another splinter of the ceramic pot zipped through his left eyebrow. Oddly enough, it was the smaller of the two - the splinter that went through his eyebrow - that left him with a scar for the rest of his life. Or maybe so it seemed, since it kept hair from growing on that particular spot.

Regardless, when the fireworks from the teapot had ceased, Elaeric slowly dropped his hands away from his face and stared at his friend. His brown, normally almond-shaped eyes were large and round.

"I appreciate you always keeping our tea warm," he told Hahn, "but this seems a bit excessive."

Hahn, who had cringed away during the small explosion, straightened. He touched his face and his hand came away with a smear of blood on his fingertips. The monk barely had time to register thanks that he had not been splattered with boiling hot tea. He might have been scalded!

"What do you mean always keeping our tea warm?" he asked.

Elaeric regarded him with surprise. "You mean to say that you did not know?" he asked. When Hahn did not answer the monk cocked his head at his friend. "Our afternoon meditations always are two, three, sometimes four hours. How did you think our tea stayed warm the whole time?"

Hahn sat back, perplexed. "I had never thought about it before. I suppose I thought that the rock, warmed by the sun, helped."

Elaeric laughed. "I am sorry," he apologized when he saw that his laughter did not bemuse his friend, it in fact it did quite the opposite. "I thought you knew."

"Knew what?"

"That it was us."

"Us?"

Elaeric nodded, still beaming. "Part of our energy, a very small part, is always focused on the tea. Like knowing the stove is on in the kitchen, while you are bathing in the next room, or pulling weeds in the garden." Hahn realized that he was right. In such situations, a small piece of the brain was always working, always paying attention, always on track. A tiny part of his attention, sometimes just a glimmer of light in the multitude of the heavens, was always on the tea. Keeping watch. He thought it had been due to how childish he was about the temperature.

"And?"

"And," Elaeric continued, "I think that we create an energy that keeps the tea warm. Tea that sits for two hours, or more, should be dead cold. You have never noticed it before?"

Hahn shook his head, slowly as if disbelieving. "Not until now. But yes, the tea is usually warm. Sometimes it is tepid," he said, making a face, "but it is never cold. It hasn't gotten cold for some months now."

Elaeric nodded. "The times when it is tepid is when I think we are deep in our meditation, and the tea less important to what we are seeing inside. But one of us, however, is usually anchored enough in the present to keep an eye on it - to keep the stove on, so to speak."

"What happened today?" Hahn asked. "Why was today different?"

Elaeric laughed. "Because it is no longer today. Look around you my friend."

Hahn did so and realized with a start that the day had gone. Not into sunset, like it often would when they were in deep meditation, or into actual twilight, like it had done a few times as well. The monk peered at a sky that was full dark, the white-gold constellations bright and mocking in the blue-black expanse above their bald heads. His almond-shaped eyes sought out the familiar group of stars that comprised the sash of Geisha and was surprised again to see it almost directly above his head. Its position in the sky told him that it was close to midnight.

"Today we were both in deep, into ourselves and into the universe, but I think part of you became cognizant of the time that had passed - either by the darkness or from the dip in temperature - and you became worried about the tea. I came back to the present, called by the whistle of steam as the tea boiled away in the pot."

"That's why we weren't sprayed with tea when the pot exploded," Hahn said softly. "It had boiled away."

Elaeric nodded, continuing. "I saw what was happening, but I was afraid to disturb you. I did not have to worry long about what to do, it all happened only seconds after I had opened my eyes."

"I killed a teapot," Hahn realized out loud, his voice cracking and disconsolate.

Elaeric laughed. "Do not worry, my friend. What can destroy, can create."

Hahn looked at his friend sitting across from him on

the rock in the darkened garden, illuminated only by the setting moon. "Are you thinking of exchanging the Zenarchist monastery for that of the Cassar Zealots?" he asked, teasing. "Trading your silky saffron robes for ones of coarse, brown linen?"

Elaeric laughed again. "Only if you think you are The One reborn, which I doubt!"

"Why would you doubt?" Hahn asked, pulling away in mock disbelief.

"Because we do not believe in The One," Elaeric said, bringing a smile to the face of his friend.

"And what is it that we believe in?" Hahn asked, as if he did not know or could not remember.

"The song of the worlds and the symphony of the universe."

"Ah, yes!" Hahn shook his head, a small smile on his face as he began to carefully pick up the pieces of shattered teapot that lay within his reach - some of the larger of which still bore the patterns of dove twigs and cherry blossoms.

"Well, I may not be The One," Hahn told him, "but I will definitely have quite a bit to meditate upon tomorrow regarding creation and destruction."

Elaeric grinned and nodded, delicately placing cream-colored shards of glass into his own open palm. "And I as well, my friend. I as well."

SEVEN

Faith, dressed in a sharply tailored skirt-suit of dove gray tweed, entered the science compound with her youngest sister by her side. Hope was also dressed professionally, though more comfortably and in what she considered more age-appropriate clothing, in black slacks and a pressed shirt that was the same green as her eyes. Her normally wild, copper-colored hair had been gathered and tied at the nape of her neck with a black band of silk.

Faith strode into the main building with her usual confident intensity and was able to hone in on their destination with the skill of a trackhound. The new lab had all the aplomb and excitement of the grand opening of an aircar dealership, though with somewhat less of an audience, and those who were there in attendance were a good deal nerdier than the ordinary folk interested in marketing giveaways and deals on nitrogen.

“This way,” Faith instructed, making a sharp turn down a corridor floored in linoleum and lit by fluorescents. She followed two young people in white lab coats wearing SE-drive glasses, the frames black and round, making them look owlish. Hope followed silently as the corridor led her and Faith to what was obviously a new wing that had been added on to the pre-existing building. The hallway was substantially wider, with tile floors and lit by hidden LEDs.

Trailing behind a number of white-coated scientists and others too young to be anything but assistants and interns, the sisters funneled into a laboratory hosting a private celebration. Faith’s brown and gold eyes swept the room, taking it all in with a single glance.

It was a run of the mill laboratory. The main area was large but not roomy. Gleaming black countertops ran the length of each wall, with one more topping an island that split the room in two. It had the usual equipment on the usual sterilized countertops and the usual high-backed stools were pushed underneath them. A row of brass hooks hung with white coats lined the entry wall.

If the lab was on the brink of harnessing Zero-Point Energy, it did not show. Then again, the lab was brand new, and Faith knew that the results would not show in the lab itself, but in what happened there.

The first thing Hope noticed was that all of the small equipment items on the long, high counters had been pushed back against the walls to make room for stacks of small plates and napkins, trays of appetizers, and rows of clear plastic cups that had been pre-filled with brightly-colored drinks.

"Ooh!" Hope exclaimed, spying the cups. "What are those?"

Faith made a face. "Geek juice. Caffeinated soda and liquor. Unless you want a racing heart now and a headache later, I wouldn't advise it."

"My heart is already racing," Hope whispered, bringing a smile to Faith's lips as she glanced around the lab, which seemed to run close to the norm for the areas expressly concerned with science. Nodes, micros, and burners took up a significant amount of space. A double centrifuge dominated one corner while another corner of the room was overrun by a pneumatic tube system that waited eagerly to shoot encapsulated samples to who knew where else in the compound or beyond.

Faith stopped a young man by gently grabbing the elbow of his white lab coat and he turned quickly, surprised as if he had been caught crashing the party. He had bright blue eyes over high cheekbones and black hair that was thick but cropped close to his head on the sides and brushed forward in the middle, framing his narrow face and accentuating his high, pointed ears

"Excuse me," Faith said, "do you work here?" The elf gave her a beguiling smile of even, white teeth.

"In part. I'm the Safety Officer for this wing."

"Really?" Faith asked before she could stop herself. He seemed awfully young to be a Safety Officer, but then pure elves always seemed younger to her than they really were. The elf nodded with a smirk, as if reading her thoughts.

"Elves always look young to humans," he told her as his smirk widened into a genuine smile, "but you can trust me, I'm a doctor - just not the medical kind. I have probably been in school longer than you have been alive."

Faith, in turn, knew that he was mistaking her for a human the way she was mistaking him for a youth. After all, her ears had been rounded to represent human ears and she was quite precocious for a human, even more so for an elf.

"I see," she said, her eyes leaving his to travel across the room that was just short of being crowded. She spied two small rooms that adjoined the one hosting the little party. A steel door on the right wall and another in the back wall led to the ancillary rooms and both were visible via reinforced glass windows. Faith recognized one as a shock chamber and another as a culture room.

What were not recognizable to Faith were the actual scientists. It was no great surprise. After all, she was in another field of science entirely – not to mention on another moon. She leaned back towards the young, elfin Safety Officer.

"And who is the Lab Commander in all this joviality?" she asked. The elf grinned from under his short curtain of dark hair.

"That one, over there," he said, motioning with his chin

before jerking his head to flick the hair away from his face.

Faith turned her head, following his gaze to see a fairly young human male with terribly short hair that was neither blonde nor brown and slightly wide-spaced eyes that were blue and piercing. Even from a distance, Faith could tell that the most distinct attribute he had was arrogance, which the group fawning around him obviously mistook for charisma.

The eldest de Rossi watched with a trace of disgust as the man shook hands and took blathers of praise as he made his way around the room.

"How capable is he?" she asked the elf. "Any idea?"

The elf shrugged. "He is either very capable, or very lucky," he answered. "Maybe a bit of both. He certainly has made some great discoveries, making more progress on the ZPE than anyone else in this system."

Faith nodded as she watched the man and his clucking flock of interns and budding scientists make their way across the room. The scientist in question finally reached her and Hope where they stood waiting with the elfin Safety Officer. The man drew to a halt, peering at them both in surprise as he had no idea who either of them might be. A shadow cloaked his features and Faith realized that the man's first impulse was to boot them out of the lab, or – better yet - call security to do it for him.

"I'm sorry," he said with a frown, "but this is..."

Faith stepped forward quickly, her face taking a pleasant expression as she offered him her hand. "Dr. Biri, I am so pleased to make your acquaintance." The man shook her hand, his blue eyes searching her face as he tried to decipher who she was. "I am Kaylee Noir," she told him, stepping aside as his face lit up in recognition of her name, "and this is Hope Walsh, the winner of our first scholarship to benefit this lab - though, I am sure, not the last." She followed her statement with a lighthearted laugh that was echoed by others in the small crowd that had followed the Lab Commander.

"Of course!" he agreed. "And thank you so much for your generous donation!" He looked at Hope, the young woman's green eyes wide and shining, and gave her a broad smile. "It is a pleasure to meet you, Miss Walsh," he told her, reaching out to grasp her hand. "Though I must say, you are much too lovely to be a physics intern!"

"Thank you," Hope gushed. "It's a pleasure to he here!"

A small line formed between Faith's brows.

"Have you found a place in the area? A place close by?" he asked.

"Yes, it's in the first burb past the main gate."

He clucked his tongue as if the place were distasteful. "At least that is close-by," he offered as consolation. "Did you just get here, or are you settling in?"

"Oh, settling in! We've, I mean I, have been here for three weeks."

"Excellent! So you will be able to start on Lunday?"

"Oh, yes!"

"Excellent!" he repeated. "May I introduce you to who we will be working with?"

"Yes, please."

Dr. Biri looked at Faith with forced politeness and she realized that his blue eyes were not just wide-spaced, but that they were off center by just a hair. She doubted that anyone but herself would notice.

"Ms. Noir, would you like to meet our laboratory staff as well?"

Faith shook her brown and gold locks, giving him an emphatic, if negative, response. "Oh no, thank you. I am terrible with names and know so little of actual science." She held out a hand, encouraging them to leave her behind. She watched, less than pleased, as the Lab Commander led Hope away, her sister already as enthralled with him as his cronies were.

Her mouth held tight in an effort not to grimace or frown, she turned to see the elfin Safety Officer grinning at her.

"Yes?" she asked.

"You don't like him, do you?"

Though Faith remained tight-lipped, her eyes changed her expression entirely. "Do you?" she asked. The elf turned his bright blue eyes to the retreating form of the Lab Commander.

"Not particularly, no," he said, keeping his voice low and watching as Dr. Biri comfortably rested a hand on Hope's shoulder while he introduced her to some of the others. Faith saw the same familiar gesture and made a face.

"Not only is he the Lab Commander," she said, "he is the only doctorate here. Other than you of course?"

"Of course. The others are all students and interns."

Faith nodded. A man that arrogant would not want to risk anyone questioning his authority. Also, he would micromanage his staff to such a degree that he would receive a co-credit, if not a full accreditation to any discoveries anyone else made in the lab. She knew a control-freak when she saw one. After all, it took one to know one – though she considered herself to be more of a purist who did not believe in compromising ideals rather than a self-centered egotist.

"What is your doctorate in?" she asked without looking away from the back of the Lab Commander. The question was more conversational than curious, but his answer caught her off guard.

"Quantum physics."

Faith's head turned sharply to face him and she looked

at him as though seeing him for the first time. It was a few seconds before she spoke.

"Do you have a lab here at the 'Plex?" she asked, trying to sound casual.

"No," he answered, still grinning. "I'm just here as a Safety Officer."

Faith's brown and gold eyes became piercing, as if trying to stare right through him and, indeed, that was exactly what she did. The responsibility of a Safety Officer, even one for an entire wing, was a grad-student job at best. Certainly not for someone with a doctorate in quantum physics. She knew then that he was no more of a mere Safety Officer than Hope was a scholarship winner. Which meant that he was probably there for the same reason - as a spy.

Though she remained guarded, Faith's body relaxed, cocking her head as she looked at him. "And how well is the pay for a Safety Officer these days?"

He shrugged. "I guess that all depends on how well I do my job."

"Mmhmm. Well, if you could use a little extra, I would really appreciate it if you could keep an eye on her," Faith said with a scarcely discernible motion of her head towards the group in the middle of the lab that was currently passing out drinks to toast their bold hero.

"Of course," he agreed. "I could always use a little extra."

Faith decided that his boyish smile was more than a bit mischievous, but she couldn't help but like him. Whether he was being dangerously honest or outright lying, she knew that he was different from all of the other phonies in the lab.

"And I trust we will keep this agreement clandestine?"

The elf's grin widened and when he spoke his voice was low again, meant only for her ears. "Your secret is safe with me, Dr. de Rossi."

Faith's only show of surprise was a brief glimmer in her gold and brown eyes. Not only had he seen though her alias and had known who she was, but had addressed her as doctor. She had just received her first doctorate only a month ago. The event had been highly publicized, but only within a relatively small medical field.

She reached into an inner pocket and pulled out her credentials card. "And I will keep yours, Doctor..." she trailed off, handing him her card. He took the card from her and retrieved his own from a pocket in his lab coat and placed them against each other. There was a flicker of light as his card retrieved from hers a small file that was commonly pre-set into credential equipment so that new acquaintances and associates may share unguarded information and contact one another.

"Galen," he said. "Just call me Galen."

8

Gwendolyn wiped her hands on her long skirts, her insides fluttering with nervous excitement. Her studio, though large, seemed crowded to her. Everyone was present, even me - the way an entire family might show up for the birth of child. It was Charity and Llewellyn, however, that would be acting as midwives.

The platinum-haired twins had brought with them dozens of pictures on their portable computes and had loaded them onto the panels in Gwendolyn's studio, or had them projected directly upon the walls, and were giving her instruction after instruction concerning the face and form of prototype B28.

The basic specifications for B28 had already been done in the HoloScuplt, making Gwendolyn's job much too easy for her taste or conscience. She had finished the broad stroke version in a single evening.

At least two weeks worth of work had it been done in clay, she thought with a trace of bitterness. *And the masters would have fought with a block of marble for months to coax such an apparition from the stone, possibly years.* She had the solace of knowing that it would take her weeks to finish the details. Though his coloring and tone would be produced from the computer, Gwen would create everything else, down to the delicate hairs on the backs of his hands.

The shape now waited, standing six and a quarter feet tall, inside Gwendolyn's HoloSculpt. Blue lines of laser light crossed over every inch of the form in a dimensional grid that relayed every point and angle to a dual compute she shared with Faith. The dyer touched a panel on the machine and it collapsed slowly, the lower portion of the body temporarily shimmering out of existence to bring the head down to a height that would make it easier and more comfortable for her to do her work.

"Don't forget he's going to need all that again," Charity teased, her voice low.

"And make sure he has all his arms and legs," Llewellyn added, making Charity giggle. They knew of Gwen's penchant for ancient art and many adorned her studio and the home she shared with Faith. God only knew why - when most of the pieces were missing their appendages.

"And certainly don't forget the most important part!" Charity said.

Llewellyn uttered a throaty chuckle, knowing what part her twin meant. It too, was often missing from the old statues Gwen favored. "That's right," she agreed. "Definitely don't forget his..."

"Girls!" Cronus commanded harshly. The elf cleared his throat and, lowering his voice, added, "you have given Gwendolyn your specifications, and she knows what she is doing. Let her work."

"Yes, Grandfather," they chimed in unison, and then hid smirks behind their hands like a pair of schoolgirls.

Faith, standing with her arms crossed over her chest, threw them a sidelong glance before looking back to where her twin was putting her hands inside the HoloSculpt. Everyone in the room, myself included, held a collective breath as Gwendolyn put her hands on the face and began to shape it.

"Give him a strong jaw line," Charity instructed immediately.

Gwendolyn drew steady fingers – one on each side of the face - along the jaw, making it straight and smooth.

"More," Llewellyn said. "Make the angle sharper."

Gwendolyn did as instructed until she heard Charity's breath catch in her throat. Smiling, filled with a deep sense of accomplishment and the excitement of having only just begun, the dyer moved on to the chin.

"Like this," Llewellyn said, illuminating a picture of a man's face that had been projected onto the wall of the studio.

When the chin had been formed to perfection, Charity lit up another picture that had been loaded onto a panel. "This is how his nose should be."

Gwen glanced at the picture and began to replicate the nose. "The cheekbones in that same picture work well with this face," she suggested.

Charity cocked her head as she examined the picture and then looked at Llewellyn, who shrugged. "If you say so, but can you make them just a tad higher? We have a pretty clear idea of what Ivana will find irresistible."

"Of course," Gwendolyn said, an indulgent smile on her own illuminated countenance as she used her thumbs to shape the nose before moving on to his cheekbones, her eyes occasionally flicking to the pictures on the wall panels that Charity and Llewellyn had provided.

"Ivana won't be the only one," Faith murmured, watching her twin mold and shape the most perfect face for a man that she had ever seen.

Gwen moved on to his brow and from there to his ears. It was probably thirty minutes gone when she finished the facial features and she began to work down to his neck. It seemed to take Gwen more time to sculpt the upper part of his chest and shoulders. We watched as she kept going back and forth between the two, trying to get the perfect balance.

Regardless of how long it took, everyone in the room was mesmerized as she worked, and most of us were near speechless when the bust was complete.

"My God," Cronus said.

I shot the elf a look of disapproval but even I had to admit that what the dyer had done was nothing short of astonishing.

"He's beautiful," Faith whispered admiring the work of her twin.

"He's just like I pictured," Charity said, her voice quiet with amazement.

Llewellyn nodded in agreement, as tongue tied as myself.

Gwen stepped back, smiling at her work and their praise, distractedly wiping her hands on her shirt only out of habit, since they were perfectly clean. "I'll work on this every day and should finish him by the end of this week," she said, "but I would like everyone to stop in whenever you can to offer me guidance on his form."

"You don't need guidance," Faith told her.

A blush crept up Gwen's cheeks. "Still," she said, "I would love to have everyone's input."

"I'm sending you the specs on hair color right now," Llewellyn continued, speaking to Faith even though her eyes were still fixed on the bust of the man suspended upright in the elongated box of the HoloSculpt. She touched a button on her portable compute, moving slowly, as if in a dream.

"And his eyes?" Faith asked. Did you finally decide on the exact color?"

Charity and Llewellyn had been going round and round for weeks trying to pick the exact shade of green.

"Yes," Charity said, also unable to tear her eyes away from the striking figure in the HoloSculpt, her voice tinged with the melancholy tone so prevalent in Madeline. "Make them this color," she said, holding up a small object with her right hand.

At first, I thought the object was a large gem - a sparkling jewel in the most beguiling shade of green that I had ever seen.

When Gwendolyn, however, stepped closer for a better look, the light caught the object and I saw that it was too smooth and uniform to be a stone of any kind.

"What is it?" she asked.

"A piece of glass," Charity answered, her eyes still glued to the face of B28. "We found it last week on the beach."

The corner of Llewellyn's mouth twitched up in a smile. "I almost cut my aaaaa!!!" she shouted as her twin stuck an elbow in her side.

"Her foot," Charity finished for her, her attention finally torn from the face of the construct. Her blue eyes darted over to their grandfather. She knew when to be discreet, even when her dyer did not.

"Yes," Llewellyn agreed, frowning at Charity for the less than gentle poke in the ribs, "my foot."

My own blue eyes followed the piece as Charity handed it over to Faith. I recognized the glass from a bottle of beer that was popular at the local fraternities these days and I suspected that Charity and Llewellyn had been at one of the notorious college bonfires by the lake.

"That really is an exquisite color," Cronus admitted. He admired the glass that had almost ended up in Llewellyn's backside as Faith held it up to the light, a small smile tucked into the corner of her mouth.

"Can you replicate that color?" Gwen asked, transfixed by the glimmering piece of glass in the same way the younger sister and her dyer seemed to be spellbound by the face of B28. "I've never seen anything quite like it."

"You bet Llewellyn's foot, I can," Faith said with a smirk.

*

It took Gwendolyn ten days rather than seven to finish B28,

but only because she was enjoying the work too much to stop. Even after Charity and Llewellyn had given every last opinion and modification they thought the construct warranted, Gwen kept at it until Faith told her to quit nit picking and move on to the next one.

The next one, E19, only took Gwen two days. Because Ynetsra Malin was after something specific, and Charity and Llewellyn were insistent that it be exactly like Ynin Malin as he had been when his daughter was a child, it left little to artistic license or creativity. Disappointed, Gwen dragged it on for a third day, making minor adjustments until once again Faith told her to stop.

She found consolation in the fact that she would be able to work on J7 for as long as she liked, within reason of course.

The buyer for J7 had not been set and, though her younger sisters were zeroing in on one, until a prospect was found and nailed down, Gwendolyn was allowed a blank slate on which to create. It made her want to lace her hands and stretch out her arms, like a great piano concertist getting ready to play.

Anxious to begin on the last of the males, but wanting to be alone, Gwen waited until the compound was closed and dark. Faith, of course, was still working in her lab and when Gwendolyn entered her studio and dimmed the lights, she found a flute of champagne waiting for her on the glass desk. It sat on a small, square napkin – white and plain save for a heart that had been drawn on it with a calamink pen.

Gwen picked up the tall, slender glass and admired the bubbles racing through the golden liquid before turning her face to the window that separated her studio from Faith's lab. Faith stood on the other side of the pane, leaning on her desk and holding an identical flute of champagne. Smiling, she lifted her glass towards Gwen in salutation, and Gwen did the same.

The dyer took a long drink of the sparkling wine and smiled as it left a trail of effervescence down her throat. She put the glass down and looked at her compute panel, already deciding on the music she would play, but found a selection already in the queue. She looked back over her shoulder at Faith and saw her twin laugh on the other side of the glass.

The song that had been highlighted was another duo composed by Turner and Bernstein but remade only recently. It was buoyant yet romantic and was the same piece that Gwendolyn would have chosen. Shaking her head in amusement at Faith's preparations, she sat down on a high stool and opened a private window on her compute screen. Earlier in the week, dawdling over the construct for Malin, Gwen had started preparing for the last male construct by loading whatever she could find regarding classical art from the Galactic Web.

The screen now had an array of photos taken of ancient sculptures, paintings, sketches, and prints that included more than just human and elfin classics. Her brown and gold eyes traveled over the pics that included what Aridians and even Golgoths considered form and beauty. If she spent enough time dissecting the figures on a linear level, she could see what the Aridians found attractive. However, no amount of time or study could get her to understand what the Golgoths considered beauty, unless it was the bright color of their exoskeletal plates. Each picture made her shudder.

Maybe classic isn't the way to go, Gwendolyn mused, looking at a restored lithograph of the human god, Adonis. *Maybe new, if not original, would be better.* She took another drink of champagne from the flute and stared dreamily at the HoloSculpt.

It had been three years now since Gwen and Faith had graduated from the Elusk University on Pram. Gwendolyn had enjoyed her time there, finding pleasure in her classes even though she missed being with Faith during the day and sometimes even at night. Faith had thrown herself into her studies with her usual vigor and their classes could hardly have been more different.

All of Gwen's studies revolved around art. Though she felt that she fell terribly short at painting, she was quite talented at sculpting with composite, clay, or even holo though she certainly did not prefer it. When she wasn't learning art technique she was studying art history. The farthest she veered away from the true craft was to dabble in literature, especially enjoying epic poetry and sagas.

Faith was quite the opposite. She immersed herself in biology and chemistry, veering away now and again only to theoretical mathematics. Once, delighted more than Gwen had ever seen her twin with an equation she had solved, she showed it to her dyer, projecting the holo in the room they shared where the calculation took up an entire wall. Her twin had looked at the seemingly endless rows of numbers, letters, slashes, and squiggly marks that looked to her like ancient, evil pictographs.

"It looks like surgery," Gwen had told her, making a face that portrayed equal amounts of distress and nausea. "If not murder."

Faith had laughed as if giddy and theatrically planted a smacking kiss on her cheek. Gwen made an exaggerated show of wiping it off, laughing as well. Though Gwendolyn often interacted with teachers and other students, the conversations were brief and to the point. She did not think of them outside of school. The only other people that occupied her thoughts were those in her family. She rarely, if ever, took actual notice of the other students on campus other than to avoid running into them physically when walking down the hallways. They were just people, and most people did not concern her. In that way she was like her twin.

One day, however, as she sat on a large stone close to the mossy pond in the middle of campus, she noticed two people sitting on a blanket they had spread out on the grass for a picnic lunch. Gwen watched them intently, her own lunch of fruit and cheese momentarily forgotten on her lap.

One was a human male, probably in his early twenties, close to Gwen's own age. The female was elfin and, though she looked like a teenager, was probably in her fifties. It seemed a common age match on campus, due to the different maturation rates of the different species. The young woman had bright blonde hair, like Charity and Llewellyn, but cut short. The young man had golden brown hair much like Faith's or, she supposed, her own. He was handsome, though not striking, and had a slight dimple in his chin.

With her sharp eyesight, Gwendolyn could discern the different colors of his deep-set hazel eyes even at a distance. The blend of his eye color was interesting, but it was the look in those eyes that captivated her. She could tell by the way he looked at the elfin female that he was unaware of anything else in the world but the woman in front of him.

He must be in love with her, the dyer thought with sudden realization, and was struck with wonder. Gwen loved all of her sisters, their mother and their grandfather, and even their father who treated them all with such indifference. But she knew that what she was witnessing was something else entirely. This was a woman with whom he had no relation. Just a person he had met somewhere and somehow. At some point this man found he could not tear his eyes from her face. A meteor could come streaming by, trailing ash and fire, and still he would only stare in wonder at the woman next to him. He listened attentively as she said something, hanging on her every word. The she laughed lightly and he smiled, either at what she said or at her delight in it.

Gwen felt something tug deep inside her body and, for the first time in her life, she began to speculate if anyone would ever love her that way. She watched him brushing a strand of hair from the woman's narrow, girlish face as she laughed and wondered if anyone would ever touch her like that.

Mesmerized, she watched them for endless minutes until he finally leaned forward and gave the young woman a long, lingering kiss on her lips. Seeing them with their eyes closed to the world in a moment of pure intimacy, Gwen had suddenly felt as though she had been invading their privacy, though the couple was sitting in a public place in the middle of campus.

Feeling her face grow hot, she averted her eyes and quickly began gathering the remains of her small lunch, tucking it into the leather and canvas satchel that Faith had given her at the beginning of the semester. She stood quickly, brushing down her skirt and hurrying from the campus park.

Faith, who had been hoping to catch her twin at the lake and share lunch, had arrived just in time to seen her twin watching the couple having their picnic and, in turn, had stopped and watched Gwendolyn, fascinated.

It was not hard to guess what her twin was seeing for the first time, though she was surprised by the way Gwen had unexpectedly packed up and hurried from the scene. Faith, a small crease between her brows, watched Gwendolyn scurry away with her cheeks flushed and then turned back to take another look at the young man with golden brown hair and hazel eyes. After a few long moments she left, returning to her own side of the campus, as deep in thought as her twin was flustered.

Gwendolyn started the music and the notes began to form from the corners of her studio, growing like smoke from small fires in the wall. She reached into the HoloSculpt and could not help but be drawn back to the image of the young man she had seen just a few years ago, brushing a strand of hair away from a woman's face. She wondered briefly if they were still together, if he still looked at the elfin female in the same way as he had that day or if they still even knew each other, but the thought was disconnected and far back in her mind. Most of her attention was busy recalling the shape of his face, the proportions of his cheekbones and the line of his brow – trying to draw out the same expression that she had seen on that sunny afternoon.

Faith watched her twin through the glass that separated her lab from the studio and before long she too was brought back to that day she had seen Gwen hurry from her favorite spot by the pond in the campus park. With a small crease between her brows, Faith sipped her champagne and wondered and watched and waited.

Gwendolyn started from the top of the forehead and worked down, something Faith had never seen her do before. Usually, her twin started with the nose and worked outwards. Curious, she watched her form the brow, and deeply set his eyes. The line in her brow deepened and she leaned forward, watching intently as Gwen molded prominent cheekbones. She drained her glass and retrieved the bottle from the chill plate on her desk without looking. Also, without looking, she refilled her flute with champagne and returned the bottle to the plate.

She watched as Gwen made his jaw sharp, like the other two she had already sculpted. A strong jaw was both classic and timeless. This one, however, was more pointed at the chin than B28, less than E19 – the elfin construct. This jaw line ended in a chin that was somewhere in between, but she had feeling it was no accident or hem hawing on Gwendolyn's part.

Faith watched her hands, hands that were identical to her own except in the fact they were far more comfortable in clay and composite than holding a beaker full of retrogacid, focusing an electroscope, or a stylus that was constantly scribbling formulas onto a compute. Her gold and brown eyes followed Gwen's right hand as it came down the jaw line of the face she was sculpting and across his square chin. It paused for a second and then pulled away. Even with the distance and through the glass, and though it was very subtle, her sharp eyes could see where Gwendolyn had given just an extra bit of pressure with her thumb, leaving a slight dimple there.

NINE

Hahn and Elaeric sat upon their favorite flat stone in the rock garden of the monastery, the sun shining down at an angle as it made its descent towards the horizon, yet still bright and warm upon their bald pates. Stunted pines grew in a perfectly planned haphazard fashion around the rocks and up the slope.

"I am sorry about your teapot," Hahn said. He had just learned that the teapot, the delicate ceramic vessel painted with dove twigs and cherry blossoms that he had caused to combust, had belonged personally to Elaeric. Quite likely something that he had brought to the monastery from his native country, his home.

His friend made a face and waved a hand at the apology the way one would wave at a foul smell in the air.

"Nonsense," he said. "And no apology is needed. It had a crack in it anyway. That being said, however, please have care regarding our current pot." He looked meaningfully at the peach-colored teapot painted with bluebirds that sat upon their flat stone, flanked by two shallow ceramic cups on saucers that matched the steaming pot.

"I will do my best," Hahn promised, bowing his head low in humble acquiescence. As his head rose and his body straightened, so did Elaeric, visibly eager.

"Now," the younger monk announced, rubbing his hands on his robe-covered knees, "what is this garden missing?"

Hahn blinked his brown eyes, thinking about the question in earnest. "Water," he answered almost immediately. "Rivers border the monastery, but there should be a stream here. Bounding over stones, chattering its way to the sea."

Elaeric smiled. "I agree. And flowers - we need more flowers. Butterflies and birds should abound, not that I am not grateful of the crickets," he added quickly. "And the occasional frog is a sign of good luck."

Hahn cocked his head, suddenly curious. He knew that Elaeric did not care for the frogs. Their croaking was the one thing that seemed to get under the skin of the usually ebullient monk.

"Having gratitude for what you already have," Elaeric explained before the other monk could ask, "lays the groundwork for what you will receive."

"In that case," Hahn said, "let me begin by saying how grateful I am for having you as my friend."

Elaeric, beaming like a ray from the sun, pressed his hands together in front of his chest and bowed to Hahn before straightening and settling into a comfortable position with his eyes closed. Hahn did the same. They had been discussing this meditation for many days over many meals and walks through the monastery.

After many talks about visualization and manifestation, they had agreed upon doing a combined meditation with the two of them directing their concentration on the same intention.

Hahn shifted his body as he also got into a comfortable position on his narrow butt bones, brushing away the slight edge of nervousness that was trying to settle on his skin. The first thing he did was to make a conscious decision not to think about the tea. *If it gets cold, I will drink it cold,* he told himself.

The monk closed his eyes and began to concentrate first on his breathing, as he always did. Slowly, he took in the environment around him - the sun on his face, the warm rock under his backside, the whisper of the wind that blew down the hill from the Temple. Then, gradually, he let them go.

The sigh of the breeze dropped away and with it went the muted sounds of combat training. Slowly but surely, the sun and the rock disappeared. He forgot the feel of the robes against his skin. Bit by bit, he lost himself. He listened to the beat of his heart, and then the pulse of the universe. Silently, he asked for forgiveness and gave forgiveness without being asked. He stretched out with the arms of his mind, throwing out his net with complete abandon.

It is not the net you must draw to you this time, but the water.

It was not a thought, but an echo that came from somewhere deep inside his consciousness. Like an echo from an underground cave. One where the walls were wet with moisture and the water dripped from the ceiling. The water.

Remember the water, the water is what you are after.

Hahn lost himself in the sea of the universe and, unknowingly and without conscious effort, drew a single deep breath and let it out over the course of an entire minute. When his outside mind became aware of a chill, he wrapped himself in a galaxy of suns, their warmth radiating into him, feeding him. It was a meditation in which he completely freed himself and gave back freely.

He breathed deeply and slowly the entire time, inhaling the dust of the stars and the water of the worlds. The water.

Not still water, a voice in his mind spoke. The reminder was so small and so faint that it seemed no more than a distant memory. The small part of Hahn that was still a conscious mind realized that the memory was not his own, the voice was not his own. As he realized this, the voice spoke again. It was soft as down, rising like a maid from a pool. *Not a pool. Moving water.*

Now Hahn swam through the universe as if it were a deep

dark lake. It surrounded his body and filled his lungs. The sound of it swished into his ears and his mind. He rose to the surface and floated on the gentle current, letting it take him to where the lake fed a waterfall. He tumbled and plunged, then he was dodging rocks with the grace of a minnow in a wide stream –beautifully deep and cold. It washed over him even as it carried him away, chattering softly and telling him secrets.

I am the dreamer and the dream maker. I am the dream itself.

Hahn felt himself float, dip, submerge – and completely lose his breath. There was no longer a need for air because his awareness had spread and become the water. He became a stream, then a river as he merged with other streams. He stretched into a yawning lake that reached long fingers into the mountains, carving caves, caverns, and wells. He stretched again until he became part of an underground ocean before he shot free, spouting from a well in a geyser of liquid that fell like rain and gathered into another pool that grew and grew, fed by the waters beneath the crust.

The pool widened and spilled, guided by gravity and the curves in the land, downhill in a rushing stream. Then Hahn contracted and became a single drop sitting upon a leaf that rode upon the stream. The drop trembled with joy, riding on the water and listening to it talk, soothe, shout and cajole.

Gurgling, lapping, dancing - the sound grew louder. He was the drop and everything else was the sound. He felt so small and yet was assured of his own significance as the sound of the water grew and grew – consuming him. The sound was all that there was until the memory came, rising like a bubble in water of course, to remind him that there were other senses. He could smell the water and he could see the water – if only he became aware.

The nascent stream spread over the ground, filling a crevice before diving down over the hill. At the bottom it hit a pebble and changed course in such a small yet violent fashion that the leaf flipped and the drop of dew that was Hahn was drowned, lost, merged with the whole. Then he was spat away, separate again, a single drop from a great stream - from rivers and oceans and lakes – a solitary fragment left quivering on a smooth round stone. He could hear the multitude of the other drops, calling to him with the sound of rushing water.

The tide of consciousness pulled back, leaving him like the survivor of a shipwreck washed up on the shore, and the universe fell away as Hahn opened his eyes so they could see what his ears were hearing.

His first thought that was that he *had* been shipwrecked. It felt as if his robes had been soaked through, his entire body ached, and his stomach clawed at his abdomen with a deep and gnawing hunger.

It took him a moment to realize that his robes were soaked with dew, and cold. He was horribly stiff from sitting for so long in the same position. And he was truly ravenous from missing a meal, maybe two.

Hahn's physical feelings, however, paled in comparison to what his eyes were feasting upon.

In the early dawn of the monastery grounds, a tiny stream burbled and bubbled its way through the garden as it followed the crevice of the hills down in search of the sea. It was caressed on each side by rows and rows of flowers, some tall and some short, all with brilliant colors and swarmed by morning butterflies and the occasional bit-bird as it darted in and out.

Hahn laughed and clapped his hands together even as he collapsed forward, catching himself with a splayed palm upon the surface of the stone where he sat. His dark, almond-shaped eyes were crusty at the corners as he looked around, exhausted. The sun had not yet crested the horizon, but its early morning light painted distant clouds a gentle pinkish orange.

"I have meditated the whole night through!" Hahn exclaimed, ecstatic. His eyes sought out his friend, sitting directly in front of him. "*We* have," he corrected himself. "We have meditated he whole night!"

Elaeric leaned forward, his saffron colored robes damp and slightly dingy. He reached out and fastened a hand around his friend's knee. "Not one night, my friend. Two!"

Hahn, too exhausted to argue, closed his eyes and listened to the brook that now ran through the monastery garden. He had been deep into his meditation, but could hardly believe that it had been an entire night. Much less...

"Two?" he inquired, his eyes fluttering open as the words of his friend sank in. "Are you sure?"

"At least!" his friend answered. "When I first opened my eyes, it was dawn. I only assumed it was the day after we started our late-afternoon meditation. The light was as it is now. Your stream was here, almost. A small pool of water had welled up and was beginning to trickle away. I ignored the rumble in my belly and went back to meditation. When I opened my eyes again, the flowers were there, not yet bloomed but huddled tight against the banks in the pre-dawn light." He paused to adjust his sparse frame about on his narrow bottom. "I will admit that I was hungry, and went to the kitchens for a bun, but I assure you that I came right back!"

Hahn grinned, though his own stomach rumbled at the thought of a bun from the kitchens. Rumbled angrily, so much that it bordered on painful. Hahn ignored it. "And?" he prodded.

"And," Elaeric continued, "here we are!"

Hahn pushed himself up, his joints and bones creaking and snapping at him in loud protest. His muscles, which had been trained to fight for days on end if need be, gave an angry squall for being held still for so long in the same position. He balled his hands into fists and put them above his sore sit-bones, arching his back and stretching.

Elaeric stood and joined him as he looked down upon what they had made.

No, the younger monk thought, correcting himself. *Not made. It was already made. We merely called it together, manifesting what already was into what could be.*

"The first thing I remember, once I was clear, was calling to the water," Hahn said suddenly, looking at all of the flowers, their myriad of color painting the banks of the stream with every shade of the rainbow.

Elaeric's smile widened. "That could have been me," he suggested.

Hahn's face turned so that he could see his friend. "And that was your voice I heard. The one that sounded like a memory!"

Elaeric shrugged, though the smile did not leave his broad face. "The first time I opened my eyes I saw the water. It was pooling, but slowly, as if it were coming from a leaky pipe. I was intent on getting it moving. It seems that it took you, or our combined efforts, to get it going down the hill."

Hahn looked at the moving water - infinitely pleased, though not with himself. With the power of the universe. He was wise enough to know that he was merely a conduit. He closed his eyes, listening to the hushed burble of the stream, stopping his own breath to hear the beat of the wings of the butterflies.

"All I knew was the water. Separation. Oneness. Separation again. It brings to light what we have always already believed. But the water - especially the sound of it. It was everything. What about you?"

"Separation and oneness, yes!" Elaeric agreed. "It was as if I were a seed. A dry seed, cradled in the soil, which needed water. But I was not alone. I was a single seed, and yet a multitude of seeds at the same time! A garden unborn. Waiting and dormant. The water was there, but far away. I yearned for it. I called to it. The other seeds called as well, infinitesimal voices joining in song. I cannot describe the feeling!"

"There is no need," Hahn told him with an ever-widening grin. "I don't know if there are words that exist to describe being a drop in the ocean. But tell me, if you can, what you felt the most."

"The colors," the younger monk replied without hesitation, watching the butterflies dance. "I actually could feel color! The darkness as it turned into light. And the smell. The rich fragrance of the soil and the sweet and cold aroma of the water as it seeped towards me. It was fresh and invigorating, almost like the smell of a freshly bleached floor I am embarrassed to say."

Hahn smiled at him. "Do not be embarrassed. That is a smell that one cannot help but associate with chlorine, and usually it is the most clean aroma that one can call to mind or associate with cleanliness, even if it is a chemical."

"And the flowers," Elaeric added. "Once the water arrived there was only the smell of life! The fresh green smell of the grasses and stems as they pushed from soil into sunlight – and I could smell the fragrance of the flowers before they had even become buds, much less blooms! It seemed to consume me."

Hahn drew in a great breath of air through his nostrils and found that the perfume of the flora was as powerful as their colors. "And here we are," he said, marveling at what they had done.

"Indeed," Elaeric said. "Though, I must say, you let our tea get cold!"

Hahn grinned at his friend as a fraction of his attention focused on the peach-colored teapot, painted with bluebirds, which sat upon their flat stone. He could see the flicker in

Elaeric's eyes and knew that his friend was doing the same thing.

Hahn laughed and stretched his arms out to either side. He lifted his chin, stretching his neck. Inwardly, he stretched the muscles of his mind and the ones of his soul. The result of their meditation might not have been impressive to anyone happening by – the tiny tributary was barely wider than his hand and the flowers were nothing but normal garden variety. But he and Elaeric had called them, and they had answered.

"I do hope you brought more than one bun from the kitchens," he said as he laced his hands together before stretching his arms out in front of his body. The bones in his back popped one at a time.

"Of course," Elaeric agreed, first kicking with one foot and then the other as he made an effort to get his blood moving as he moved back towards their flat stone. "I even pinched a few small muffins, knowing that you would be as famished as I, or more."

Hahn stretched and flexed and joined his friend on their stone, sitting back down in front of the peach-colored teapot that held tea that was, once again and quite suddenly, piping hot. Hahn lifted it gently as steam rushed from its slender spout.

"Shall I pour?" he asked.

Elaeric smiled his seemingly never-ending smile. "If you would be so kind," he said.

ONE ZERO

I ran my hand across my head, pushing the blonde hair back from my eyes. The cut was fashionable but longer than what I was used to, certainly long enough to make my grandmother cluck her tongue at me had she been there. The thought of her made me smile as I tucked the foldout computer under my arm.

I walked down the sterile hallway of the compound with more spring in my step than usual. I had to admit that I was excited about starting the lessons for the day. Though I had been unsure of a lot from the start, the first being working with manufactured humans (and one manufactured elf) and the last being that I hadn't spoken French in almost a decade, both worries turned out to be fruitless.

The constructs turned out to be almost as normal as could be. They were a bit naïve and curious, but no more than a tourist to a new planet. They each had a singular beauty about them that was breathtaking, refined and exotic, even after seeing them every day for almost a year. That Gwendolyn had done amazing work, there was no doubt. Especially on M9-PA1.

I tried to tell myself that it was because she was an apt student, much more so than the others. The other PA and E19 gave proper attention, but seemed less enthusiastic. J7 tried hard in a strange, clinical way, and B28 made it obvious he could care less. The tall, handsome blonde clearly had other classes he was more interested in, and French was just something to get through.

The truth of it regarding M9, I had realized just one week earlier and had only finally admitted to myself the day before, was that I was attracted to her. Not just attracted - it felt like a silly, teenage crush. It was strange because that was something I hadn't fallen prey to even as a teenager. There had been some pretty hot screen stars when I was in high school but my feelings for them didn't go farther than the hard-on in my pants, which I dealt with myself as often as I possibly could and sometimes more than necessary. Hell, I was a teen and only human.

Once I hit twenty, I found that sex with a real woman was even better than with myself in the shower - and a lot easier to come by once I had more money than acne. I had gone out plenty since I had moved to Esodire, but I had only seen a few girls more than once and certainly had never gotten serious with any of them. My first red flag about M9 happened when I realized that I had stopped dating altogether, only three months after I had started working as a French tutor to her and the other constructs.

Under normal circumstances, I would have put it out of my mind. I knew what she was and what she was meant for – and it wasn't me. I could have patiently borne my silly crush except she made it impossible. It could have been my imagination, or just my ego, but I had the feeling that she was attracted to me as well. I told myself time and again that it could simply be the fact that the constructs were programmed to be obliging and eager to please, but I still thought that she was different from the others. It was in the way she talked and the way she moved, but mostly what was in those dark eyes of hers.

Something else, I realized later, was that being young sometimes made you feel invisible – like a ghost. But it also gave you the illusion that, like said phantom, you were invulnerable and invincible.

I held my palm against the metal panel next to the door and it slid open without a sound. The area inside was called

Classroom One. Like the other classrooms and almost every other area in the compound, it was as warm and friendly as an operating room. But the person sitting at the single table lit up the space as if it had been a day at the beach, or a glamorous club, or a steamy jungle. I tried not to look sheepish and daydreamy as I put the computer down on the Formica tabletop and I dipped my chin in a quick nod of greeting while I tried to find my voice.

Her face brightened when she saw me, and she welcomed me with a smile that almost split her perfect face in two. Large brown eyes were framed with dark lashes so long and thick that they reminded me of butterfly wings. Her thick, dark brown hair fell in ringlets past her shoulders and down her back. Of all the constructs, I thought she looked the most like a doll. Something perfect and made only to be looked at, not touched. But, especially over the last week or two, touching her was exactly what I wanted to do.

"Bonjour, Mason!" she announced as I sat myself in the chair across from her. "Comment allez-vous?" she asked.

"Je vais bien, merci" I answered, returning her smile. "Et vous?

"Je vais bien, aussi."

"Je vais aussi bien," I corrected.

She repeated the phrase, correctly this time. I gave her a smile and a nod at the proper grammar and she beamed at me. I unfolded the computer and pushed it into a position so we could both see the screen.

I found her lesson record and cued up the language program. She went over what she had learned on her own in the past forty-eight hours while I corrected her pronunciation now and then. It wasn't often and I could tell that she had practiced. She was always prepared for our class, much more than the others. I was sure that B28 didn't practice at all unless he was having a lesson, and he still stubbornly read French words phonetically, like they were Anglicus. It drove me crazy. Even more so because I knew that he had already learned how to pilot jets, planes, and helis – and he could speak fluent Russish having learned it from a program.

I went through the lesson and she gave it back almost to perfection. I probably would not have noticed anything other than gross mispronunciation at that point. I was too concerned about the smell of her skin, and the attempt to cover my erection. Because of the latter, I had her repeat the last quarter page, just so I could get myself back under control.

I did so, but barely. Her brown eyes were luminous, and not just from her progress. I watched all of the constructs from time to time, and maybe I watched her just a bit more than the others (or maybe I just watched the others at all to make it understandable that she was on my compute screen quite a few times during the day) and I knew that her eyes only looked that way when they were looking at me.

I looked at my watch even though there was a digit console on the wall by the door. Habit and nervousness always seem to go hand in hand. She was done for the day but I didn't want to leave until our time was officially up.

"Excellent," I told her in Anglicus. "You are actually ahead of schedule. Are there any questions you would like to ask me?"

She leaned back in her seat, sitting up straight, her hands clasped tightly in front of her. "Yes!" she exclaimed as if she had been waiting for such an occasion.

I smiled at her excitement. "What?" I asked.

"Why do you wear a timepiece on your arm? Everyone else here wears a comset, or jewelry."

I shrugged. "Habit," I answered, echoing my thought from just a few seconds past. "I've worn one since I was a kid. Now I feel naked if I don't have it on."

Her eyes went wide at my statement and then she smiled

that smile of hers again. “Why do you wear those pants? Everyone else wears different pants.”

Now I laughed and she blushed a little bit.

“Am I not supposed to ask such questions?” she posed, her voice quieter.

“No,” I said, “it’s fine. I just didn’t expect you to ask questions about me. I was expecting you to have questions about your lessons.”

“Oh.”

I could tell by her voice and expression that she was crestfallen and unsure. “It’s okay,” I told her. “I was just surprised. You can ask me anything.”

She brightened again. “Your pants.”

I almost laughed again but I held it back. “My jeans?” I asked with a smile. “What about them?”

“Jeans,” she said as if tasting the word. I wondered what it would be like to taste her mouth. She cocked her head at me and I crossed my legs. “Nobody else wears pants like that,” she told me, as if I didn’t already know. “They are so...different.”

I nodded, still smiling. She was comparing me to others. Or just noticing differences. I wasn’t sure but I wondered what it meant. I was sure Faith would know but I wasn’t about to ask her.

“They are a workingman’s pants,” I told her, realizing as I said it that I was quoting my grandmother.

“The other men here at the center,” she asked, perplexed, “they don’t work?”

God, how she made me want to laugh. And *Jesus* she was beautiful. Those dark curls fell perfectly around her perfectly shaped face.

“They work plenty,” I assured her, “I’m just out of date. Like wearing my watch, I suppose. The material is from Earth.

The name itself, denim, says where it came from – de Nimes, meaning from Nimes, France. The fabric was always shipped to America from Genoa, Italy. The wooden boxes were marked 'de Nimes, Gen.' – giving them their name – denim jeans."

Her expression, at first surprised, became a mixture of sly and shy.

"May I touch?"

My breath caught in my throat and, after a very short pause, I nodded. I slid my chair back from the table as she rose eagerly and circled around to my side where she knelt down and ran a hand over my denim-clad knee.

I do not know if I have the words to express what I felt, or what passed between us. I had heard the word "chemistry" used to describe the connection between two people, but it was much more than that. Electricity would be better. Or magnetism. Or electro-magnetism.

All I know was that it was something that was both natural and unreal.

The caress was so innocent and yet so exquisitely erotic that I bit my tongue hard enough to draw blood. I hardly noticed.

"The fabric is so coarse," she remarked in a voice full of wonder. "It is thickly woven, and heavy."

"A man from the French region of Germany by the name of Strauss made pants like these for gold-miners on Earth a long time ago," I said stupidly.

"Why?" she asked, looking up at me with those luminous eyes. Despite how thick the damned fabric was, I could still feel her fingers right through it as if they were touching my bare skin.

I had a terrifying moment when I thought I was going to simply bolt from the room but somehow I managed to stay in my chair.

"The pants the miners had been wearing did not last. They tore everywhere and came apart at the seams. Strauss used a heavy stitching and metal rivets. Along with the tough cloth, they were made to last even with their rough work."

I breathed a sigh of relief at my verbal recovery but it was short-lived. Her curious eyes traveled over my leg and she ran her hand up along my outer thigh, feeling the seam and running her thumb in a circle around the copper rivet on the pocket under my hip. I silently blessed Strauss and his ridiculously durable pants because I was sure I was about to explode in them.

I looked at my watch and had no idea what I was looking at. "Time to go!" I announced in a rush, as pleasantly as I possibly could.

Her full lips pursed in a resigned but cheerful acceptance. "Thank you for the lesson, Mason," she told me, rising. I caught one of her hands in my own, instinctively, helping her to her feet as I rose as well. "I like your...jeans," she said, pausing on the last word to make sure she got it right.

"Well," I told her, my smile returning as I scooped up the computer, "besides me, you are the only one."

She laughed and I left, giving her a smile that I hoped was not sheepish. The sound of her laugh echoed in my ears like a song you can't get out of your head, and the feel of where she ran her hand along my leg burned all through me.

I walked down the hallway, past half a dozen more rooms, then stopped before my next destination to collect myself. I tugged down on the crotch of my jeans, took a few deep breaths, and waited for my heartbeat to slow and my mind to clear a little. Finally, I placed my palm on the panel next to the door on the end. It slid open to reveal a classroom like the one I had left only moments ago. J7 sat at the table instead of M9-PA1, along with Gwendolyn.

J7 was strikingly handsome, even I could tell that, though he looked a bit different than B28 and of course very different from the elf they had manufactured. His features were not as severe as those of B28, but the young man had a radiance all his own. His skin was a golden tan, his hair the color of honey, and he even had glints of gold in his green and brown eyes.

Gwendolyn glanced up at me and laughed, almost embarrassingly – probably because her lesson had overrun its normal time – and rose up and said goodbye to J7 as she gathered up her portable compute.

J7 stood up politely and murmured a goodbye as she turned to leave.

"Bonjour, J7!" I greeted, putting my own foldout computer (the older and bulkier version of the new ones they simply called computes) down on the table.

I began to open the thing but when there was no response from the construct I looked up at him, curious. He was watching Gwendolyn exit the room, his eyes as intent as a Golgoth sniper. I had been boiling over with heat after my lesson with M9, but a sudden chill overtook me. It wasn't until the door had slid shut behind her, the latch snicking shut, that he turned his strange hazel eyes to me.

"Bonjour, Mason," he said, as if suddenly realizing that I was there. "Comment allez-vous?"

"Je vais bien," I said, slowly sitting down, watching him warily. "Merci."

He sank back down in his seat and I had the oddest feeling that I was in the room with an animal. An animal that was wild only a second ago, or one that had been trained to attack. Yet the second that Gwendolyn was gone, he was one that was as docile as a house cat.

My grandmother had told me once that the cat, from the great lion to the small tabby, had been the greatest predator on Earth. It killed more than any other animal. I scoffed at the idea, at first. We had a gray and black striped cat and he was the most loving, if haughty, animal I had ever encountered. One day, however, I watched as he crunched down on his latest acquisition. It was a rat, a big one. I realized then that my grandmother had not been joking. That cat certainly ate more mice than I did steak, and I surely never had to hunt it.

I think it had surprised me because I had always thought the cat was lazy. After that day, I knew that it was only his disguise. His body was always ready to spring, and his eyes were never still.

The memory came to me in sharp relief as I watched J7 sit down and greet me with a disarming smile. It was as if he was slipping on his disguise.

I began our lesson and, though he was intent and polite, I could feel that his mind – or maybe his heart – was elsewhere. Once he started reading his lesson, I know that mine was.

ONE ONE

"There's something wrong with number seven."

Faith turned slowly, with all the grace of a ballerina doing a delicate pirouette. Only Gwen could see that every muscle in her twin's body had gone taut, and that her fingers were white at the knuckles where they wrapped around the edges of the compute pad in her hands. Her eyes were just wide enough to show white around the irises. She drew a slow breath in through her nose.

"I beg your pardon?"

"There's something wrong with number seven," Gwen repeated. A line formed between Faith's brows, mirroring the line already in Gwendolyn's brow.

"Can you be more specific?"

Gwen sighed and sank down into the chair that faced Faith's desk and cupped her face with a hand. "Not really." Her chin dipped until it was her forehead that was resting in her splayed palm.

Faith's frown deepened and she leaned back on the edge of her desk, observing her twin's strange behavior. "What's wrong?" she asked, even more intent as she realized that there might be something wrong with Gwendolyn rather than, or in addition to, the construct. "Are you okay?"

Gwendolyn laughed nervously. "I think so, just a little unsettled. I guess."

"Unsettled?" Faith put her mini-compute down and leaned forward with her weight on her hands. "What happened? What did he do?"

"Oh no! Nothing like that!" She tittered nervously again. "He just acts different from the others. Talks to me differently, I guess."

Faith shrugged. "They are all going to have their own unique personalities. None of them will be the same." She stared intently at her twin, silently encouraging her to continue.

"It's not just a different personality," Gwen told her, searching for a way to explain. "Its..." she trailed off and sighed in exasperation. "He's different mentally. Sharper somehow. I can't put my finger on it exactly, except for the fact that he knows that I am not you."

A gush of air poured from Faith's lungs and she laughed and shook her head, flooded with relief. "Is that all?" She had already been faced with some minor setbacks along the way, but anything that kept her from her predetermined schedule was starting to set her teeth on edge. A personality quirk of a construct was nothing to get upset over, but if Gwen was obviously agitated it warranted her attention.

"Don't make light of it!" Gwen scolded. "No one has been able to do that, not ever."

Faith bit the corner of her lip, holding back a smile. "So you're saying that we made a construct that is more perceptive than a human? I can't say I'm surprised."

"Quit tooting your own horn!" Gwendolyn reprimanded, which made her twin laugh out loud again.

"Where in the world did you pick up *that* expression?" Faith asked. "Mason?"

"I can't remember," her twin replied, annoyed. "But

even elves are not that perceptive, even ones that know us!" Gwendolyn added emphatically. "Even Grandfather had a time of it. I think he still does!"

"Oh, I know he still does," Faith agreed. She picked her compute pad back up, the rings on her left hand clicking against the metal casing. "But I don't think it's any cause for alarm. Is there anything else?"

"Yes." Gwen glanced away as if embarrassed and then back to her twin. "He looks at me funny."

Faith's frown returned. "There's something wrong with his eyes?"

"No, dammit! His eyes are fine! It's the *way* he looks at me."

Faith regarded her twin with genuine surprise. "And what way is that?"

"Like he can see through me. No one else looks at me like that - except you. I always figured it was because you are the only person in the universe other than myself that really knows who is who."

Faith pressed her lips together to keep from smiling, eliciting another frown from her twin. "I still think there is something wrong with him!" Gwen insisted. "You should bring him in and do a scan."

Faith regarded her for a few moments, tapping her finger on the top of her compute pad, rings clicking. "Hmm."

"Hmm, what?" Gwen demanded.

In answer, Faith stood and pulled off the white lab coat she always wore over her dress. "Have you seen him yet today?" she asked.

Gwen shook her head. "I was on my way, but I lost my nerve and decided to come here first."

Faith nodded and handed Gwen her lab coat. "Put this

on." She pulled off her high-heeled shoes and held them out as Gwen put her arms into the loose white jacket and pulled it up over her shoulders. "These too," Faith instructed as she handed the shoes over as well.

"What are you going to do?" Gwen asked, kicking off her comfortable shoes to exchange them for Faith's heels.

Faith grinned. "An experiment. What else?" Faith held out the portable compute to her twin and Gwen took it, eyeing her with suspicion. Faith scowled and made a twirling motion with her fingers and Gwen immediately switched the compute to her other hand. Faith's grin resurfaced. "Like looking into a mirror," she approved. "Classroom Three?" she asked as she slipped her feet into Gwendolyn's shoes.

Gwen nodded and followed Faith as she straightened and left her office. She walked down the hall, her twin at her side, taking the corridor that connected the offices to the section of the compound that housed the constructs and their classrooms. After a single turn into an adjoining hall, Faith paused before a door with no handle and looked at Gwen, making sure she was ready.

Gwen was not exactly sure what her twin had in mind, but she had a good idea. She shrugged and Faith gave her a conspiratorial smirk before she put her hand to the small metal panel on the wall and the door slid open. The smirk dissolved into a pleasant smile as she walked through the door. Gwen, in turn, tried to fix a serious expression on her own face as she followed.

The room beyond was more utilitarian than cozy, four folding chairs around a square holo table made out of black perspex. J7 stood up quickly as they entered, his chair skittering back from his thighs. His hazel eyes were sharp, and they flashed back and forth between the two women. He smiled at them as he let them take their seats before he sat back down.

"Good morning, Seven," Faith greeted, her tone much warmer than the one she normally used, as she sat in a chair and crossed her ankles rather than her legs in the manner that Gwendolyn usually did.

"Good morning, Faith," Seven replied before turning his face to look at her twin. "Good morning, Gwen," he told her, favoring her with a broad smile before looking back at Faith. "Why is Gwen wearing your coat?"

If Faith was surprised it did not show on her face. "What makes you think that is Gwen and I am Faith?"

Seven looked back and forth between the women again. "Are you serious?" he asked, looking from one to the other. His gaze did not linger on either young woman, showing that he was not questioning who they were, just curious as to what they were doing. "Is this humor?" he asked. "Is that what this is?" He gave Faith a slight smile, showing even white teeth. "Or is it a test of some kind?" He looked at Gwen, his smile growing. Faith ran her left thumbnail along the bottom edge of her lip as she watched him.

"I am surprised that you can distinguish one of us from the other," she said. "Most people cannot."

Seven made a face. "*Are* you being funny? I'm not sure I understand."

"I'm not intending to be funny. Gwen is the exact image of me."

"No, she isn't an exact image of you," Seven corrected, a small line forming between his brows even though the edges of his lips were still upturned in a smile. "She is a mirror image of you."

This time a jolt of surprise did show on Faith's normally stoic face. It had taken her years of genetic studies, an entire decade if truth be told, to come to that conclusion - though her comprehension had been on a scientific scale. It had been quite the breakthrough for her to realize that her grandfather had not replicated her genes to create Gwen, but had mirrored them. She stared at the construct, speechless for the moment.

"But it's more than that," Seven told Faith, looking down and away as he thought. "She is completely different from you." He frowned as he considered his next words then continued. "She is different from everyone." Though it only lasted a second, the understanding on Faith's countenance glimmered and then was gone. She sat back in her chair, her left thumbnail tracing the bottom of her lower lip.

"Tell me how," she said.

Seven shrugged and shook his head. "I don't know. At least, I don't know how to explain."

"Try," she encouraged. "Give me an example."

The gentle crease returned between his smooth brows as he turned his gaze to examine the woman in Faith's lab coat. "The way she looks, I guess." His face softened. "The way she talks to people?" He watched Gwen roll her eyes in exaggerated exasperation. Seven's expression brightened and he looked back at Faith. "Like that! The way she is funny without trying to be."

Faith stared at him for long seconds as a clock on the wall ticked away divergent numbers. Then she stood up. Seven stood, a courtesy he had learned from the start. Gwen stood as well, clearly confused as Faith made hand motions to encourage the return of her lab coat. Gwendolyn took it off and handed it back to her twin.

"There's nothing wrong with him," Faith told her in elfin.

"Are you sure?" She took off one heeled shoe and then the other, then held the pair out to Faith who was stepping out of her own shoes.

Faith looked at her, slipping on one shoe at a time, deciding how much she should tell her. She knew that eventually she would tell her everything - Gwendolyn was the one person in the universe that Faith shared everything with - she could not keep anything from her for long. Still, she thought it might be prudent to keep her suspicions untold for the nonce.

"Maybe it's time for him to start his lessons with Charity," she suggested. Though Gwendolyn never so much as flinched, Faith could read everything in the second that her twin hesitated before she spoke.

"I think we should wait until he has finished his core classes, first. Don't you?"

"I do," Faith agreed, taking her compute from Gwen. "But I don't want you to be uncomfortable. Do you want to keep teaching him? We can get a tutor from Elusk if you feel awkward or if you are too busy."

"I'm not too busy," Gwendolyn told her, then frowned, considering. "Are you sure there's nothing wrong with him?"

Faith's thin eyebrows raised and her gold and brown eyes shifted as she thought. "Well, nothing wrong with him, per se," she assured Gwen, though she could not keep the smile from her face. Gwen's face pinched.

"What is that supposed to mean?"

"That yes he may be different, and yes I want to run some tests on him - but otherwise he is fine. We can talk more about it later. For now, I think you should stay."

Gwendolyn crossed her arms in front of her chest and tapped the toe of her right foot. She thought for a second, then two. "Alright. I'll stay."

Faith's smile widened into a grin as she glanced at the

construct before she turned to go. He was still standing, watching them. "Seven," she said, switching back to Anglicus. "I will have some questions for you later."

Some, Gwen thought with a wry smile. *She'll have a hundred compiled before she gets back to her office.*

"It was good to see you Faith," he replied, watching her flick a smile at her twin and leave the classroom. He turned back to Gwen after the door had closed and smiled. "I'm glad you decided to stay."

Gwendolyn laughed. "Who taught you elfin? I thought you were still learning French from Mason!"

Seven laughed. "No one, but there is a lot I can understand just by the way you act." He held out a hand, inviting her to retake her seat. When she did, he sat in the chair next to hers. "And French," he complained, "is not easy."

Gwen laughed lightly. "It's a beautiful language. And much easier than Anglicus. Or elfin."

"At least French has a flow," he conceded. "Though I like the sound of Italian better."

"What does elfin sound like?"

Seven smiled as he took a moment to think about it. "Like mice eating cheese," he decided. Gwen laughed and leaned forward to turn on the holo table.

Faith, on her way back to her office, watched the exchange on her compute pad via the relay from the security camera in the classroom. She saw the way Seven's eyes tracked Gwendolyn's every move and expression. She felt the hairs on her neck rise and did not know if it was excitement or fear.

*

Hope, light years away but wearing a white lab-coat almost exactly like the one Faith wore (though she also wore safety glasses), held her cylinder close to the burner. She turned the vacuum tube slowly and carefully. She went even slower than normal, since the Lab Commander stood at her shoulder, watching. He made her so nervous, but not in her job. She knew what she was doing in the lab.

Part of the nervousness was caused by his smell, most likely from whatever soap or shaving cream that he used, and it drove her crazy. Like his eyes. His eyes were a perfect blue and they seemed to stare right through her. She tried to keep her voice on a professional level though her heart was kicking frantically in her chest.

"Still nothing," she told Dr. Biri, with unfeigned despondency. "Is the other team having more success that I am?"

The young human doctor shook his head. "No, though I was optimistic about their progress. It has been known for a long time that liquid helium will not freeze at any temperature when in atmospheric conditions because of its Zero-Point Energy. I thought that we could replicate the results with other elements if we changed the conditions relative to their atomic weight. So far, no luck."

Hope knew that Faith would have sneered at the man for using the word "luck" in a laboratory and would have told her youngest sister that the responsibility of success and failure of the lab fell upon the shoulders of the Commander. But, to her great satisfaction, Faith was not there.

"I'm sure you will find the answer," she assured him before she dared a furtive glance in his direction. She saw his muscles move beneath his lab coat as he turned and moved to grab the next tube and hold it ready for her.

Muscles! she thought, her heartbeat racing even faster. *He's not the normal lab rat. He has a real body.*

Just a few days ago they had coincidentally entered the lab at the same time and she had seen him take off his light jacket that he wore over his civilian clothes to put on his lab coat. He had been wearing a short-sleeved shirt underneath and she could see in plain sight that his biceps were round and well defined – his triceps muscle a thick fork of strong flesh cupping the back of his arm. She had gasped slightly and turned her face away. Since then, she was careful to be somewhere else in the lab when he came in. A place where she could watch him take off his civilian jacket and put on his lab coat.

The Safety Officer came in to take a quick look around, which he usually did at least five times a day. His sharp eyes did not miss the unusually nervous intern and the way the man next to her was looking at her. It had nothing to do with the vacuum tube that she held. He watched them warily.

"Would you like to have dinner with me tonight?" Dr. Biri asked.

"I would love to!" Hope gushed before giving herself a mental kick in the ass. She didn't want to seem so eager but she couldn't help it.

She would ring Madeline the first chance she got, though she knew her manufactured twin was not likely to care what time Hope came home. Madeline had just gotten her vegetable garden going and now spent hours pouring over articles on the Galactic Web concerning what flowers she should plant to attract butterflies. The only butterflies that concerned Hope were the ones in her stomach every time she was around the Lab Commander.

You have the key, she thought, recalling her last dream of the Lab Commander. Her excitement rose even more. *You are the key. I'm sure of it.*

"Then what do you say about us cutting out a little early tonight? I know a great place, not far from campus. We can go as soon as you have logged your results."

"You're the boss," Hope told him with an unrepressed grin, giving him a glimpse of her green eyes as they darted to his face for the briefest of seconds.

"Yes," he agreed. "I am."

He gave her a smile and her heart skipped a beat. She had seen his smile many times, but it was not ever like this. This was a real and genuine smile. And just for her.

The Safety Officer, finishing his rounds, had other ideas about what that smile might mean. But, for the time being, he kept his opinions to himself.

ONETWO

"Mes deux garçons sont.... grands?" M9 only paused on the last word because she was stretching her neck to see it.

"Oui," I said, "mais, attendez un moment." I turned the computer so that it was facing her and moved my chair around to her side of the table and sat next to her. She took a deep breath, not sharp enough to be a gasp, more like a backwards sigh. I could feel a warmth radiating off of her along with a sweet smell. I think it was honeysuckle, though it smelled like the whole plant – leaves and stems and wet earth - as well as the flower.

It was a strange scent for me to recognize – I was raised in a city in an apartment pod almost half a mile from the ground and the only vegetation I saw on a regular basis went into the pot on my mother's stove. I had a friend though, whose family was a bit more well off than my own. Though he lived on the same floor as I did, his parents had a pod that faced the outside of the building and they had a window. Under the window his mother had two potted plants. One was a small rosebush, the other was a honeysuckle. I never did see a rose bloom, but I saw the honeysuckle blossoms plenty of times. They looked like alien jewels – bright spots of color in my ghostly gray world.

I had smelled honeysuckle once again since those days, on the day I arrived on Esodire. I had just disembarked from the ship that had brought me to where my new job was lined up and a rainstorm had just blown through. After being assaulted with the metal reek of ship for so long, I imagine anything would have been better. But the aroma of wet asphalt, fresh rain and damp earth was like magic. I stepped away from the line of departing passengers so I could close my eyes and enjoy it. The wind freshened and brought me another smell and my eyes popped open, surprised. I looked around and spied it - a long, lonely vine of honeysuckle growing along the edge of the tarmac. Those white and gold flowers mixed with the rain and the fresh atmosphere smelled as sweet as anything I had ever smelled, until M9-PA1 that was.

Lessons had progressed with the constructs though most were done with me. The only two I still instructed were M9-PA1 and N7-PA2 since they both had to be fluent and have a good accent. The tension between M9 and myself had not subsided over the past few weeks like I had hoped it would. Instead, it had only gotten worse. Our words and actions around one another became more and more forced, short, and acutely polite. It was as if we were terrified of one another.

I made myself start dating again, thinking it would help, and quit almost immediately. The girls in town and at the college were suddenly and hopelessly dull and lackluster. Their conversations were now unbearably stupid and they smelled like cheap cosmetics. Most dates after those were just me, myself, and I. At home. A movie and shower. I was okay with it – there was still a lot to do at the compound.

"Meilleur?" I asked as I inched my chair closer to hers.

"Oui," she said, blushing a little. I had never seen her do that before.

We continued the lesson, her reading rapidly and me stopping her only occasionally to change her pronunciation. She finished the unit in half the time it normally took and turned to face me with a triumphant grin.

"Très bon!" I exclaimed, giving her a congratulatory pat on her leg, just above her knee. She was wearing a long skirt, but through the fabric I could feel the hard muscle and soft skin that covered her thigh. "Would you like to stop for the day?" I asked in Anglicus but she shook her head emphatically, her dark curls wild around her face.

"Can we keep going?" she asked. "I haven't practiced past this part, but I would like to keep going – if you have the time."

"Bien sûr!" I assured her, bringing that bright smile back to her beautiful face. I reached out with my left hand to start the next unit on the computer.

I guess I forgot that my right hand was still on her leg. Or I just wanted to. I was rewarded with another rush of warmth and that sweet, earthy smell. That smell, along with the feel of her body under my hand was almost overwhelming. Though her reading for the next unit was halting and full of mistakes, I hardly corrected her. All my attention was focused on keeping still. My hand was dying to explore that leg but I kept it frozen to the spot.

Without my constant corrections, she was able to finish the unit, clapping her hands with a child-like sense of victory. I nodded dumbly.

"Très bon!" I told her and she squealed and wrapped her arms around my neck, hugging me. My arms did the same though the rest of my body seemed determined to take another, more single-mindedly aggressive route. Instead, I patted her on the back as patronly as I could. "Très bon!" I repeated. "Bon travail aujourd'hui!"

She pulled away, but not far enough. For one aching second I thought she was gong to kiss me when the computer beeped loudly, like an angry parent, and shut down. We both laughed, like teenagers almost caught.

"It is time for my next lesson," I told her in Anglicus, pulling away as gently as I could, and I could see her disappointment despite the fact that she tried to veil it. "But," I added, "I will show you how close acquaintances in France both greet and say goodbye."

Her eyes lit up and I leaned close, putting my lips on her cheek. She held very still, waiting, though I could feel the warmth from her body rise.

"You kiss my cheek at the same time," I instructed, my lips along side her smooth face. She turned her head just the slightest bit so that she could press her lips against my cheek. "Now the same on the other side," I told her. She pulled away and leaned back as I turned so that we could kiss on the opposite cheeks. Then I held her at arms length. "Très bon!" I appraised.

She let go of me and clapped her hands. "I like that!" she said. "Good acquaintances do that every time?"

"Yes," I agreed, already feeling the delicate chill that replaced where her hands had been. "But only close acquaintances. Good friends. In greeting and parting. You would not want to do that with someone you were not close with."

"Well, we must be good friends, and very close. I have known you practically my whole life!"

"That sounds a little creepy," I said, laughing and making her laugh as well, "but it is true."

"Alors," she said and leaned forward to repeat the gesture. We kissed each other on one cheek and then the other. "Au revoir, Mason."

"Au revoir, M," I said. I folded up the computer and headed for the door. I looked back as it slid open and M had her hands clasped between her breasts and looked like she was on the verge of joyous laughter. I smiled and left, my whole body burning up.

I stopped at the first window I passed, looking at my reflection. My first thought was that I might now have dimples on my cheeks where she had kissed me, but no. They were the same smooth cheeks I had always had. Yet I felt that I would somehow forever feel the spots where she had placed her perfect lips. If I lived to be a hundred or even five hundred, I hoped that I would still feel those kisses upon my face.

ONE THREE

The petite elfin hostess led Cronus through the still quiet restaurant where only a few patrons were sitting down to an early lunch. Considerably taller than the hostess, the slim, gray-haired elf followed her bobbing, blonde ponytail outside and into dazzling sunshine. The flagstone patio was surrounded by a low, flowering hedge that showcased an emerald lawn descending gently into a lake where swans paddled around in lazy circles and figure eights.

The hostess stopped next to a table where Faith stood quickly to embrace her grandfather and give him a kiss on either cheek. The hostess placed what looked like a fist-sized diamond on the edge of their table that projected a holographic menu directly above it in turquoise light.

"Your waiter will be with you shortly," she informed, gave them a short bow, and returned to the interior of the restaurant.

"Where is Gwendolyn?" Cronus asked, looking around. He knew that the two of them were never far apart.

"Working," Faith told him. "It's just the two of us for today."

"How lovely!" Cronus exclaimed. He always enjoyed Gwendolyn's company, but very rarely had his eldest granddaughter all to himself. His gray eyes narrowed over the handsome smile in his slender face. "You must have something quite important, quite private, that you want to discuss with me."

Faith gave him an innocent smile. "Isn't there a chance that

I might want to have lunch with you?"

Cronus grinned. "Of course there is a chance. In this universe, anything is possible and most things are probable - but few things are actual. Is that what this really is? A friendly lunch? A chance to catch up on our personal lives?" Cronus laughed, unable to help himself, and the sound was young and warm on the sweet air. "No. And do you know how I know that?" He continued without waiting for her to answer. "Because we have no personal lives, you and I."

Faith's laughter joined his as the waiter approached their table. "I'll have a glass of champagne," Faith told him before he could ask.

Cronus arched a gray eyebrow at her for the audacity of ordering a drink so early and then shrugged. "I'll have a glass water with a splash of absinthe. Cold, but no ice."

The waiter bowed and left without uttering a word. Cronus looked back to his granddaughter, who had a sly smile tucked into the left side of her mouth. "I figured if you need a drink for this meeting, I probably will too."

Faith laughed. "I don't need a drink, I just thought I would enjoy one. Just because I have a mind to talk business, does not mean I cannot enjoy your company and act like we are ordinary people having an ordinary lunch."

Cronus tipped his head back till it rested on the back of his chair, shaking with quiet laughter. "Ordinary people!" He chided, looking down again. "Very well, let's play your charade and act like ordinary people. What shall we discuss? What do ordinary people talk about? Shoe sales? The weather? I hardly think they discuss ribonucleic infraction!" He threw back his head again and laughed, louder this time.

Faith scowled at him, her lips pressed tightly together, though it was in amusement rather than consternation. She had never seen her grandfather so tickled. He was usually so stoic. Like herself. "Alright, funnypants, you've had your laugh."

Cronus gathered himself, clearing his throat as the waiter approached with their drinks and set them on the table.

The waiter looked back and forth between them, expectant. "Have you had a chance to look at the menu?" he queried.

"Ah!" Faith exclaimed, glancing at the turquoise square of light that hovered over the diamond on their table. "I'll have the bowl of spring berries," she said. "No cream." The waiter gave her a curt nod and turned to Cronus, who was still examining the choices.

"I will have the field greens," he instructed. "No cheese and no dressing." The waiter gave him the same nod and touched the diamond, making the menu of light disappear before turning and walking briskly back into the restaurant.

Faith picked up her flute of champagne and touched the rim to her grandfather's glass. "To your health."

"And to yours," he returned.

Faith took a sip and put the glass back on the table. "I'm taking J7 offline." Gray brows went up over gray eyes.

"Whatever for? Did something go wrong?"

Faith shook her head and took another sip from her glass. "No, nothing like that. He has...developed some interesting qualities that I would like to study further. I'll make another to take his place."

Cronus pursed his lips. "Care to elucidate on those qualities?"

Faith shrugged and looked at the swans on the lake. "His mental acuity is normal, maybe a bit ahead of B28 and E19. But his EQ is advancing rapidly – much more than any of the others."

"His emotion?" Cronus asked, piqued. "That could be a blessing or a curse. Or both. What did you do different with his proto?"

"That's the thing," Faith said, looking back at her grandfather. "Nothing other than the C-pec splicing of his DNA."

"That shouldn't make a difference in EQ or IQ."

"I know. That's why I'd like to study him further. I'll make another so we still have six to go on the market as we had planned."

The gray brows came down over eyes that gleamed. "I will still expect payment for him." Now it was Faith's turn to look surprised.

"Our agreement was that you would get payment for the prototypes that are sold. You will get payment for the one I use to replace him."

"I did not invest my money in a research lab for you to experiment in, I invested in a business. If you want to keep him, you can buy him yourself. And I want the same as what you get for the others."

Faith's brown and gold eyes narrowed. "Do you know how much Charity is planning to ask?"

Cronus took a sip of his water and grinned, showing strong, straight teeth that were only starting to show his age with a slight mineral build-up at the gums. "I do, though I advised her to set it lower. Do you think she will get it?"

Faith tapped her glass with a manicured fingernail, her eyes far away as she considered, then looked at her grandfather and nodded. "Most likely. You can't put a price on loneliness or elitism, though Charity is counting quite a bit on the depravity of our customers."

"She should know," her grandfather said, making a face before taking a long drink from his glass. Faith hid her smile in a sip of champagne. The waiter returned and set a plate before Cronus and a bowl before Faith. She dropped a few berries into her sparkling wine and picked up the tiny silver fork provided to eat the rest.

"And you expect me to pay the same price?" she asked, continuing their previous conversation.

"I do," Cronus replied after he finished chewing a mouthful of salad. "And, speaking of sales, you need to incorporate. I can't believe you haven't done so yet."

"I'm waiting for Hope to return. She is as much a part of this as any of us. She should be here for that."

"I think that is very admirable," Cronus conceded, "though I don't know how you have been able to function as a business so far. How do you purchase anything?"

Faith bit into a pink and purple berry, smiling. "Charity writes up false purchase orders as Cryotech, an entity of TASER."

Cronus coughed, placing a hand over his mouth as he choked on his greens. TASER was the company he had retired from, and of which he owned a large part.

"Don't worry," Faith assured him. "There is nothing that can lead back to you. But if something should go wrong, or any sort of lawsuit come into play early in the game, I intend to disappear like a spark of quartz into a diminishing black hole."

Cronus wiped his mouth with a napkin and admired his granddaughter across the table. "Where in the universe did you learn to be so wily and shrewd?"

"I wonder," Faith replied, smiling at him.

"Speaking of Hope," Cronus said, returning to his greens, "how is her progress going? I'm not seeing much of anything that is useful in her reports. Has she passed anything along to you that has eluded me?"

Faith selected another large berry and popped it into her mouth to give herself a few seconds to answer. It was a subject much more dicey than pulling a five billion credit prototype offline.

"I get the same report from her that you do, but I agree - that lab does not seem to be making a whole lot of progress."

It wasn't a lie, everything she said was true. She did receive the same report as her grandfather did. It was just that she received an extra one from Galen, though that info was mostly about Hope rather than the progress in the lab.

Cronus wiped his mouth again and sat back, a small sigh escaping his lips. "If that is the case, maybe we should just bring her back. I miss her terribly, and worry about her even more. Madeline, too," he added with a fond smile. "But I have heard it through the grapevine that one group is close to breaking the barrier," he added, straightening in his seat. "I just don't know which. OpeiOne has the most advanced lab in the system. It must be them! Do you know of anyone else?"

Faith shook her head, making her brown and gold hair tremble around her face. "Unfortunately, no. But Hope's reports are quite detailed. They make some progress, but it is little and slow."

Cronus frowned. "You don't think she would hold anything back from us, do you?"

"Not about lab work," Faith said caustically before she could stop herself - regretting it instantly but showing nothing in her own composure.

Cronus, however, stiffened as if poked. "In some other area?" he asked. "Do you think something is happening and she is not telling us?"

Faith waved a hand at him, recovering quickly. "Don't be silly," she admonished. "I just meant that she is sometimes frustrated by Madeline, but does not want to share that with us."

Cronus relaxed noticeably. He sat back in his chair and

stroked his smooth chin as the waiter returned to clear their dishes. "Yes," he agreed. "The fault, there, is mine."

Faith shrugged. "It is not your fault. You had no way of knowing."

Gray eyes fixed on her, sharp and keen. "And what was it that I did not know?"

Faith shrugged again. "You made Gwendolyn when I was five, you made Llewellyn when Charity was five, and Madeline when Hope was three. Genes are genes, but when you reproduce a brain that is not yet fully developed..." she trailed off, leaving her sentence unfinished and hanging in the air over the table between them.

Cronus nodded. "I extrapolated as much myself," he admitted.

"Do not fault yourself," Faith told him, "in your eagerness to make us happy." Her grandfather gave her a smile so warm that she knew it came from his heart.

"I won't, then. Thank you."

The waiter returned to see if they would be in need of anything else. When they declined, both ready to return to their work, the waiter bowed and touched the diamond on the table before he departed. The cost of lunch was projected onto the table and Faith reached into her wallet for her credentials card.

"Don't be ridiculous!" Cronus admonished, waving her off. "When a client is promising as much as you are, the least I could do is pay for a small lunch." He zipped his card through the turquoise light and was rewarded with a gentle chime as the light turned from a bluish-green to a bright green.

Faith gave him a wry smile. "I'm glad my credit is still good."

Cronus gave her a small chuckle in return as they stood to leave. "That is because, even if you did disappear, I would know where to find you." Faith laughed and, on impulse, gave him a hug.

They parted ways in front of the restaurant, Cronus getting into a sleek airlimousine and Faith taking an aircab. Her comset buzzed the second she climbed inside. She saw that it was Galen and took the call.

"Well?" he asked, after they had said their hellos. "Do you want the good news first, or the bad news?"

"Ugh," Faith grunted. "I hate being given that choice."

"Well, your sister is definitely seeing the Lab Commander out of the lab. If she isn't sleeping with him now, she will be soon."

Faith closed her eyes and shook her head. "What's the good news?"

"Oh," Galen said. "That wasn't the bad news, it was just... news. I didn't think it would be that surprising since it was what we had both expected."

Faith sighed and looked outside to where a meadow streamed by. "Then what's the bad news?"

"That he is a hack. His progress before must have been luck alone. And that Hope is infatuated with him, if not in love, though he doesn't seem to be interested in an actual relationship."

Faith put a hand over her eyes, blocking out the scenery. "Of course she is and of course he isn't. The good news?"

The doctor was light years away but she could hear the grin in Galen's voice when he spoke. "I found the group that actually *is* on to harnessing the ZPE."

"How do you know that they aren't hacks as well?"

Again she could hear the smile in his voice and could picture the glint in his blue eyes. "Because they've already done it."

ONE FOUR

M9 finished her unit in record time and I praised her for it. I asked if she would like to go on to the next lesson and she shook her dark curls and, to my surprise, closed the computer.

"I want to know what else close acquaintances do, Mason," she told me in Anglicus, fixing her dark eyes on me.

I can hardly explain what happened next, but I will try.

First, my adrenaline spiked as if I had been stabbed, though not in a bad way. The look she gave me with her request was unmistakable – it near stopped my heart. The consequences of such implications would be catastrophic – which got it thudding again.

Nonetheless, I was unable to keep the grin off my face. "Well, first of all," I told her "we call each other by our Christian names. Our first names."

The look of bewilderment that came across her face was so genuine that I wanted to grab her and kiss her.

"I thought Mason was your name," she said. "No?"

"No," I said. "It's my job." I did not explain the significance right away; it was more fun to watch her face as she tried to figure it out.

"Like a doctor?" she asked with a slight but beautiful frown. "He *is* a doctor and everyone *calls* him doctor?"

I could not help but chuckle at that one. "Not quite as lofty as all that," I assured her, "but I suppose it is along the same lines."

"Then what is your first name?" she inquired, eager once again.

"Fletcher," I said and waited for her reaction. What I was not expecting was the reaction I would have when she called me by my given name.

"Fletcher," she said, tasting the word in that way she had, and liking it. "Fletcher," she repeated, marveling at the sound of it and looking at me like she was seeing me for the first time.

I felt as if I had been struck. Suckerpunched. Hard. The colors of the room went garish and the lights were equally bright. Sounds wrapped my body with an abrasive familiarity, making my skin tingle from my scalp to my toes. For me, hearing her say my name was like being born.

For the first time in my life, I left the ghosts behind. I began to live.

"How would you like to go for a walk?" I asked.

"Outside?" she asked, breathless.

I nodded.

The gleam in her eyes was all the answer I needed.

*

About the same time that Faith and her grandfather were having their private luncheon, Hahn and Elaeric were at the same galaxy fair that Cronus had taken Hope to when it had circled the nebulous Flower.

It had been more than six turns of the moon since Hahn and Elaeric had begun to change the landscape where they meditated. Hahn Chi, a Fighting Master self-cast from the Temple, had thrown himself into meditation. But his friend could see that the other monk saw it as a challenge to be conquered rather than something to embrace with his soul.

Their newfound discovery of manipulating fields and energy had become an obsession for Hahn. It replaced fighting for him in a way that simple meditation had not.

Elaeric had become worried and had suggested the trip with the knowledge that his friend could use a change of scene, without changing the scenery of the monastery, even if it was only for a day.

All of the monks at the monastery had chores they were responsible for to keep the place running smoothly. The usual duties that Elaeric opted for always involved working in the kitchens and the young monk had been well aware that the Abon had been keen on restocking the monastery's diminishing supply of spices for quite some time. Upon hearing of the approach of the Lavender Spin, he had been quick to inform the Abon that Spice Grevins could always be found at galaxy fairs. He asked the Abon if he would like for Hahn and himself to make the day trip that would fill the spice pantry for years to come.

The idea was considered, then welcomed and approved. The very next day the two monks were given paper money and sent on their way to catch the most affordable shuttle that serviced the small, mostly monastic planet.

Hahn was not entirely pleased to be pulled from what he now considered a new type of training, but relented quickly. Elaeric was a friend and a mentor, and Hahn was not about to let the gentle monk travel alone.

Though both men were each nearly a century old (Hahn much closer than Elaeric), the monks, clad in yellow robes and worn leather sandals, walked two hours to a village hub. It was the place nearest the monastery grounds where they could board an engine-powered vehicle, which in turn took them to the closest port where they could catch a space-clipper. The clipper was the least expensive mode of short-range space travel, and was full of the poorer class of the small planet's denizens.

Elaeric made room for a farmer with two goats and Hahn shifted closer to his friend to avoid being jostled by a small swarm of Gobli teenagers from one of the city's hostels, no doubt part of a group backpacking through the galaxy.

The ride was turbulent but swift, since the lavender bubble of the fair was drifting just outside the atmosphere of the planet. The two exited the shuttle with the normal manner of a pair of aging monks, to emerge into the effervescence of a sunset in reverse. The sky was going from purple to pink and that, along with the carnivale ambiance, immediately brought out the child-like nature housed within them.

"I would very much like to have some spun sugar," Elaeric said as his dark, almond-shaped eyes darted about, trying to see all that he could. "Blue. No, pink – like the sky. And I want to have a ride on the ferry-wheel."

Hahn's eyes took in everything at once without having to look around, as was his practice. "I want to have a hawker guess my age," he shared.

Elaeric laughed. "No you don't! You want one to try to guess your age, so you can laugh yourself silly at his response."

"I cannot help if his guess is inaccurate," Hahn said in mock defense, "nor can I help my own amusement at his laughable lack of knowledge."

Both monks chuckled, their hands tucked into the sleeves of their belted robes, as they walked over the sawdust-covered ground of the midway. "First things first, " Elaeric said amiably, ignoring the hawkers that were plying at his ears and the sugary smells assaulting his nostrils. He looked around as they left the sultry pavilion. "That way, I believe," he said, motioning with his chin. "The Grevins are usually beyond the Street of Souls."

The two walked down a lane that was lined with narrow

tents covered with brightly striped silk. They knew that it was here that the elves of Pangaea, with their dark skin and clairvoyant abilities, set up shop to tell the futures of willing patrons that had a bit of expendable income.

"Do you think they can really see the future?" Elaeric asked conversationally.

Hahn's shoulders went up under his saffron-colored robes. "They are called charlatans by many, but I do not remember hearing of one being disproved."

"I know that," Elaeric responded, looking at the rows of tents, some with their owners sitting out front, calling out to prospective patrons. "What I want to know is if you believe it, and why – or why not."

Hahn smiled at his friend. "Alright," he conceded, "but the why, first."

Elaeric smiled and nodded in acquiescence, showing he was fine with the backwards order of the discussion.

"Many people," Hahn told him, "say that it is their dark skin that gives them the ability to commune with the unknown. I have heard that the darker their skin, the closer they are to the universe because they share the same color. Others say that it has to do with their freckles, and that the freckles upon the skin represent stars. I think both ideas are nonsense."

Elaeric smiled and almost nodded in agreement before he was distracted by the buttery smell of popped corn and looked away, trying to find the source. Thus distracted, it was by chance alone that he missed stepping into a purple wad of taffy that was half-melted into the sawdust and waiting for a ride on the shoe, or sandal, of an innocent passerby.

"The Pangaeans," Hahn continued, "are supposedly the most ancient race in the universe. A supposition that I believe to be correct. I deem that it is their age that gives them wisdom."

"You only say that because you are older than me," Elaeric

told his friend. "Older does not always mean wiser."

"It doesn't?" Hahn asked, feigning surprise.

Elaeric grinned. "And what else?" he asked. "I know you are holding something back, my friend. Please share."

Hahn smiled at his friend's knowing. "I believe that they still hear the song of the universe," he told him. "The first verse that was ever sung."

Elaeric nodded, in understanding if not agreement. "So to answer the first part of my question, do you believe that they can truly see..."

The monk was cut off mid sentence as one of the dark elves in question emerged from his tent in a billow of smoke. As he did, the toe of the man's sandal caught on a stone, making him lurch forward ungainly, his arms pin-wheeling erratically in an effort to keep his balance.

The tall man pitched precariously to the left but, before Elaeric could blink an eye, Hahn was there. The fighter monk caught the teller deftly in his wiry arms and with a fluid movement pulled the man upright. He held the taller man firm for a moment until he had regained his balance and then stepped away with care, one strong hand still on the man's elbow. The whole ordeal lasted less than three seconds.

"There you are!" Hahn exclaimed as he waited for the elf to be steady on his feet once again.

When the black elf had recovered his composure he gave the monk a broad smile, breathing out a sigh of relief.

"Thank ya!" the teller told Hahn. "I might have had quite the spill!"

Hahn let go of the elf, suddenly aware that the man's long fingers were on his own skin along his inner arm, feeling an odd sort of energy pass between their touch. He resisted the urge to brush at his arm where the man had touched him.

"Not to worry," the monk assured him, "I was glad to help."

He watched the teller's smile widen into a grin. Hahn paused, pursing his lips as he regarded the elf's knowing leer. Finally, he sighed. "Very well," he conceded. "I can see by your look that you saw something when you touched me. Is it something you would like to share?"

The black elf nodded, still grinning. "Indeed, I know your fate. And because you may have saved my front teeth, I will tell you for free."

Hahn bowed at the proffered gift of a telling and straightened, waiting. His patient expression was one as if indulging a baby with a toy, or a child in nonsense.

"You will be torn between two women," the black elf said simply.

Hahn, who had never lain with a woman and had no memory of the one that had birthed him, bowed to the man.

"Thank you, sir," he said, polite and formal. "And may you not be torn in two by your footwear, or your errant step."

The man gave a chuckle that slowly evolved into a guffaw. Hahn smiled, straightened, and continued on his way. Elaeric, who had been staring at the teller in surprise, hastened for a moment to return to his side.

"And now," Hahn said with grin as he kept his eyes on the oncoming alley enclosed by fragrant stalls, "do you have an answer to your question? Do you think I truly believe that they can see the future?"

Elaeric laughed, knowing that the possibility of even one woman affecting the life of his friend was impossible, much less two.

"I do. But if a hawker can guess your age to the inside of two decades, you buy me a cone of spun sugar!"

"It's a deal!" Hahn agreed. Behind them, both could hear a booming laugh echoing down the midway. Neither monk had to turn and see to know that it came from the black elf that had told Hahn's future.

ONE FIVE

Faith leaned back in the chair behind her desk and sighed. She had spent an entire day – a day she should have spent refining the cerebral cortexes of the female constructs – running tests on J7. Before she called him into her office to bombard him with more questions, she summoned me.

Like any scientist with cutthroat aspirations, Faith had logged her research over the past three years with the IGC Board of Science and Medicine and had been awarded her second doctorate, this time in genetics, as soon as the constructs were finished and scrutinized by a team of IGC eggheads.

"Yes?" I asked, standing in her doorway and expecting to be sent off to fix something. "You called for me, Dr. de Rossi?"

She looked up at me across the expanse of her laboratory from the desk that was squelched into the back corner.

"Come in, Mason. Please, have a seat."

I crossed the floor, evading overloaded but organized tables and machinery that I found downright terrifying. What she did with most of the equipment I had no idea. I took my seat with a bit of trepidation. I had never been fired from a job, but I knew that being called into the big man's office (or big woman's in this case) was not a good sign. Losing employment, however, was the furthest from my mind. I was suddenly terrified that I would never see M9-PA1 again. Terrified that we had been found out. Terrified of what might happen to M9 herself.

I had never taken her from the compound. Not the grounds

anyway. I was crazy in love, but not downright crazy. I never broke any rules, per se, but I had been bending them in various ways – ways that I always thought I could explain my way out of if caught. Now I wasn't sure. Faith's tawny eyes glittered dangerously and I could tell that she was far from pleased.

I swallowed hard and sat down. Dr. de Rossi folded her hands and placed them on her desk, leaning forward.

"Tell me about J7."

The question caught me by complete surprise.

"J7?"

"Yes. I'm pretty sure we have only one."

"Ah…well…what would you like to know?"

"Does he act different than the others?"

I swallowed hard again, thinking now that she might be trying a roundabout method of inquiry regarding the different way that M9 acted, around me anyhow.

"Well," I said, "they all act different."

This seemed to surprise her and it dawned on me that she never spent any time with the constructs on a personal level, not the way I did. With her I'm sure it was always Q and A. Routine examinations. Tests and results.

"Explain."

"Well," I told her, "B28 never gives me problems, but I can tell that he doesn't like French lessons. I feel like he gets through them as quickly as possible. E19 is very intense. G1 is very timid though I don't see her much because she is the only one not taking lessons with me. N7-PA2…"

"And J7?"

I was inwardly relieved that M9 was truly no concern, but still hesitant in my response about J7. I shifted in my seat. "I know you are not going to like this," I said - and here I could see her body and her eyes go hard like stone, as if she were bracing herself for a blow, "but only because of the way it sounds."

"Go on."

I knew that she wanted the truth, at least in a clinical way. On a personal level I was not quite sure.

Tell the truth and shame the devil, my grandmother would say. But I had the abrupt and horrid sensation at that moment that it was *Faith* that was the devil.

"He seems...the most robotic out of all of them," I said quickly. "But not like a droid," I assured her, trying to find the best way to explain. "He seems the most...the most... calculating!" I exclaimed, finding the right word. "It's like he is thinking of a million things at once in the background, while still being able to carry on a conversation."

Dr. de Rossi relaxed the slightest bit, which was probably why I opened my mouth again.

"In that way," I started without thinking, "he's kind of like..." then my brain caught up with my mouth and I snapped it shut.

"Like what?" she demanded.

I bit my lip and thought better of what I had been about to say, but I went ahead and said it anyway. "Like you."

Instead of being offended like any normal person might, Faith smiled as if complimented. I breathed a sigh of relief and something else occurred to me. It was something I had noticed before, but not really thought about.

"But, now that I think of it, he is not like that all the time."

"Really?" she asked, piqued. I nodded.

"When Miss Gwendolyn is around, he seems quite the opposite. His focus is singular – and his focus is on her."

Dr. de Rossi nodded as if this was something she had already known. When she offered nothing else I thought that maybe I was done, but her golden and brown eyes fixed on me, pinning me to my chair. And when she spoke, her words were as sharp and pointed as daggers.

"Do you think that he could be dangerous? Even the slightest bit?"

I took a moment to consider. The way that the construct always watched the eldest dyer had always unnerved me. I was brought back to the thought I had before, about our cat back home, watching mice in the same manner – with that quick, sharp intensity. Right before he pounced on them and snapped their necks with his small but powerful jaws. But did that mean J7 was a killer? A predator?

"I honestly can't say, Dr. de Rossi."

She nodded quickly, wrapping up our interview.

"Thank you, Mason. That will be all."

I gave her a nod and was rising from my chair with immense relief when her face moved suddenly to follow me.

"Mason?" she asked.

"Yes?"

"I've heard a few of the constructs call you Fletcher. What is the significance?"

My heart jumped at the significance, but I smiled. "It's my name."

The blank look on her face was comical, only because she was a person that was almost never caught off her guard. I doubt much of anything ever got by that woman. But I had to hand it to her, she put it all together with lightning speed. She probably even thought herself a fool for thinking that her grandfather might call someone by their given name. Especially the help.

"Of course," she said.

"I thought I should be on a first name basis with people I was working with everyday," I explained. She nodded.

"Which is also why you address them by their first initial," she observed aloud. "It sounds more like a name."

"Yes," I said, though it was only partially true and I was startled that she knew. I had started calling M9-PA1 by her first initial because it was more human. I hadn't even noticed what I had been calling the others though, now that I thought of it, I did call J7 simply Jay. I had already noticed that the de Rossi's called them by their number, which I found did the opposite, making them less human. I never knew if it was intentional or just clinical.

"Well," she continued, "of course we should do the same, since we work together every day as well. Please call me Faith."

I opened my mouth to protest, since I could not see myself doing such a thing, but nodded instead. "Yes, ma'am," I replied.

Faith gave me a half smile and shook her head in amused irritation, effectively dismissing me. "Send in J7," she said.

I left the office to go find the construct, only to find that he was waiting outside the door. I was startled but he gave me a disarming smile.

"She's not going to cut open my head, is she?" he asked. The overhead fluorescents washed out the golden tones of his hair but his honey-colored skin was still smooth and perfect.

I smiled and shook my head. "Not literally," I said, clapping him on the shoulder. "At least I don't think so."

He rolled his eyes and took a deep breath before he pushed open the door. I headed the opposite direction, glad to be gone and intending to leave the compound and hit a bar. I needed a drink.

J7 had hardly taken his seat across from Faith at her desk when she began bombarding him with questions.

"What is your favorite class?"

"Human mythology."

“Greek, Roman, Christian, or Norse? Hindu? Or one of the Asian cultures?”

“Greek.”

“Is it because it is one of the classes that Gwen teaches you?”

“No.”

Faith gave him a look that was heavy with suspicion and J7 sighed.

“She teaches me art history too but it is as boring as...” there was a pause as he searched for the right metaphor. “French,” he finished.

Had I known that, I might have kicked him.

Faith smiled. “M9-PA1 doesn’t seem to be bored by French. In fact, she told me last week that it was her favorite class.”

“That’s because she likes Fletcher.”

Had I known *that*, I would have gladly strangled him.

Faith straightened in her chair. “Is that so?”

J7 shrugged.

Dr. de Rossi continued her barrage of questions for nearly an hour. They mostly revolved around emotion, response, and Gwendolyn. J7 bore everything with an assured air of patience and a gentle smile. He answered plain and honest every time. At least, as far as she could ascertain. I had been right. Though his speech was straightforward, she could see it was as though his mind was constantly running on overdrive and that the conversation they were having was inconsequential. Also, it was laced with thinly veiled sarcasm. She made a mental note to find out what vids he was watching during his downtime.

She ended the day not feeling much more decided than when she had begun.

“Well,” she announced finally with a sigh of exasperation,

"I want to run a scan on your brain, but it's getting late – it can wait until morning. The only thing I can tell you now is that I am taking you offline." She massaged her eyebrows with the tips of her fingers.

"I won't be sold like the others?" he asked, brightening.

"No. Not for now."

His smile widened. "I'm glad. I like being here. I wouldn't like to leave…you all."

Faith's lips twitched. "You are already guarding your answers."

"Am I?"

"Yes. Don't think that I don't know what is on your mind."

"Then why ask me questions at all?"

Faith shrugged, smiling. "I like the idea of possibility."

"Not if it is the possibility that you could be wrong."

Faith's smile vanished. "Then let's cut to the quick, shall we? It's been a long day and I'm getting tired."

"I agree. First of all…"

Faith gaped at the handsome construct, startled by his tone, and cocked her head, unsure. "Are you about to start making demands of me?"

J7 shrugged with lean yet muscular shoulders. "If I have no wants, then what am I?"

Faith sucked a breath in through her teeth and then nodded, both annoyed and pleased. She crossed her arms in front of her chest as she leaned back in her chair and lifted her chin. "All right then, let's hear them."

"I want a name. No more letter and number."

Faith dipped her chin in acquiescence and regarded him from under her thin, raised brows. "Is that all?"

"No, but it's a start."

"Then give yourself a name. It is of no matter to me what you call yourself."

The construct sat back, startled. "It had not occurred to me that I could name myself. I thought that naming was something that was done for you."

Faith smiled. "Well, you are a special circumstance." Her left hand came to her mouth and she absently traced her bottom lip with her thumbnail as she watched him.

J7 put a finger to his own lips as he thought. "Though I do not like it very much, being a letter and a number, it has created a sound that is associated with me and one that I have become quite comfortable with, so I would like to stay in that area, if I may."

"Very well, do you have anything in mind?"

J7 bit down on his right thumbnail as he considered the possibilities. "What about Evan?" he asked, brightening. "Evan is a name, right?"

Faith nodded. "It certainly is."

"And it's kind of short for seven, right?"

Faith nodded again, smiling. "Only phonetically, but yes."

The construct bit down on his nail again, just for a second. "That's it, then. I'm Evan," he said proudly.

"It's a pleasure to meet you Evan. Now get the fuck out of here so I can talk to Gwen."

Evan was not put off in the slightest. "Of course," he said rising from his chair. "Thank you for your time, Faith."

Faith looked away, moderately annoyed, as he took his leave but the door to her lab swung open before he could get to it. Gwendolyn had been in an obvious hurry and yet pulled up short, surprised to find the construct there.

He caught up her hand and kissed her fingers. “You must be Gwendolyn,” he said, grinning. “I'm Evan.”

Gwen watched him, too shocked for words, but when he held onto her hand she snatched it away and turned her brown and gold eyes to her twin.

“What the hell is going on?” she demanded. “What are you two up to?”

“That will be all, Evan,” Faith said.

Evan made his way to the door, still grinning at Gwen. Once the door swung shut she whirled on Faith. “We're naming the constructs now? “ she asked, circumventing a steel table and taking long strides through the lab. “When was this decided? And why wasn't I included?”

“We are not naming the constructs. Sit down.”

“No.”

It was so infrequent that Gwendolyn got this riled up that Faith now had to bite the insides of her lips to keep from smiling. Gwen, however, did not miss a beat. It only made her more upset. She gripped the back of the chair that faced Faith's desk but she could feel the warmth from where J7's body had been, and his scent lingered in the air. She pulled her hand back and drummed her nails along the edge, waiting impatiently.

“I'm taking him offline,” Faith stated.

Gwen took a careful step forward and sank into the chair, a hand coming up to cover her mouth. “I knew it,” she whispered. “What happened?”

“Nothing happened,” Faith said. “Nothing's wrong. He's in love with you.”

Gwen's hand dropped like a stone and she stared at her twin in shock. “He's what?”

“In love with you,” Faith said, matter of fact, then smiled

at the look on Gwendolyn's face. "Don't be so surprised," she scolded. "You're a wonderful person, I'm actually surprised it didn't happen sooner."

Gwen's expression became tight and when she spoke her voice was like the strings of an over wound instrument. "What are you saying? You did this?"

Faith gave her a look of mild disgust. "I most certainly did not. I just meant that I can't believe anyone hasn't fallen in love with you yet, other than the fact that you never socialize with anyone outside of our family."

"You don't either," Gwen said, indignant.

"I don't have the time and I wouldn't if I did." Faith fixed her gold and brown eyes on Gwendolyn's. "Regardless, you need to decide what you want to do from this point. Will you still be comfortable teaching him, or do you want to reassign his lessons to someone else?"

"I don't know," Gwen mused, looking pouty at having to make such a decision. "I had suspected there was something in the way he looked at me, but now that I know what it is, it feels awkward."

"Well, his feelings don't need to dictate yours."

"Still, I don't think I would like to pass him off because of it. It wouldn't be fair."

"Fair?" Faith asked, leaning forward and gaping at Gwen.

"Yes, fair," Gwen repeated, cross. "Just give me a second to think."

Faith, brows arched high, leaned back in her chair with her hands raised up in mock surrender.

Gwen let out a short breath and took a few seconds to consider. A program could probably continue along the same lines, but she knew that Seven would get shortchanged on more than one subject, and he had seemed genuinely interested in some of his classes. Maybe not art history, but there were aspects of human history in which he had appeared deeply engrossed. And B28 had shown hardly any interest at all beyond the fact that he wanted to know simply enough to be considered a cultured individual. Especially since Charity had begun other lessons with him. Gwen was suddenly glad that Charity had not yet gotten her hooks into Seven.

Why is that? Gwen thought. *Do I feel something for him as well? How would I know?* She wrung her hands in her lap and tried to push the idea away, deciding to think on it later. Faith would certainly grill her about it at some point and help her figure it out. *Actually, she could probably help me now. The right question might set me straight. Faith would most likely get it out with a single question. She is like a troll, that way, not wasting time by knowing exactly what to ask.*

"I don't know how I feel," she told Faith.

"Of course you do."

"No, I mean I don't know how I feel about him."

Faith sighed. "How would you feel if I put him on ice and dissected his brain?"

Gwen cried out, her hand leaping to cover her mouth. "I don't think I would like that at all," she finally whispered.

Faith held perfectly still, but her eyes were easy enough for Gwendolyn to read as if they were the large holoprint on an aircab.

"I'll keep going," she said.

Faith smiled. "Good. I want to see how this turns out." Gwen could feel the bottoms of her cheeks get hot.

"I don't want to be one of your experiments," she warned.

"I'm just an observer," Faith promised.

Gwen's lip twisted down into a smirk as she rose from her seat. "Do you really think you can do just that? Without interfering or suggesting things that you think might alter the outcome?"

Faith bit her bottom lip and shook her head.

Gwen sighed. "Do you think you can try?"

Faith, still biting her lip, nodded her head vigorously as she rose to her feet.

"Alright," Gwen agreed and found herself tight in Faith's embrace. Gwen hugged her back. "We'll keep going, and see what happens."

Faith broke the hug and held her twin at arm's length by the shoulders. "Can I make a suggestion?"

"Faith!"

"It's completely innocent, I swear. Do you remember how we were talking a few days ago about how we need to get someone to start helping with the things we don't have time for?"

Gwen dipped her chin in a nod. "Yes, we discussed getting a PA for reception, but we also need someone for more than just answering the com. You need lab assistants, an RN, a dresa droid. I need help for..."

"I think Seven might be ideal," Faith interrupted. "He can split his time with continuing his courses and helping out here at the compound – whether it be setting up reception or hauling clay for you."

A smile made its way across Gwendolyn's face. "That's actually a great idea. He's already familiar with everything and everyone, and Charity will do a back flip if she can get the extra pair of hands without having to shell out any money."

"I wouldn't count on that," Faith said caustically, sitting on the edge of her desk.

Gwen grinned. "On what? Charity not doing a back flip?"

"About not having to pay Seven. It seems he has a bit of an agenda." *The demanding little cuss,* Faith thought with a wry smile.

"Is that so?"

"Yes, and on another note, I want to keep him from the other constructs. I don't want them to know what became of him."

Gwendolyn tilted her head, curious. "Why is that?"

"I'm not sure," Faith said, almost to herself.

Gwen shrugged. Trusting Faith was something she had always done.

ONE SIX

When the compound was first constructed, Dr. de Rossi's personal office was a designated area that took up almost a third of her lab. Now, it was just an angled desk and half a dozen compute panels of various sizes confined to the corner.

Gwen was sitting across the desk from Faith in her twin's shrinking administrative space when a ping sounded over the com system. The system that I had installed had been a necessity, since Faith was regularly on the move around the complex and had thus far refused to wear a com in her ear.

She touched a blue light on the small silver disc that sat precariously close to the edge of her desk. "Yes, Thomas?"

Thomas was the first real assistant they had hired. J7, the construct that had been taken offline, had been working tirelessly to help everyone, including me, and did everything and anything that was asked of him. Still, a point was reached where he couldn't do it all. Personally, I think he was immensely relieved when Faith hired Thomas. It gave him time to return to his studies and more time to dote on Gwendolyn. Though the construct was never anything less than what was entirely proper, his infatuation with Faith's twin was obvious – to me at least.

Thomas, however, had him beat hands down on being the perfect gentleman. The PA was tall and lean, with deep olive-tan skin, black hair and dark eyes, and was a complete Godsend as far as the girls were concerned. He capably stepped in and immediately began to handle all of the little details that the sisters no longer had time for, from making sure the bills were paid and the compound was running smoothly to handling all of their calls and making sure they had food to eat. There was no longer a place where anyone could turn to look for something without finding him there in his narrow-cut suit and tie, hands clasped politely, ready to provide anything – whether it be a meal, a com number, or a solution to practically anything.

Though I never considered myself an integral part of the company, Thomas also made sure that the fridge in the break room – my preferred place to dine during the week - was always stocked. How he knew what I liked, or how the heck he found pâté in Avviare, I will never know. It took me over a month to find a bakery that could make a decent baguette and of course it was nowhere near where I lived.

"Your mother is here," Thomas replied. His voice, which usually carried a prim authority over such matters, sounded a bit befuddled. Faith looked at Gwen, seeing her own surprise mirrored on her twin's features.

"My mother?"

There was the sound of Thomas gently clearing his throat before continuing. "Well," he said, "there is a woman here who says that she is your mother."

Faith laughed. "I really don't think anyone would claim to be my mother who was not. I'm sorry, Thomas, you just caught me by surprise."

"Should I show her in?"

"By all means. See that she is comfortable and let Charity and Llewellyn know that she is here. We're on our way." Faith and Gwen rose as one, smiling at each other curiously as they left the room.

"Mother?" Gwen asked. A twinge of worry made her voice

sound reedy. "What is she doing here? Do you think everything is okay?"

Faith walked next to her down the hallway, their steps as identical as their faces. "I'm sure everything is fine," she assured. "We would have received word via holo if anything was wrong."

The two made a right-hand turn and Faith touched the wall panel to open the doors to the reception room of the complex where Thomas was already setting up a tray with a cup and saucer for a petite elfin lady with bright blue eyes and white-blonde hair. She caught sight of them as they entered and stood, gracefully sidestepping Thomas who was putting a sugar bowl down next to a small pitcher of cream and a saucer arrayed with slices of lemon.

"Girls!" she exclaimed, embracing Faith and Gwen with one arm around each of their shoulders, holding them tight as tears filled her bright eyes. "It is so good to see you!" Kisses on cheeks were given all around and she let them go just as Charity and Llewellyn entered the room. Christa de Rossi repeated the scene with the newcomers with equal vigor. She was a head shorter than both her daughters and their dyers and had a child-like petiteness that was both dazzling and dainty.

"We should sit," Llewellyn said, looking around the pristine but rather small reception area. "But where? Certainly not here."

"The conference room?" Faith suggested.

"It's too businessy," Gwen remarked.

"Maybe we should go out?" Charity asked.

"Oh no!" Christa exclaimed. "I will be fine in the conference room. I just want to see and talk to you all! Besides, Thomas was just preparing tea. Perhaps I can take it in there?"

Thomas looked to Faith who nodded. "Certainly," he told

Christa. He retrieved the tray in a brusque and businesslike manner and led the way to the conference room, carefully opening each door by touching the wall panels with his elbow.

"Hope and Madeline?" Christa inquired, as she followed, looking around curiously as they passed through a hallway of darkened windows and entered the brightly lit conference room.

"Are not here, unfortunately," Faith said, holding out a hand towards a chair, inviting her mother to sit at the head of the table. Christa took a seat and the girls sat down on either side. "Hope was working in a lab, though her and Madeline are on their way back now."

"Is that so?" she asked, shooing Thomas's hand away from the silver tray. "I can pour my own tea, Thomas," she assured him, smiling.

"Well," he said, looking around the group with his hands clasped in front of his lean form, "is there anything else I can provide for you ladies?"

"We're fine, thank you Thomas," Faith told him, but Thomas was not so easily put off.

"Some sandwiches perhaps?" He knew that it was lunchtime and that they had not yet eaten.

Faith smiled at him. "That would be wonderful, thank you."

"Something to drink, perhaps?" he asked, this time looking at Charity and Llewellyn. He knew they each usually had a cocktail in hand by noon, if not sooner. Charity's blue eyes flicked toward her mother, who was selecting a tea from the box of pods, and back at the young man. Llewellyn drummed her manicured fingers on the glass table, looking away. "A glass of juice?" he suggested.

Charity and Llewellyn both beamed at him. "That would be perfect, thank you," Charity replied.

Thomas gave them a short bow and left the room.

"It is so nice to see you, Mother," Faith said. "Is there a special reason for your visit? Everything is fine at home?"

"Oh yes," Christa said, selecting a pod of Darjeeling and dropping it into the dainty mug before dousing it with steaming hot water from the pot. "I was just lonely, is all. Your father left on an extended trip and I thought it would be nice to surprise you with a visit. I'm not troubling you, am I?"

"Of course not!"

"Don't be silly!"

"The idea!"

Christa smiled at their shared reaction. "And Hope is working elsewhere? I thought for sure she would be here, collaborating with you. Thick as thieves you always were, the six of you." All eyes looked to Faith, each girl wondering how much the eldest of them would divulge.

"Hope was after a little excitement, so she took a dangerous job on another moon," Faith told her mother. "As a spy in a restricted lab."

Gwen bit her tongue, always surprised at what Faith considered humor, as three pairs of eyes widened and then looked at their mother, who was squeezing a slice of lemon into her porcelain cup.

"Faith!" Christa admonished. "Don't pull my leg just because I'm not as tall as you! Besides, I'm sure you would never let her do anything that was dangerous." She removed the pod from the mug with a pair of silver tongs and placed it on the tray before taking a tentative sip. She smiled approvingly and set the cup down on a matching saucer.

Faith smiled at the elfin lady and shook her head. "You know me too well, Mother," she admitted.

"I know all of you," Christa told them, "and how protective you are of Hope. You always have been. Madeline, too, of course."

"Of course," Faith murmured.

The doors to the conference room swung open and Thomas entered, guiding an air cart laden with food and drinks. He set bottles of sparkling water in front of Faith and Gwendolyn, and tall glasses full of a bright orange liquid over ice before Charity and Llewellyn.

"What is that?" Christa asked, curious.

"Apperol juice," Thomas answered, transferring plates of miniature sandwiches, fruits, and crudités from the cart to the table in front of the ladies.

"Apperol?" Christa asked, drawing away. "I'm horribly allergic to the fruit."

"We will keep them at quite a safe distance," Charity assured her as she and Llewellyn slid their heavily spiked glasses of juice a safe distance away, giving Thomas twin smiles of gratitude.

"So," Christa continued as Thomas left, closing the doors behind him. "How is work going here?"

Faith and Gwen each selected a sandwich and Faith took a bite of hers and chewed thoughtfully before she replied. "Good, other than a few snags, but that is to be expected when starting a business, especially one on a scale as large as this one."

"Oh?" Christa asked, placing a few crudités on a small porcelain plate that matched the tea set. "What kind of snags? Maybe I can help."

Faith smiled indulgently at her mother, a woman that she regarded with much love and fondness, as well as with a touch of sorrow and pity. The woman was not loved by her husband, and Faith believed that she did not have much more wits than Madeline, which probably made everything easier, or at least cheerfully bearable. But the woman took solace in her religion, as she always had. Her mother was quite a devout follower of The One, a Zealot in heart if not in fact. She had told her girls, proudly and quite often, that she had very nearly been marked as a Zealot. She had met her husband only days before she was to take her vows.

"Well," Charity answered honestly, "lining up buyers has not been a walk in the park - considering that we are selling an item that has never been offered before, and we are asking prices that are quite astronomical."

"And we are unsure of how to complete their training," Llewellyn continued. "Who might pay what we are asking just to have a gorgeous chauffeur taking them from place to place? Or for the best cook in the galaxies? We can't predict what will be most profitable, or most popular."

"As soon as we get over the hump of the first six sales, we can better engineer and plan for the next run," Faith said, more for her sisters than for their mother. She did not mention that they had also pulled one of the prototypes offline and now needed another. The others knew that she had, but not why. Evan had been capable help around the compound but Charity and Llewellyn were lost as to what had led Faith to such a decision. But, like Gwen, they trusted Faith and her decisions implicitly.

Christa's blue eyes went wide over the brim of her teacup and she put it down quickly. "I have an idea that might help!"

"Really?" Charity asked. Faith nibbled her sandwich and smiled adoringly at their mother.

Christa nodded. "These new dyers, you can make them to be fast? Make them strong?"

"We can make them just about anything," Faith answered, tilting her head. "What did you have in mind?"

"Can you train them to do anything?"

"Just about, Mother," Gwen said, darting a quick look at Faith who confirmed with a quick nod. They were all becoming curious.

Christa folded her hands over the table and took all four of the young women in with one look of her bright blue eyes. "Recently, there have been threats against the Bauam's life."

Llewellyn snorted and Charity pressed her lips together, swatting Llewellyn's leg under the table. Their mother did not seem to notice.

"There are always threats on his life," Faith said. "And usually every year there is an attempt or two."

"Oh, I know! But the threats have grown, as well as the attacks. And, even though the last attacker came very close to ending the Bauam's life, His Grace is still planning on doing a galactic tour, visiting every Zealot church in the 'Drom, finishing up with a visit to the human galaxy, to bless it." Christa finished her sentence by marking the air in front of her with the sign of the Holy Circles.

"Hmm," Faith grunted. Gwen gave her a nudge under the table as their mother continued.

"Anyway," Christa said, her tone strangely dismissive though only a moment before it had been quite reverent, "along with his usual security contingent, there is talk that the Predict will be looking for a personal bodyguard for the Bauam."

"I thought the Bauam already has a bodyguard," Gwen said.

"He has a whole team of them," Christa assured her. "But the church wants better for him. It is widely known that they are looking for something, or someone, special." Christa leaned forward to deliver her next tidbit of information in a conspiratorial whisper. "There were even rumors that the Predict was looking into rogue Golgoths!"

Llewellyn snorted and took a pull from her libation. "A Golgoth would just as soon cut open the Bauam's throat and drink his blood."

"I'm sure the church thought the same," Christa agreed, placing her now empty cup back on its saucer. "But it just shows that they really are searching for something very different." She leaned forward, this time to prepare another cup of tea, just as Thomas entered and replaced her current pot with a fresh one, steam still rising from the spout. "Thank you, Thomas."

She did not notice, though Thomas did, how every other body at the table had gone rigid. Each of the younger de Rossi women had gone so still that they could have been carved from stone. Only their eyes moved, glancing at one another before they all looked to Charity, whose blue eyes glittered.

"Thank you, Mother," she said. "That is quite helpful. Thomas?" she asked, though her eyes stayed fixed upon her mother.

"Yes Ma'am?"

"I need the number for the head Thauam of the One Church."

"Yes Ma'am!"

"I can contact my Sauam if you need help, Thomas," Christa offered.

"Thank you, ma'am, I will let you know if I have any trouble."

He exited the room while Christa prepared herself another cup of tea and Charity and Llewellyn took long drinks from their tumblers of Apperol, their blue eyes peering at each other over the rims of the glasses. If there was anyone in the universe with more than enough money to pay the prices they were asking, it was The One Church.

"Well, Mother," Faith said, "the universe certainly conspired to send you on a visit right when we needed you."

Her mother made a tsking sound as she put lemon in her tea. "It was The One True that did that, Faith. I shouldn't have to tell you that."

"Then you must thank him for us."

"I certainly will, of course. You might thank him now and then yourself, you know."

"We were actually going to start on the newest prototype today," Faith said, changing the subject. "Would you like to watch Gwen sculpt? It's really quite amazing and I am sure she would love your input on the course we are now considering."

Christa put down her teacup and clapped her hands a single time like an excited child. "I would love to!"

"Well then," Gwendolyn said, wiping her mouth with a napkin. "I should get started." She looked at Charity and Llewellyn, who were whispering excitedly to each other, when Thomas's voice sounded through the room's com system.

"Miss Charity? I have the number you requested. I'm sending it through to the contact file on the compute in your office."

"Thank you, Thomas," Charity called out with a smile.

"My pleasure," he answered before the com went silent.

Llewellyn lowered her head and grinned. "I absolutely love him!" she whispered.

"I don't know how we survived without him," Charity agreed.

"Do you two have some specs for me?" Gwen asked.

"Actually," Charity said, "I think Mother might be more help, now." She drained her glass, chunks of ice clinking softly against her teeth, and stood up. "Besides," she said, giving Gwen a broad smile as she set her glass back down on the table, "I believe we have some calls to make." Llewellyn also finished her drink and left the empty glass on the table and stood to follow her twin out of the room, both of them stopping to give their mother a kiss on the cheek. "We should all stay at Faith and Gwen's tonight," Charity suggested. "An old-fashioned girls sleepover!"

"That would be lovely!" Christa agreed.

"Come, Mother," Gwen said, rising from her seat. She was suddenly eager to get started. "Thomas can bring your tea."

"Certainly," Christa said, placing her cup on the tray as Thomas entered the room. He arranged the tray with the tea and two small plates piled high with the miniature sandwiches and crudités before lifting the tray and leading the way for the ladies towards Gwendolyn's studio, skillfully managing to open each door for them as they went along.

Faith raised the lights in the studio as they entered and Gwendolyn crossed the room, weaving her way between high tables and raised stools, and stood in her favorite spot in the room - the place between her large compute screen and the HoloSculpt.

From this vantage the eldest of the dyers could reach and see everything she needed. When standing in that spot, Gwen knew she was the most at one with the universe. She felt singular yet so complete. She could feel her soul stretch in every direction, never ending. It was there that she became aware of a mass of creativity welling up inside herself, so much so that she could sense an almost impossible amount of energy that came right out of the tips of her fingers like electricity.

She turned to Christa, who was looking about the area fraught with art and technology with her blue eyes wide open. "Well, Mother," Gwen said with a smile, "how do you want him to look?"

Christa inhaled sharply, clasping her hands between her small breasts as Gwen called her attention back to the present. "Make him look like an angel," she breathed.

Gwen looked at the large compute screen that bore streaks of dried sculpting clay. "Images of angels," she commanded. The screen flared to life and was filled with pictures, mostly of babes with round, flushed cheeks, though a few others looked more war-like, brandishing swords or flames. All had huge, spreading wings.

"Here!" Christa exclaimed, pointing. "Mikeal! Make him look like Mikeal!" With a flick of her eyes, Gwendolyn projected the picture of the warrior angel brandishing a flaming sword onto the wall in front of her. "And Delok!" Christa said pointing to the picture on the compute screen of the elfin angel that had struck down Knolwin with a bolt of lightning. Gwendolyn's eyes moved and Delok's image hovered in the air to her right. She enlarged a few more images at her mother's request and went to work, hands deep into the HoloSculpt.

Evan walked into the studio, done with his morning lessons. His hazel eyes swept across the room, taking in the three women but seeking out Gwen, though she was too engrossed in her work to notice him. He spied Faith and it was obvious that her body had stiffened at his entrance. Next to her stood a small elfin woman with platinum blonde hair and an expression of rapture on her face as she watched Gwendolyn sculpt.

He approached them warily, not wanting to disturb them, and noticed Faith become more tense with every step. "Good morning, ladies," he offered.

Christa turned to him and took an unexpected gulp of air. "Good morning!" she exclaimed. "What a handsome young man you are! Do you work here?"

"You could say that." He paused for a moment, unsure. "I'm Evan," he said after a second of indecision, offering his hand. "And," he continued, "by the grace of The One, you must be Mrs. de Rossi." From the corner of his eye he could see Faith's body nearly collapse with relief.

Christa grasped his hand and gave a small curtsy. "I am!" she agreed. "I was just helping..." she started as she looked back towards Gwendolyn. Flushing a bright pink, Christa turned her face away as she spied the body parts that Gwen was working on, though it was only the portion of his upper chest. "Just visiting my daughters," she finished quickly.

"Evan," Faith greeted.

"Dr. de Rossi," he responded politely. "Thomas wanted to know if there is anything you need," he said, lying coolly and making Faith smile. He and Faith both knew that Thomas would check with her personally.

"No, I'm doing fine. Thank you."

"And Gwendolyn?"

"Is fine as well," Faith assured him, amused by his subterfuge. "I'll have her call to the front if she needs anything."

"In that case," Evan said, "I'll return to my...office."

Faith almost laughed but kept her composure. "Thank you, Evan."

"It was a pleasure to meet you, Evan," Christa offered.

"And you as well," he replied with a short bow before he turned and left the room, darting a glance and smile at Gwen whose own eyes were fixed upon her work. Christa, too flustered by the naked bust, looked instead at her eldest daughter.

"Give him blue eyes," she whispered, "like Charity's."

"Like yours, you mean?" Faith asked, her lips twisting into a wry smile. Her mother beamed at her.

"You think that Charity has my eyes?"

Well, Faith thought, *considering Father's eyes are the color of sick shit, yes. Or, as Hope says, duh.* She smiled at her mother. "Of course she does!" she assured her. "The same color and the same sparkle!" Her mother looked as if she might melt under the praise. *Although the sparkle in Charity's eyes, unlike yours, is not from the ecstasy of the light of The One. Quite the opposite, I'm sure.*

Faith perched herself atop one of Gwendolyn's stools and, keeping her thoughts to herself, reached out to a small screen next to the large one that Gwen had running, and opened a program that showed an enormous sphere of gradient color. She moved her finger over the area, selecting the right shade of blue.

"And give him freckles!" Mother said. "Like Hope! But maybe not as many." She laughed girlishly and turned back towards Gwendolyn, smiling at the figure that was forming inside the HoloSculpt, carefully keeping her line of sight above his neck.

"Are there any of Faith's qualities that you would like him to have?" Gwendolyn asked over her shoulder.

"Can you make him as smart as Faith?" Christa asked.

Gwendolyn laughed. "That might be a dangerous thing to do, Mother. And that would be Faith's department anyway."

Faith smiled to herself as she worked the color program. "Do you think he should have ginger hair?" she asked, "to go with the freckles?"

Christa laughed. "Yes, but not like Hope's."

Faith nodded as the tip of her finger moved across the color sphere. She didn't want some would-be bodyguard looking too much like her youngest sister. Madeline was enough. She selected a shade that would equate to a deep auburn when finished rather than a burnt orange.

Gwen had returned to the construct's face, fine tuning his cheeks and chin. Christa clapped her hands, delighted as the figure took shape before her eyes. He was average height and slender (if one could tell from the chest upwards), and his boyish features had an elegant grace.

"Throw a holo," Gwen instructed her twin as she stepped back from the bust inside the HoloSculpt. "So she can see more of how he'll look."

Faith touched the small screen and projected a hologram onto the bust. The blue grid lines that had made the head and shoulders of the next construct gave way to white skin with a ruddy tone under a spray of freckles. A sweep of auburn hair shaded bright blue eyes. Christa gasped.

"He is utterly beautiful," she breathed. "He really is just like an angel! I'm sure the Bauam will absolutely love him!"

More than you could ever imagine, Faith thought. She looked at Gwen and her twin shot a glance back that showed that the dyer's thoughts mirrored her own. Faith stood and embraced Christa.

"Thank you Mother!" she exclaimed, her tone quite sincere. "You have been a great help to us!"

"I have?" Mother answered, hugging her daughter.

"Yes," Faith told her. "And now, just like us, you will be changing the future of the galaxies!"

Christa, her mouth hanging slightly open, clasped her hands together in front of her thin chest. "Do you really think so?"

Faith looked at the figure in the HoloSculpt and a frisson of premonition ran up her spine. She dismissed it immediately. Premonitions held no scientific ground with her. She forced a grin. "I know so."

ONE SEVEN

The Abon's office was quite an unexpected sight. For the head monk, known for leading a minimalistic life as a leader of simplistic people, his workspace seemed nothing but chaos. There were papers, paper books, notes, slippers, boxes and more papers, all crammed into and laying over what little space was available. Not to mention that the desk, as well as the room, was comparatively tiny for a man so large. Nothing adorned the cracked plaster walls save for a long single scroll scrawled with a plain ideogram text.

"Well!" the Abon boomed, making Elaeric jump. Hahn turned coolly, surveying the mammoth-sized man with golden skin and a tonsured head that was now blocking the only exit. Old habits died hard. "If it isn't my budding terraformers!"

He opened his arms wide and ushered the two monks from the doorway and into the room where they dropped their narrow bottoms into the two small chairs that faced the desk. Proportionately, they looked like two schoolboys awaiting punishment in the office of the school principal.

Elaeric cringed at his words, unable to help himself. Since their first experimental tributary, he and Hahn had enlarged the stream and given it companionable brooks and creeks, created more gardens, raised boulders and trees. From the time when they had returned from their trip to the galaxy fair they had done more, and had most recently produced a miniature volcano – just to see if they could. They had watched it with fascination for the past three evenings after they had meditated. The knee-high crater coughed out gouts of lava that inched down the sides to hiss in the widening stream where it cooled into black, porous rocks.

The Abon wedged his body behind the desk and sank into the wide chair that crouched there in patient fear, groaning under his oppressive bulk. Behind the authority of his meager metal desk, as if being the Abon wasn't already enough, the man's face contorted into a stern and patronly expression.

"I have been meaning to talk with you both for some time," he said. "And speak on your antics of late."

Hahn Chi bristled. He didn't know if it was the man himself, his manner or his attitude. Though his fatherly tone was, as it always was outside of the Temple, gentler, it still rubbed Hahn the wrong way. Everything about the Abon seemed to put Hahn on the defensive, as it had done so for the better part of a century. *Maybe I simply do not like to be rebuked,* he thought. He did not need to look at his friend to see the hangdog expression that he knew was on Elaeric's face. Just the knowledge of it made Hahn bristle even more.

"Antics?" Hahn asked. "I am not sure that I know what you mean."

"Do not play the fool with me, Hahn Chi," the Abon scolded softly. "You may be a Master in the Temple, but you do not lie well, or play a good fool."

"That is a compliment," Elaeric assured quietly, leaning towards his friend.

Hahn could not help the look of gratitude for his friend that overtook the contempt he felt for the Abon.

"Though I appreciate your effort in the aesthetics of our grounds here, you two need to think through your plan first, or follow up afterwards. The stream you created was quite pleasing to the eye, and so was the lake it formed in the basin of the hill below – until it overran its banks and flooded the farm paddies underneath!"

Elaeric looked up sharply, though his whole body clenched with shame. Even Hahn could not keep the astonishment from his face. His mind tried to calculate how far the paddies were from the spot in the monastery where he and Elaeric liked to meditate, along with how large the basin on the hill below must be.

Quite large. And to flood the paddies!

So much water!

He tried to squash the feeling of pride that welled up inside him.

The Abon looked at him with exasperation as if reading his feelings. "Energy fields are not something to be toyed with," he admonished. Though his tone was still mild, his voice had deepened in a threatening manner.

Elaeric bowed his head while Hahn Chi lifted his chin the slightest bit. He could feel something strange welling within his body. Filling him and surrounding him. It felt like an electrical charge, similar to the time when he was a boy and had been goaded into putting his tongue onto a velite battery. The shock was unpleasant and yet, somehow tasty.

The Abon opened his mouth to deliver what Hahn was sure to be a scathing remark but, before he could utter a word, a smoothly shaved head popped in through the doorway.

"Abon!" the monk called without waiting for recognition or welcome. "There are some men here to see you!"

The features of the Abon's wide face grimaced with displeasure. "And who might these men be?" he demanded. "So important to disturb a meeting with my brother monks!"

The messenger did not even spare a glance for Elaeric or Hahn. "Two men from the IGC," he said, swallowing. "And another. A Zealot of The One." He swallowed again, his almond-shaped eyes darting about. "A Cassar Zealot!" he whispered as if it would be unseemly to speak the words aloud.

"Bah!" the Abon denounced.

The monk in the doorway fidgeted, too agitated to leave. "But they are demanding an audience!"

"It is not for mortals to demand," the Abon replied, though he was already raising his great weight from the chair. "Where are they?"

"The voriste, down by the fountain."

The Abon nodded as he navigated his substantial girth around his desk and through the doorway. He paused there as if listening, or simply considering, then motioned for Hahn and Elaeric to follow. The monks looked at each other, surprised, then rose to follow the Abon and the messenger.

The four left the small building that housed the Abon's office and walked out into a courtyard filled with sunshine. Their saffron-colored robes flapped in the breeze, producing the sound of a small but cheery audience as their slippered feet crossed the flat, bluish stones that had been set into the grass. To their right rose the edifice of the Temple and from beyond came the heavy clicking sound from the monks in the fight yard, battling with copra-staffs.

To their left were manicured lawns and spreading aca trees that shaded wide, still ponds. The ponds were filled with Komi - golden whiskered fish, known to devour men or any other living thing dropped into their waters, though they had no teeth.

The monks made their way down the path to where three men waited at the far end of the voriste. Two wore blue suits complete with jackets, rumpled from traveling. The third was dressed in all black but wore a vest over his shirt rather than a coat. As the monks approached, Hahn could see a scar on the man's neck and knew that he was a Cassar Zealot. The Cassars were the militant branch of The One Church, Zealots who had dedicated their lives to enforcing the Church's laws. Though he could not see a weapon, Hahn sensed that the man was armed.

The Cassar leered at them from a thin, pockmarked face as the monks stopped in front of them.

"Gentlemen," the Abon greeted, bowing to the men.

One of the blue-suited men stepped forward, his watery eyes fixed on the Abon. "Zhang Li!" he demanded.

Hahn had to bite his tongue. He had never known the Abon's name.

"You should address the Abon by his title!" corrected the monk that had announced their arrival.

"You are still the leader here?" the man asked, ignoring the agitated monk.

"I am," the Abon agreed.

"You are in arrears for taxes due to the IGC. Five years to be exact!"

The Abon spread his hands apologetically. "The monastery is self-sustaining, but does not earn any income," he explained.

The other blue-suited man made a phbbing noise with his lips. "We know that new monks enter the monastery with donations, some of them quite large."

"Some," the Abon agreed, "though some come with nothing and are accepted just the same. The monies that we do receive are spent on things that we cannot grow or supply on our own."

"Well," the man said, "I certainly hope you have some saved up."

"I do not," the Abon said.

"Then you will be remanded into custody," the man with the watery eyes told the Abon.

"Me?"

"Yes. After five years, non-payment of taxes becomes a criminal offense."

"What?" Elaeric demanded, finally spurred from his

silence. “That is nonsense! And how is it that you direct the punishment on a single man?”

The man in black watched the conversation with a look of satisfaction on his pock-scarred face, but so far had said nothing. Hahn watched everyone and everything, that strange buzzing beginning to surround him again.

“We do not seek to punish just one man,” a blue suit informed him, “but we will imprison anyone who can be directly found at fault. You all, however, will lose these lands if you cannot pay the taxes on them.”

“Who would want them?” the monk who had played messenger asked, truly curious.

The blue-suited man glanced at the man in black before he continued. “If the church of The One True pays the taxes,” blue suit informed them, “the land will be theirs.”

“But why?” Elaeric asked. “We don’t use all the land on this moon, and there are still moons that are totally unpopulated! There is more than enough for everyone!”

“It is not the land they want,” the Abon said quietly.

The grin widened in the pocked face. Hahn could feel the buzzing all over his skin and inside of his head. It felt as if he were covered with an invisible swarm of bees yet he was strangely calm.

“Not today,” the man in black agreed. “Today, we just want you.”

“No,” Hahn told him. The man in black turned his grin to Hahn, welcoming the challenge.

“Hahn Chi!” the Abon commanded. “Hold your ground!”

Hahn bowed his head in acquiescence and it felt to him as if the invisible swarm lifted from his body and moved away, forming a barrier between the men in robes and the men in suits.

The blue-suited man with bleary eyes reached into a pocket and produced a pair of plastique hand restraints. "Zhang Li!" he announced, moving towards the enormous monk. "You are!" He stopped short, puzzled.

There was a mild pause. The Abon cocked his head. "I am...?"

"You are," the man said again, moving forward and again stopping short. The man in black and the other blue suit looked at him, puzzled. The man with the bleary eyes reached out a hand and it went flat as if pressed against a wall of glass.

"Devils!" the black-suited Cassar shouted. He reached behind his body with both hands and produced two small hot-round pistols, training both of them on the monks.

The Abon's assistant shrieked while the Abon himself held perfectly still. Elaeric tilted his head, curious about the welling he felt inside his body and what the outcome might be. For Hahn the effort was less than the electrical impulse needed to relay thought, much less matter.

The pistols melted from the man's hands, making him cry out in surprise and pain. The liquefied steel pooled on the path, save for a single drop that clung to the edge of his thumb. He shook it desperately, howling in pain until it was flung away.

The men in the blue suits backed away, staring.

The Cassar looked scathingly at the monks, clutching his injured hand. "Devils!" he shouted again. "May The One..!"

"See you safely home," the Abon finished for him. "I think it is best that you leave now."

There was a moment of prickling silence induced from indecision and fear. "We will be back," one of the blue-suited men warned, finally pulling his bleary eyes away from the pooled metal on the ground to fix upon the Abon. "Unless you pay your taxes within thirty days, standard time."

"It would be a terrible thing to risk," Hahn said coolly,

drawing everyone's attention, "if the same thing were to happen to your ships, should you return." He glanced meaningfully at the melted pistols and back up at the men.

All eyes widened. The IGC men in the blue suits, like Hahn Chi's fellow monks, were too dumbstruck to speak. They grabbed the elbow of the man in black and forcefully turned him and led him away. They passed through an archway between the small lavatory buildings at the end of the voriste and were gone.

The four monks bowed, more out of habit than courtesy. As they all straightened, the Abon turned his dark narrow eyes to Hahn.

"Was that you, Master Hahn Chi?" he asked, his voice grave.

Hahn opened his mouth to ask the Abon what he was talking about and then snapped it shut and bowed his head. "I cannot be sure, Abon. But I think so, yes."

"What will we do?" the messenger cried, not understanding their exchange, only their situation. He wrung his hands inside the folds of his robe, despairing at their predicament. "If they return?"

"Return they will," the Abon assured him. "Fear is a great deterrent, but it stands no chance against hatred and greed. The IGC wants money and the followers of The One want us dead, or at the very least scattered to the ends of the galaxies." He looked at the distraught monk and his gaze softened. "We will find a solution, or a solution will find us," he assured him. "For now, please see if the kitchens are in need of anything, it is almost lunchtime."

The monk bowed and hurried away as the Abon rubbed the top of his double chin with a stubby finger.

"Will they really take the monastery from us?" Elaeric asked when the monk had departed for the kitchens.

"It is always a possibility," the Abon replied, his finger now tracing the folds between his chins. "But perhaps not." He dropped his hand and fixed his gaze upon Hahn and Elaeric. Elaeric shifted under his heavy stare but Hahn held perfectly still, suddenly wary. "I was actually contacted some time ago about you two," he told them.

"Us?" Elaeric asked, his brows high over his dark, almond-shaped eyes.

"Yes," the Abon said. "It seems that someone, somehow, has learned of your newfound abilities. I disregarded it at the time, and another time after, as I often do when it comes to matters of money." The Abon sighed heavily. "It seems that I was ignoring the whispers of the universe when it was not even my message to ignore. I should have asked the both of you instead."

"Asked us what, Abon?" Elaeric asked.

The great man folded his hands into the sleeves of his robe and straightened. "What you two have been up to – harnessing energy fields - would either of you be interested in doing it for money? I never would have asked before, it is both unseemly and universally unethical, but the times seem to demand more than just decorum."

The two monks looked abashed, but each held still, considering. Something about it seemed wrong. Not what they were doing, but doing it for money. Their meditations were deeply personal, part of their religion and their deep connection to the universe. Doing it for pay made it seem tawdry, like a cheap parlor trick. Still, they knew they could not deny help if help was needed.

Finally they both sighed, almost in unison.

"If it would mean saving the monastery..." Elaeric started.

"...we would help in any way we could," Hahn finished.

The Abon nodded. "There is someone who wants to meet you." Now he sighed as well. "Just for meeting with her and showing her what you can do, she is willing to pay enough that would cover everything that we owe." Elaeric gasped and the Abon nodded sagely. "Should she desire one or both of you to work for her, even for a short time, the monastery would be secure for as close to forever as I could imagine."

The monks looked at each other for a long moment and then back at the Abon.

"When would we go?" Hahn asked.

"As soon as possible. You could take the light-lonorail to the city and a clipper to the Thermopylae on Redclava. From there, to the farthest moon possible from the center. From there, I believe I could get you transport on the Pearl Dragon."

"A Dragon!" Elaeric exclaimed.

The Abon nodded. "Dragons are certainly not used for conveyance, but the Captain is a friend. Do not expect them to bend time for your journey, and they take their own course, but it will still be the fastest way to cross the galaxy."

"A Dragon," Elaeric breathed in wonder.

Hahn drew himself up, smiled and bowed to his friend before turning to the Abon and doing the same.

"I do not think I will need more than a few clean robes and personal items?" he asked the Abon.

The Abon nodded and bowed. "What is most important, you take within you," he told the monk. Hahn dipped his head in understanding, then took his leave and turned to walk back past the Komi ponds.

"I should pack as well," Elaeric said quickly, nearly overcome with the situation and the turn of events. He started to bow but the Abon stopped him smartly with a fleshy hand. Elaeric looked at him, surprised, but the man was watching the departing form of Master Hahn Chi as it passed through the east archway of the voriste.

"Can I trust him?" the Abon asked, his voice grave.

Elaeric was filled with relief and smiled broadly, knowing that it was the one thing of which he was certain. "You can," he assured the Abon. The giant monk turned to give him a look of suspicion but Elaeric only grinned. "I'd bet my eyes on it," he told him, giving him a wink before he bowed low, already thinking about the adventure on which he was about to embark.

ONE 8

Evan began his new life helping Gwen at the compound. It was small tasks at first since she was reticent about asking for his aid - unless it was for things she couldn't do, such as carrying something that was too heavy for her to lift.

Gwen never thought she would need any kind of an assistant, especially now that they had Thomas, but she found it was not just a relief not to lug in blocks of clay by herself, but she really enjoyed Evan's company. He was the first one who had ever listened, not just patiently but *attentively*, to her talk about art. She shared with him everything she knew about the history and growth of painting and sculpture, human and elfin, as well as what she knew of the other races of the galaxies, both living and dead. Finally having an avid audience, the floodgates opened.

She was rattling on to him one day in her studio after a column of rugged marble that she had been waiting for had finally been delivered. Not only that, but next to it, wrapped in a piece of hand-tooled leather, was a set of small hammers and chisels, made especially for working the granite she had just received. Gwendolyn had squealed with delight, practically bursting out of her own skin as Evan helped her unveil the block of dusty stone and she showed him the tools, explaining the purpose of each one. Suddenly, she stopped her babble in mid-sentence.

His smile was a little more broad than usual, his hazel eyes sparkling. Instead of warming her, it made her cold.

"If I asked you a question, would you be honest with me?"

Evan's smile widened the tiniest bit. "I would be anything you asked," he said.

"Does this interest you at all?"

Evan cocked his head. "What do you mean?"

"I just realized that I have been babbling away this whole time, like I do every time, and I've never asked you if this interests you in the slightest. So tell me, honestly, does this interest you at all?"

His smile widened just a bit more, showing his perfect teeth. "No."

Gwen felt her shoulders slump. "Then why?" she asked. "Why do you listen to me go on and on?"

" I love listening to you talk," he said. "It wouldn't matter to me if you were just rattling off random numbers."

"I don't know if that makes me feel better or worse," she murmured.

"You should feel better," he said, his voice deep and sincere.

"Is it..." Gwendolyn asked, looking away, "does it have something to do with the way you were...you are..."

Evan laughed and shook his dark blonde head, anticipating her question. "No," he answered, "I don't think it has anything to do with how I was made. I don't feel like I'm trying to oblige or to please you. It's just, what I think is, my natural response. I might not love art, but I love to hear you talk about it. I love the way you light up when you talk about brush strokes, or The Age of Elfish Impressionism. It lights me up too." Gwen gave him a doubtful look but it was trimmed with a smile. "But," he argued, "in a broader sense, I am very interested when your talk about art coincides with stories about the rise and fall of empires."

"You've always shown a proclivity for history," Gwen

admitted with a smirk.

"And," he continued, picking up her hand, "I can't wait to see you work." He massaged her palm with his thumb and the feeling was intensely intimate. It made her insides feel like jelly. She stared at him for a moment and, for a second, she wanted to move his hand onto her body. "Especially with that," he said, jerking his chin and bringing her out of her short reverie.

Gwen followed his gaze to the machine near her worktable and made a face as she carefully drew her hand away from his. "I don't like the HoloSculpt," she admitted out loud for the first time. "I don't think technology should play so deeply into art."

Evan cocked an eyebrow at her. "What am I, then?" he asked.

Gwendolyn laughed. "You are exactly that," she admitted.

"Show me how it works," Evan encouraged.

Gwen sighed and then nodded. "Alright." The dyer abandoned her precious column of rock for the moment and approached her technical workstation. She powered up the machine and cleared it, giving her a three-dimensional empty canvas. Scooting her body in close, she put her hands inside the laser beams that crossed into a grid and drew them across, down, and across again at the bottom, forming a sphere. Then she gave the sphere ears and stood back, chuckling. "You see? It's too easy, especially when you compare it to chiseling rock."

"Can I try?" Evan asked.

"Of course!" Gwen exclaimed, though she was surprised, and stepped aside. Evan put his hands into the machine and hesitated, his fingertips brushing the surface, and then he gently grasped the sphere and began to change it. It was awkward at first, but he soon got the hang of it.

Gwen glanced at the sculpture in progress from time to time, but her focus stayed mostly on Evan. She was more fascinated by him than what he was working on. She watched his expressions change, so varied sometimes between joy and consternation that it made her laugh more than once. After what was near an hour he pulled his hands out and, she was amused to see, wiped them on his shirt in the same manner she did after using the machine, though the sculpting left no physical residue.

"What do you think?" Evan asked, expectant. Gwen turned her face to the freshly sculpted visage and her eyes lit up.

"Evan! That is amazing! It...it..." Her smile and voice faltered at the same time as she realized what she was looking at. Who she was looking at.

"It's you," he said, quickly, as if she was not already aware. Even without the hair, skin tone, or irises in the eyes - it was like looking into a mirror. Or like looking at Faith.

"How did you do that?" Gwendolyn whispered.

"It wasn't so hard, once I got started and figured out how to make it work."

"No. How did you make my face?" She realized that while he had been sculpting he had not looked at her. Not once.

Evan gave her a soft smile. "It's the face that I see when I close my eyes. It's the face I dream about." He reached out and touched her cheek with his fingertip. Gwen closed her eyes for a moment and then shook off his touch.

"Evan, no. I don't think..."

Evan, sensing her discomfort, switched off the machine. Gwen was glad. She was afraid she wasn't going to be able to tear her eyes from the likeness he had made of her. "Enough art for the day!" he announced, changing the subject in an instant. "Why don't you show me the vid you were telling me about last week? The one from Earth?"

Gwen chuckled, her mood already lightened. "That is actually about art, though," she said, and then laughed at Evan's sour expression.

"But you said it was an action vid!"

"It is," she agreed. "It's about someone who steals art. It has fights and chase scenes that I think you might like."

Evan rubbed his hands together in anticipation. "Alright! Do you want..." to get something to eat for the movie, he was going to offer but Gwendolyn interrupted him, shaking her head.

"I'm sorry, Evan, but we can't."

"Why?" he asked, his excitement dissipating like air from a punctured balloon.

"It's a flat chip," Gwen explained. "It won't run on anything here, it's too outdated."

"How did you watch it?"

Gwen shrugged. "I have a chip-player at the cottage."

"Then why don't we go there?"

Gwen looked at him, abashed. "Well," she said finally, slowly, "I guess we could." Evan had left the compound with her plenty of times, day and night. But going to her home seemed different. Especially after a simple touch on her hand had elicited such a response from her own body. Even more so after he had carved her image out of thin air. She glanced at the HoloSculpt, expecting to see it there, but he moved his body to block her view of the now dark machine.

"Come on!" he chided, poking her ribs with his finger. "It's the least you can do after making me lug in all that clay!"

Gwen laughed. "Alright, alright. You're right, it's the least I could do." Evan gave her his best grin, the one that made her feel warm all the way to her bones. Gwen touched the pad on the glass desk under her compute screen.

"Yes, Miss Gwendolyn?" Thomas answered at once.

"Could you please have a car brought around? Evan and I... will be going to the cottage."

"Yes, Miss Gwendolyn. Would you like anything waiting there for you upon your arrival?"

"Champagne," Evan said firmly only to be swatted at by Gwen.

"I can assure you, Mr. Evan, the cottage is plenty well stocked on that front. But I will see to it that the house is opened up, and a chilled bottle is waiting. Something to nosh on as well."

"Thank you, Thomas," Gwen replied before cutting the com. "Champagne?" she asked Evan with raised eyebrows.

He gave her an exaggerated shrug. "It was worth a try!"

Gwen laughed as she headed for the door. "Well, tonight may be your night. Maybe I'll let you try some."

"I hope so," he answered, looking back over his shoulder at the glass that separated Gwen's studio from Faith's office. It was dark now, but Evan could sense her eyes on them as they left.

The aircar drove for nearly an hour, though the time seemed to pass quickly as Gwendolyn admonished Evan for his pretentiousness and he teased her equally about her obsessiveness.

Finally, it dropped them off neatly in front of the white, picket fence that ran around the cottage gardens and Evan was quick to circle the car to help Gwendolyn out. He held onto her hand a moment longer, making sure she was steady on her feet, and not wanting to let it go.

She led him through the gate and up the path. "It's a beautiful night," she said softly, her hand still in his as her eyes slid across the heavens.

"It is?"

"Yes. I forget how bright the stars are out here, away from the glow of the city."

Evan's hazel eyes swept across the sky as they reached the door and Gwen opened it. Though the building had a rustic charm, it had a fingerprint reader on the door handle. He followed her in to the living room and, as she turned to remark laughingly on the champagne that was already waiting for them in a bucket of ice, he pulled her close and kissed her.

She kissed him back, but only for a moment. Then she was pulling away and shaking her head.

"Please." Evan implored, though it was more statement than question and his face was drawn, as if in pain. He leaned forward and kissed her again. "Please," he said, and kissed her on the cheek. He cupped her face and looked at her beseechingly. "I've wanted to kiss you for so long," he said and kissed her chin.

Gwendolyn closed her eyes and smiled at the feel of his lips just under her own. His mouth slid down her chin and he kissed the top of her throat, making her breath hitch. "Then why didn't you?"

Evan laughed softly and kissed the line of her jaw. "Are you serious? Where there are cameras everywhere and Faith watching all the time?"

Gwen laughed lightly, understanding quite well. Evan kissed her ear and it sent a shiver through her so hard that she pulled away. "Evan, I don't know about this."

He cupped her face again in his hands and his hazel eyes bore into her. "Please?" he asked and, when she only stared at him, saying nothing, he kissed her cheek. "Please," he said again, kissing her eyebrow and then the hollow of her temple, his lips lingering there for what seemed to Gwen like a long time and yet not enough. "Please." His lips touched under her ear and she gasped.

"No," Gwendolyn said, pushing him back. "Evan, we can't."

Evan cupped her face in his hands and his hazel eyes stared into her hers, pleading. "Please, Gwen. I love you. I love you so much I can hardly stand it." Gwen stared back as he leaned forward and kissed her cheek again. "Please." He kissed the corner of her mouth and then the corner of her jaw. "Please," he whispered, kissing her neck and pulling her body tight against his own.

The feel of his body, hard and strong against hers, ignited a fire within her. She wanted to respond in kind, and kiss him back, but she turned her face away, unsure and torn with indecision.

"I'm sorry Evan," she said, amongst his entreaties and kisses. "I don't know what to do." She laughed a little at the absurdity but Evan leaned back and took her face into his hands again.

"Start by kissing me."

Gwen closed her eyes and did so. Softly at first, then gradually more insistently. Not because he did, but because her body and soul seemed to demand it. She kissed him and then kissed him more. His gentle touch and her apprehensive kisses seemed to last for moments only before the fire of their passion curled about their bodies like flames and consumed them.

Gwen was astounded by the ferocity in which they clung to one another - as if an unstoppable force was pulling them together, like two moons being crushed by gravity into a single planet, her mouth opening now to search out his tongue, his teeth, his breath.

When he unfastened the back of her dress she did not stop him, but instead helped him from his shirt as they kissed their way to the couch, losing their shoes as they went. Evan slipped her dress from her shoulders and stopped kissing her long enough so he could lean back and look at her. A sigh tore through him and escaped his lips and then they were kissing again as she pulled him to the couch, her hands tangled in his hair and he cradling her neck with one hand.

Gwen worried that it would be awkward or uncomfortable, but it was far from both. Just when she had decided that deep kisses were not enough, he was deep inside her and she cried out, arching her back.

She moved with him as their passion seemingly, unbelievingly grew and grew, moaning into his relentless mouth. He kissed her all the way till the end, till she broke the kiss as her body was racked with convulsions, each one as intense, if not more, than the first. She shouted his name over and over as her body clenched and unclenched, her shouts tapering off into cries until the body-racking shudders subsided.

They lay together on the couch after, slick with sweat and breathless.

Finally, Evan propped himself up on his hands, grinning at her. She reached up and held his face between her palms.

"I never had any idea that would be so wonderful. You?" she asked, still breathless. "What do you think?"

Evan laughed and looked at the bottle of champagne as it shifted in the melting ice. The steel bucket was beaded with condensation. "I think we should open that," he said and then looked back at Gwen to touch his damp forehead to hers, "and then I think we should do *that* again."

Gwen, thirsty and sweaty, could not agree more.

She could feel his legs entwined with her own and thought, *that's what we are – entwined. I suppose we always were. He was always in my heart, long before he was made.*

As if echoing her thoughts, Evan grasped her hand in his own, entwining her fingers in his as he kissed her.

ONE NINE

Hope rolled over in the bed, sweaty and agitated though the night was gentle and full of moonlight. She threw a leg out of the covers and let the breeze from the open window blow over her pale, freckled skin, cooling it. She stayed that way for a few moments, and then rolled back over. Madeline, sharing the large bed in Faith and Gwendolyn's guest room at the cottage, reached over and gently swatted at Hope's damp, copper-colored curls in an attempt to offer some comfort without having to actually wake up.

Hope tried to be still, for Madeline's sake, but after a few moments she rolled back the other way again, scrunching the pillow angrily under her face and hating Faith. She hated her sister so much that she would not have agreed to stay at the cottage at all had Gwen not assured her that Faith never came home anymore.

He loved me, Hope thought. *He really loved me.* She felt a sob rise like a gorge in her throat and she clamped her teeth down on the corner of the quilted coverlet, muffling the sound.

Then why didn't he say goodbye?

Tears welled in her eyes and slipped sideways across her face, disappearing into the folds of the pillow.

Maybe it was too painful for him, she thought, her heart swelling in empathy.

It wasn't too painful for me. Not too much to find him. Even though we never got to say goodbye.

She thought of how she had rushed to the airfield that day, twisting an ankle as she left the aircab bobbing and waiting and unpaid as she limped through the gate and onto the broken tarmac.

She had made her way past a row of jets waiting for deployment and then stopped short as she saw the chalk that was next in line to depart. The dirty wind whipped her already wild hair all over her face and she brushed at it angrily. There had to be fifty meters between them but she knew the shape of his body too well. The air was rank with diesel fuel and the sun was being pulled to the horizon through a haze of smog but his face turned and she knew his blue eyes were looking directly at her.

She had waited, holding her foot slightly off the ground to favor the inured ankle that was already beginning to swell, her breath coming in painful hitches. And she waited. She had still been wearing her lab coat, her wild, copper-colored curls being thrown and twisted by the hot dry wind. There could be no doubt as to who she was, especially with his keen sight. She held his gaze a moment longer, his expression clouded by shadow, then he turned and climbed into the jet.

Hope bit down on the coverlet again as she felt her breath start to hitch in her chest, determined to wait out the storm inside. Her blurred vision caught sight of her dream journal sitting on the nightstand. The dark leather cover jutted out over the edge just a bit and she reached out to touch it.

Johnny told me, she thought, running a fingertip along the binding and thinking of the dream that she had dreamed not just once, but twice. *He told me and I didn't listen. I didn't want to listen because I was in love with him. I am in love with him.*

A cold poured into her then as her memories overran her thoughts.

And then there was that horrible dream with the sand. In the dream he was forcing me to eat the sand, so I thought. But it was really me – feeding myself lies. He didn't love me and he wasn't the key. I knew even then but I didn't want to listen, even to myself. I'm a fool. A stubborn fool.

The tears kept flowing hot and wet on her face, turning cool and damp after they had soaked into her pillow. At least the hitching in her chest had stopped. The storm was passing.

Later, after the large blue moon had drifted higher into the sky and then a small purple one had risen (both visible through the cottage window), Hope slept.

She thought her sleep would be dreamless now that she was deprived of her dream love, or tormented by nightmares, but she was wrong.

When she awoke in the morning there was bright blue sky and birdsong outside the cottage window. She sat up, rubbed her eyes with her fists, then yawned and stretched. The dream that had come after last night's emotional storm still clung to her with an amorphous embrace. The man who had pulled her from the riverbank in a previous dream had come back to save her again.

She retrieved her dream journal from the nightstand and dropped it into her lap, opening it to the first blank page. Her purple pen waited there, wedged between the last dream and the blank space.

Hope uncapped the pen and started to write but it produced nothing but scratch marks on the paper. She looked at it quizzically then realized it had run dry.

What does it mean? she thought, staring at the tip of the dry stylus. She sighed and returned the book and now defunct pen to the night table. *Probably just means that I need a new pen.*

She pushed back the covers and headed for the bathroom. After a shower she felt better, especially since Gwen had old-fashioned towels instead of a body dryer. Dryers turned her already wild hair into an unmanageable mane. She used the heavy terry cloth to scrub her skin even more, a cathartic exfoliation that left her skin pink and her heart much lighter.

Her lifted mood took a considerable dip as she caught the bleeping sound of a call coming over a comset somewhere in the cottage.

Hope squeezed water from her hair with the towel, rubbing it as dry as she could while the bleeping continued. Finally, she threw down the towel and stormed into the living room. She could see Madeline beyond the dining room and through the door that led to the kitchen. The comset was on a book-laden table in the living room, bleating noise and flashing blue light.

"Why don't you answer it?" Hope demanded in a tone just short of a shout.

"I don't know how," Madeline called from the kitchen.

"There's a light flashing on the button! You just press the button! Duh!"

"I wouldn't know where to put it."

"I'll tell you where to put it," Hope muttered, picking up the device and hooking it over her right ear as she pressed the button. "Hello?"

"Please hold for Miss Gwendolyn," a male voice said amiably before disappearing altogether. Hope rolled her green eyes towards the ceiling. At least it was Gwen. Had it been Faith she would have closed the line and tossed the comset in the toilet. She still might.

"Hello?" Gwendolyn's voice asked over the com. "Hope, is that you?"

"You called me," Hope said, though she was already smiling at the sound of Gwen's voice. "Of course it's me." She could hear Gwen sigh over the com, but it was a good sigh, almost a laugh.

"Hope! I am so sorry I wasn't there to welcome you home

last night. I'm the only one here at the center, well not the only one, but the only one of us. You have to come see me. I'm dying to see you!"

"It's okay," Hope told her, sitting down on a couch. "I needed the alone-time to adjust anyway." She could see Madeline going from the kitchen to the dining room with steaming plates of food. She could feel and hear her stomach rumble.

"Will you?" Gwendolyn asked. "Come to the center?"

"Faith's not there?" Hope asked.

"No, she's not even on Esodire right now. And Charity and Llewellyn are...well, I don't know where they are."

Hope laughed. "Some things never change," she said and could hear Gwendolyn's laugh echo over the com. "Yes, I'll come see you. Give me an hour or so. I need to eat and get ready."

"I'll send a car in an hour," Gwen said, delighted, "but take as much time as you need. I can't wait to see you!"

"Me too," Hope agreed and knew that it was true. She had missed Gwen, everyone, she now realized. She pressed the button on the com at her ear, cutting the link.

Except Faith. Hope decided. *I could do without her controlling bullshit for a Dragon's age.*

She pulled the comset off and put it back on the table before joining Madeline in the dining room where her twin was settling down to breakfast. "Thanks," Hope told her, sitting herself down behind a plate of eggs that had been scrambled together with chives and spinach.

"I couldn't find any coffee," Madeline apologized, nodding at the pot of tea on the table. "But there is juice in the fridge."

"That's okay," Hope said, pouring tea even though she had come to prefer coffee. "I'm sure there will be plenty at the center. Would you like to come with me?"

Madeline smiled and shook her head as she wiped her mouth with a napkin. "I would love to, but Gwendolyn has let the garden run wild! I like the way it looks, a bit jungle-like, but it really should be tamed. I have lots of work to do here."

Hope nodded and quickly ate her breakfast, anxious to see Gwen and what had been going on while she had been gone.

By the time she reached the compound, it was an hour before noon. The young de Rossi woman was amazed to see what had progressed at the center, marveled at the polite and fastidious Thomas, and laughed heartily at how overjoyed Gwendolyn was to see her and introduce her to Evan.

"It's a pleasure to meet you in person, Evan," Hope told him, visually appraising the construct that Charity had said was in love with Gwen. He had beautiful features, with blonde-brown hair and bright hazel eyes. He had a lean form but Hope could see a fine musculature that moved beneath his clothes.

"And you as well," he said, shaking her hand. "Gwendolyn says that you and Faith are the smartest people she knows, so you should know I am already both intrigued and intimidated by you."

Hope beamed at him and turned to Gwen, scrunching her nose in delight at the praise. Her sisters usually described her as being cute or darling, making her feel that she was about as useful as a bunny rabbit.

"And very bold," Evan continued as Gwendolyn turned to lead them from the lobby of the center. "Gwen says you traveled to another moon to look into the prospect of the ZPE harnessing."

"Yes," Hope agreed as they followed her eldest sister's dyer, ignoring the tug in her chest at the reminder of her recent aspirations. "And, I am told, that my talents are needed again."

Gwen glanced at her youngest sister and Hope could see the apology in her brown and gold eyes, an apology that should have been coming from Faith. One that Hope doubted she would ever get.

"Yes," Gwen said. "Faith has another, ahem, mission lined up for you." She led them through a series of corridors to a small room with two rows of four chairs each. She sat in the first row and motioned for Evan and Hope to join her.

The chairs faced a large window that looked into an even larger room. The room beyond the glass was empty save for a young man with auburn hair in drab clothing, kneeling on the bare floor. As Hope and Evan sat down, the door to the viewing room opened again to admit Thomas and a butler droid.

Thomas carried a tray of drinks and a foldout stand. Without losing an ounce of poise, he dropped the stand and kicked it open. The droid's body flattened out and landed carefully on the tray, its cargo of refreshments rattling quietly as they settled. Thomas handed Gwen and Evan tall glasses filled with sparkling water poured over ice broken by thick slices of lime.

"You know what I could actually use..." Hope started as the tall young man turned to her, handing her a large cup atop an oversized saucer. She could smell the heady aroma of strong espresso that had been topped with creamy foam. "How did you know?" Hope asked, incredulous.

Thomas gave her a hint of a smile. "It is my business to know, Miss Hope."

"Miss Hope?" she asked.

"He does the same for all of us,'" Gwen told her. "Except for Faith, of course. She's Dr. de Rossi."

"How else would you know to whom I was addressing?" he asked before turning to Hope without waiting for an answer from Gwen. "There is cream and sugar on the tray," he told her. "Please let me know if there is anything else you require."

"This will be fine," Hope responded. "Thank you." Ignoring

the delicate silver tongs, she plucked a lump of sugar with her fingers from the bowl and dropped it into her cup. Thomas pretended not to notice. He bowed and left the room, closing the door behind him.

The droid had reduced itself to not much more than a silver platter with café condiments and a few delicate pastries upon its back. Hope selected a small silver spoon from its offerings and stirred her coffee, mixing the sugar and the foam down into the espresso.

"What is this place?" she asked as Gwen raised a hand and pointed to the glass. Hope directed her attention to the other room where a door was opening and the young man was rising to his feet. Hope saw for the first time that he held a weapon – a long blade of hammered steel.

Through the door on the other side floated three ellipsoidal half-droids. Though they were only half the size of the normal humanoid drone, they had more than twice the speed. They were often used in military training. Hope had heard of the type but had never actually seen one.

Most droids she had ever seen were servant droids. They were glittering, gentle, floating things. The things that had entered the room on the other side of the glass were bulky and looked malevolent.

"He's never fought three before," Gwen said, watching the droids encircle the young man who stood straight and tall, keeping his weapon low along the line of his leg.

"He's one of the constructs?" Hope asked.

"Yes," Gwen said. "BG-Syn. The last of the first se..six."

"You can say seven," Hope told her, sipping her coffee and watching the glass. "It's no secret that Faith took Evan off the line."

Gwen cleared her throat in a nervous manner but Evan only grinned. "I know," she agreed quietly, "but Faith would like to keep that under wraps."

"I don't give a fuck what Faith wants," Hope retorted calmly.

Gwen's face went white and Evan chortled into his hand. Hope sipped her cappuccino and lifted her chin at the glass.

"They're starting," she said.

The first droid, a meter tall and hovering a meter off the ground, came at the young man, zooming in from behind. The construct spun and cut away the knife the droid was brandishing as the next droid came, pointing a mock-photon pistol.

BG-Syn ducked and swerved as a shot was fired, blurring the air with real heat. He rose back up, swinging his weapon so fast that it was even less visible than the heat mirage from the dummy gun. There was merely a flash of light as the overhead fluorescents burst dully off the blade and the droid fell to the ground in two pieces.

"He's pretty," Hope remarked.

"You like him?" Gwen asked, expectant. "Mother actually had a lot to do with his exterior design."

Hope snorted, seeing the hand of their mother now that it was brought to her attention. "I should have known. He looks like a character from one of her stories."

"From her One Bible?"

"What else?"

The last droid engaged as the first one returned, both attacking at once. The knife was knocked away again as well as the makeshift club that was swung by the third droid. The young man jammed his blade into the third attacker and it fell to the ground in a gout of blue sparks as the first one returned once again with the knife.

The auburn-haired fighter batted the knife away with ease and cut the droid in half on the return stroke. The man straightened with confidence as it fell to the ground in two pieces. Then, from his blindside, what was left of the third droid shot up with a piece of pipe and smashed it against the side of the young man's head.

The construct crumpled to the ground.

Gwen stood up from her seat, her hand covering her mouth. Then the shock melted away and her hand dropped. "Get him to medical!" she shouted over the open com, a frown-line creasing her brows.

Hope looked at the twin of her sister and gave her a rueful grin. "You sound more like Faith every day," she said.

*

Half of an hour later they stood outside the room where BG-Syn was housed at the small medical center at the compound.

"What do I do?" Gwen asked, not for the first time. "We are presenting him in nearly a month and he has to be infallible. I have him on an accelerated training level but it is clearly not enough."

"You have to ask Faith," Hope told her, which was also not the first time.

"Faith isn't here!" Gwen cried. "And I did everything that she told me to do! All the numbers, all the sequences! I had everything set and I had Evan double check!"

Hope glanced at the handsome construct and he nodded. Hope shrugged. "Then adjust his differentials. I'm sure Faith rigged his nervous system to mimic a human because they have faster reflexes than elves due to more fast-twitch muscles. But you can tell by the way he fights that he is *too* human - he expects what a human expects. He should be more like a machine, with no expectations – making him ready for anything."

"How am I supposed to do that?"

Hope considered for a moment then her green eyes looked up, glinting. "Is it too late to change his DNA?"

Gwen shook her head slowly, hesitant. "I don't think so." Her right hand went to her mouth and she traced her lips with the edge of her thumbnail as she tried to think like Faith. It was something she had to do more and more lately. "We can change a single strand," she mused aloud, "and then program it for dominance. Once in, it would replicate and replace the other strands in his cells in about twenty-four hours. But I wouldn't know how to do it."

"Can you pull up his schematics on Faith's computer?"

Gwen nodded. "I think so."

"I can take care of the rest," Hope told her sister's twin, who sagged with relief. Hope thought she might have fallen over had Evan not been there with an arm to put around her. "Can I go in and see him first?" Gwen nodded quickly. "How do I open this thing?" Hope asked, looking at the door and not seeing a handle or a palm pad – but as she spoke the word "open," the door slid into the wall with a shush.

"Voice command helps keep everything as sterile as possible," Gwen explained. Hope nodded and walked through the opening. "We'll meet you back in Faith's lab," she said. Hope's only acquiescence was the dip and bob of her copper-colored curls as she nodded absently while entering the room. Gwendolyn gave the door a soft command to close and it did so.

The room inside was brightly lit but had the same scrubbed-down industrial look as the rest of the compound, other than the lobby and Gwen's studio. Hope pulled the only chair in the room up to the bed and sat in it, making a mental note to ask Thomas about putting something on the walls.

The construct had a beautiful face. She could appreciate it more now that she was up close. His skin was like alabaster, with a spattering of dark freckles. The bandage around his head had pushed a lock of his auburn hair down over his left eyebrow and Hope reached out and gently brushed it back. His eyes fluttered open at her touch and she saw that his eyes were a brilliant blue. Not the same achingly blue as the Lab Commander, in her opinion, but still breathtaking.

His eyes saw Hope, her freckled face surrounded by a halo of gold and copper, and the construct felt a hitching in his chest. He wondered briefly if he had been injured there as well as his head.

"I don't know you," he said. "Are you new?"

Hope laughed and laid a hand on his arm. The touch was warm and reassuring, just like her laugh. "No," she said. "I'm just late to the party." BG-Syn was apparently confused at her remark and she laughed again. The sound of it made him smile. "Do you know where you are?" she asked, making his smile disappear.

"Yes. I've been here before."

"Do you remember what happened?"

BG-Syn nodded, looking even more disconsolate. "I wasn't fast enough."

"That's okay," Hope reassured him, brushing his hair away from his porcelain features once again. "I'm going to make you faster."

"You are?" BG-Syn asked, his face lighting up. He didn't know what made him feel better - her assurance, her voice, or her touch. No one had ever touched him like that before. With that tenderness. No one really touched him at all outside of the normal poking and prodding as they looked him over in a clinical manner. And no one had talked to him in the same way either. It was always questions, mostly from Faith, cold and calculated. Or demands from his trainer. He didn't mind either one, but being talked to with care and concern was entirely different. It was like cool water being given to a man that had no idea he had been dying of thirst.

"I am," Hope told him with a smile. "But first, you need to rest. I need to look over some figures but I'll be back later."

"You will?"

Hope nodded. "Yes...I'll be back in a little while to give you an injection. Will that be okay?"

"Of course. I won't mind at all."

Hope put her hand along his face. "Get some rest, then," she said standing up and taking her hand away as she went. "I should be back in an hour or two."

"Wait!" he called as she turned away to leave. Hope looked back, curious, her copper curls swaying around her small face. "I don't know your name," he said.

BG-Syn had never asked anyone at the compound for their name before. It was always given to him straight away or he figured it out on his own after a time. But this was the first time that he cared. The beautiful girl with the bronze hair smiled at him.

"Hope," she said. "I'm Hope."

BG-Syn watched her leave and then, once the door had swooshed closed, he closed his eyes.

Hope.

★

Hope joined Gwen and Evan in Faith's lab where Gwendolyn already had everything she needed up and running. Hope took the seat behind the desk and moved her index finger along the glass trackpad, her gaze intent upon the compute screen. She enlarged the picture of the DNA strand and her green eyes became slightly unfocused as they traveled over the double helix. She didn't try to read all the code, it would take forever anyway, but by relaxing her eyes she could find what she wanted - pattern repetition in the blocks of fast-twitch muscle control.

"I can't really make him faster, per se," she admitted while she scrolled through the code, stopping when she found what she wanted. "But I can take what slows him down and snip it, making his reflex and response times faster. A lot faster."

Gwen and Evan watched the screen, mesmerized. "How did you learn to do this?" Gwen asked. "You didn't know this when you left, did you?"

Hope shook her head, zooming in on the sequence she was after. "I learned a lot in the lab. Their whole program was based on breaking things down into smaller and smaller particles to find the Zero-Point Energy. And the Safety Officer for our wing got me into quantum thinking."

Hope opened a square over the part of the enlarged strand that she wanted to remove but, when she clicked on it, the program notified her of legal rights and demanded a password to continue. She harrumphed.

"What is it?" Evan asked.

"Faith has more business sense than I thought," Hope replied. "She copyrights all of the DNA she writes before it is ever published. Pretty smart. Do you know her password?"

Gwen shook her head, disappointed. "Does that mean you can't change it?" she asked, unable to hide the desperation in her voice.

Hope turned her face to look at the dyer for a moment and then turned her face back to the compute screen that was demanding a nine-digit code. She typed *Gwendolyn* on the ghostboard. The legal warning disappeared, allowing her access to change the program. "Smart," she murmured, "but not that clever."

She removed the coding she had selected from the DNA strand, then kept scrolling, looking for other places where she could improve. A half an hour later she had done enough to the framework to start it running a seek and repeat sequence. She got the computer to recognize what she was looking for and make the required adjustments, but even with the lightning speed of the c-drive, it was another hour before it finished. Hope saved the changes, updated the copyright, and sat back and stretched.

Evan and Gwen had tired of standing at some point and were sitting in the two chairs opposite the desk, sharing a late lunch and talking quietly. Gwen straightened and covered her filled mouth so she could start talking right away.

"All done?"

"With this part. Does Faith have a reverse centrifuge in here?"

The blank look she received told Hope that Gwen had no idea. Hope stood up and looked around, stretching once again, putting her fists in the small of her back as she arched it. She spied the device in the corner.

"I'll need 10 cc's of saline," she told Gwen.

Gwendolyn nodded as if she knew what she meant and then clicked on her com to call Thomas. He would know whom to ask. She pointed to the plate next to the compute screen while she waited for his answer, though he picked up the line before it had rung twice.

Hope saw the plate, topped with two baked sandwiches and picked one up. They were still warm. "When did you guys get these?" she asked Evan as Gwen spoke to Thomas on her comset. She bit into it, carefully keeping any flakes away from the compute area. It was filled with melted cheese and vegetables.

"Thomas," Evan answered, meaning that they had been

delivered via the super-assistant. Hope nodded in appreciation and reached for a bottle of cold tea.

They finished their lunch while one of Faith's lab assistants came in and fitted the machine with the requested vial and Hope started it up via the master computer. When it was done, Hope removed the vial from the fuge and socked it into a syringe. She held it up and contemplated the fluid inside. The strand was too small for her eyes to detect, but they would know soon enough if they were successful.

"Where do you inject him?" Gwen asked.

Hope smiled. "It doesn't matter, since it has the program for dominance, but I'll have one of the med guys put it into a brachial vein."

Gwen embraced her. "Thank you so much! I didn't want to call Faith again and we certainly couldn't wait. You are a lifesaver!"

Hope smiled as she hugged Gwen. "I don't know about that," she said, "but I was glad to help." *Especially since Faith wasn't here.* "I'm going back to his room to supervise the injection and maybe stay with him awhile. He seems so lonely."

"You are so sweet," Gwen said.

Hope shrugged. "Do you think you could put some pictures in there? Maybe a holo screen?"

Now it was Gwen's turn to shrug. "I don't see why not. We can put in a flat screen if there isn't a holo available. Though he's not ever in there for very long."

Hope's eyes looked wistful. "A short time can be an eternity when you're alone."

Gwen and Evan looked at each other before they looked back at Hope, who was already leaving. Twenty minutes later, I was installing a flat screen in the narrow room at the compound's small Medical Center. We called it the "Recovery Room." So far, the new construct was the only one who used it.

I looked over my shoulder as the medical assistant, who was also Faith's lab assistant, came in and administered a shot to the construct. The young man in question was talking to Hope and hardly seemed to notice the needle, much less my presence. I finished the install and, after checking the screen to make sure it worked, put the remote on the bed stand. The construct and Hope were just saying goodbye.

"Eighty-eight sometimes has good movies," Hope told him. "Though, a lot of the time, they're old."

"Thank you, Hope," he said. She smiled at him as she turned to leave and I followed her, pausing just for a second as I noticed the way he looked at her. The gleam in his eyes was unmistakable.

It was the way that M9 looked at me. And, I realized, must be the same way I looked back at her.

TWO ZERO

Faith drummed her nails on the conference room table, her lips pressed together in a line. Hope was still not speaking to her. Thomas poured Faith a glass of champagne before placing napkins down in front of Charity and Llewellyn and topping them with tall glasses full of some red liqueur that Faith did not recognize. He served Hope coffee and Madeline tea. When he was done he left quietly, closing the door behind him as he went.

Faith's eyes went again to Hope, who was too busy with her coffee to meet her sister's eyes. Dr. de Rossi sighed.

"Well," she started, "we have a few things to discuss, that hopefully won't take too long. Charity?"

"Hmm?" Charity's blue eyes peered over the rim of her glass, surprised. "I'm first?" she asked, putting the glass back down. When Faith nodded, she daintily wiped her lip with a napkin and cleared her throat. "Fabulous. Well, the only thing I have on the docket is that we have run our course as simply a research facility and before we move to sales we will need to incorporate."

Faith shrugged. "So incorporate. I'm sure you have the funds." Charity's smile was mirrored on Llewellyn's face.

"We need a name," she said.

"Oh. Well, what do you suggest?"

Charity looked abashed. "Me? I don't have the first idea!"

Faith shrugged and looked at her twin. "How about

Gwendolyn Incorporated?"

Gwendolyn herself blushed as Charity and Llewellyn snorted laughter. "How original!" Llewellyn hooted.

"Creativity is not my strong suit," Faith retorted, her brows creased though she was half-smiling as well. "Gwendolyn made them, why not name the company after her? It's not like it matters."

Gwendolyn shook her head. "I most certainly did nothing on my own. We did all of this together."

"Then give everybody a credit, without having to list all of our names," Charity suggested.

"The de Rossi Federation," Madeline suggested.

Hope made a face. "Too militant."

"Does Grandfather want to be included?" Llewellyn asked.

"Absolutely not," Faith answered. "He wants to stay completely out of this."

"Except where payment is concerned," Llewellyn muttered.

"Hush!" Gwen told her. "We're only here because he funded the entire operation. He should get the return on his investment and then some."

Llewellyn snorted. "Oh, it'll be quite more than some."

"The Sisterhood Six?" Charity suggested, changing the subject. "Makes us sound like crime fighters."

"Sisterhood?" A voice asked as the door swung open. "Six?" Evan walked in, flashed a smile at Faith as he ambled past her, and leaned down to kiss Gwendolyn on the cheek before he looked up at the others with a grin. "And what am I? Chopped sim-strate?"

I had been aware that J7 had been named Evan, but hardly saw him. I knew that he had been taken offline and replaced, but not why. I didn't care. I was done ghosting their meetings.

I had living to do, and their meetings gave M9 and I time to be alone. It helped that I knew where every camera in the compound was located.

Llewellyn picked up her glass and swirled it, making the ice clink against the sides. "Do you think we should name the company after you?" she asked, teasing. Evan shrugged as he straightened, his hands grasping Gwen's shoulders, and Charity giggled.

"Gwen's Evan?" Charity and Llewellyn said in unison and then leaned into each other, laughing.

"Why not?" he asked.

"Why not indeed?" Faith mused aloud.

Llewellyn, who happened to be drinking, at that moment, choked on her cocktail. Charity, also drinking, promptly spit her drink back into her glass and thumped her twin on the back. Llewellyn waved her away and fixed her blue eyes on Faith.

"You want to name the company Gwen's Evan?" she asked, incredulous.

Faith shrugged. "In a manner of speaking."

"What manner?" Charity asked, equally incredulous.

Faith smiled and glanced at Madeline and Hope. "A manner of pronunciation," she answered. "What would you think about GwenSeven? I think that gives credit where credit is due and includes us all."

Smiles crept onto all the faces around the table.

"I like it," Llewellyn announced with an air of finality.

Charity nodded. "Me too."

All eyes went to the two youngest sisters.

Madeline nodded, solemn. "There truly are seven of us," she said. "Evan has a role here, just as much as any of us. I can feel it."

The room was silent and still for a moment before Hope shrugged. "I'm fine with it," she said.

Five pairs of eyes turned to where Gwen sat with Evan standing behind her, his hands still on her shoulders.

Gwen sighed. "I'm not entirely comfortable being the only one named, I certainly don't feel like I deserve it, but as long as it does include us all, I won't argue."

Five pairs of eyes rose to fasten on Evan. "Don't look at me," he told them with a beguiling smile. "I am here at your whim, my darling de Rossis. But it does seem fitting, since I will follow Gwen everywhere for as long as I am alive." Gwendolyn blushed and reached up with one of her slender hands to grasp one of Evan's.

"Then it is settled," Faith announced, looking around the table. "GwenSeven it is."

"We are," Madeline said.

"Forever and ever, amen," Llewellyn added. Charity snorted into her drink and Gwendolyn blushed again. Though Evan couldn't see her face, he gave her shoulders a reassuring squeeze and then leaned down and gave her a kiss on the corner of her jaw just under her ear.

Charity grinned at Faith, her glass balanced delicately at the edge of her lips. "I feel like you should bang a gavel."

"I feel like you should bang any..." Llewellyn started before Charity jabbed her in the ribs with an elbow, cutting off her air as well as the rest of her sentence. She bent over with a gasp and Charity glanced about the table, innocently batting her eyelashes.

"Well!" Hope said, dropping her palms down on top of her thighs. "It was wonderful to see you all, but I need to be getting to the lab."

"Where have I heard that before?" Gwen asked, glancing at her twin.

"And the last shall be the first," Llewellyn said.

"Is that how it goes?" Charity asked as she laughed into her glass, shaking her head.

"I told BG-Syn that I'd look over his readouts before he trains today," Hope explained, her body tense and her hands clasped together. She obviously wanted to go. Faith gave her a nod and Hope disappeared. Madeline finished her tea and smiled at the group before following Hope.

"Well!" Gwendolyn breathed. "That went well!" Charity and Llewellyn both made sounds that equated to non-committal grunts.

Faith looked at them in exasperation. "Don't you two have work to do, or cantina seats to warm?"

"Yes to the latter," Charity said, draining the rest of her cocktail.

"If you think you can manage without us," Llewellyn quipped, also as she finished her drink.

"I'm sure we will manage," Faith confided. "Somehow."

With nudges, giggles, and goodbyes, Charity and her dyer left the conference room of the newly incorporated company. With an exaggerated sigh that was deep enough to be classified as a groan, Faith turned to Gwen and looked up at the construct that stood behind her twin.

"Thank you," she said.

Evan smiled in the lopsided way he sometimes had when he was not entirely sure of himself or his situation. "You're welcome," he replied.

Gwen looked from one to the other. "Thank you for what?" she asked.

Faith cocked her head at her twin. "For his contribution.

For suggesting the name of the company."

Gwen frowned at Evan. "Did she put you up to it? The name?" She turned her fierce gaze on her twin.

Faith sighed, in earnest this time. "I didn't put him up to anything. I was just worried that suggestions might have gone round the table for hours. Stop being so suspicious. I just don't want to be wasting time when I could be working."

Gwendolyn rolled her eyes dramatically and Evan bit his lip. Faith drummed her fingertips on the glass, agitated.

"All of the time?" Faith demanded, looking from one to the other. "That's what you are both thinking, isn't it? That I am working all of the time?" Evan chuckled and Gwen laughed aloud.

"Sorry, Faith," Evan apologized and Faith shook her head.

"Don't be sorry, Evan. I know that I get so stuck on thinking about some things that I forget about others." She pressed her lips together and looked away and then, almost as quickly, looked back with an expression that had become intrigued. "What name would you have come up with, before suggesting that Charity and Llewellyn proceed with their joke?"

Evan gave her a shrug that was barely discernible. "In that category, I have as much imagination as you. I was ready to go along with just about anything that gave Gwendolyn credit. Are you sure I didn't do the wrong thing?"

Faith shook her head. "No, Evan. You did just the right thing. Just like Gwen always does."

Evan smiled, relieved. "You do the right thing too," he told her "You're just so absorbed with your work."

"You can't think of everything," Gwen assured her.

"Why not?" Faith demanded.

Gwen laughed. "You are too hard on yourself, and you work too hard. I'd love for you to take a trip with us. We are planning a vacation for after the sales. A celebration!"

Faith smiled. "Why don't we just go to the cottage instead, and you can tell me all about it?"

"Why don't you take just one day off? You haven't left the compound for more than a business meeting in the city for over a year."

"I can go to the cottage for the night," Faith argued. "We can have a holo fire and you can tell me everything you have been doing and I'll tell you everything I've been up to. It will be just like when we were in school. Except instead of cheap wine we'll open a bottle of cava."

Gwen, who had been hoping to talk Faith into a day off or two, made a face and looked at Evan for support but he only shrugged.

"It's the best you're going to get from her," he advised. "I'd take her up on it."

"Alright, alright," Gwen conceded. "A few hours are better than none at all." Faith grinned, victorious.

Evan smiled at Gwendolyn. "I'll have Thomas send over that bottle of cava, and make sure another is on ice for you two."

"Where are you going?" Gwen asked, surprised. "Won't you be joining us?"

"Oh no," Faith said, shaking her brown and gold hair. "Evan, I didn't mean for it just to be me and Gwen."

"Don't be ridiculous," he told her. "All of your girl talk would bore me to tears. Besides, there are some vids that Gwen has already seen that I've been meaning to watch - this will give me a chance to catch up. Is my room still here at the compound?" He had been staying at the cottage with Gwen for some time now.

Faith, who knew that he would never be bored with anything Gwen had to say, smiled at him and nodded her head. “Just the way you left it,” she assured him.

Evan grimaced. “I hope not. I think I left an unfinished calzone in there.”

Faith laughed and shook her head and Gwen rose with him as he stood, slipping her hands inside his. “Are you sure?” she asked as her brown and gold eyes searched his face. It was the first night they would be apart since their first night together two months ago.

“Of course,” he said, giving her a quick kiss on her cheek. “Have a good time. I’m going to find Thomas to help get us all settled and I’ll see you in the morning.” Gwendolyn gave him a kiss on the cheek and a lingering hug before letting him go.

“Thank you Evan,” Faith said, rising to her feet and giving him a hug as well.

“It’s not a big deal,” he told them, a blush spreading along his jaw. “You girls have fun.”

The door to the conference room swung shut behind him and Gwendolyn turned to her sister. “What did you do to his composite, to make him blush like that?”

Faith tipped her head back and a smile ran across her lips before she looked back at Gwen. “I didn’t do that,” she told her. “You did.”

“Me?”

“Yes, when you selected his skin type.”

Gwendolyn, surprised, looked at the closed door of the conference room. “I wasn’t aware that was a package deal,” she said.

Faith cocked her head. “You don’t like it?”

Gwen grinned at her sister. “Are you kidding? I love it.” She sighed. “I love everything about him.”

Faith mirrored her grin and grabbed Gwendolyn’s elbow,

wrapping her arm around it and giving her twin a playful shake. "Let's go get drunk!" she suggested enthusiastically.

"Well," Gwendolyn acquiesced, laying her head on Faith's shoulder. "Only if we have to."

TWO ONE

Charity walked down the hallway of the compound, her four-inch diamond-tipped heels clicking on the polished tile floor. She wore a smart, sleeveless, pinstriped gray suit that had been tailored for her figure. She had given herself a nod of approval in the mirror that morning, deciding that business attire really could be sexy. She never would have guessed, since Faith dressed for business every day and had yet to pull it off. Charity decided that next time she would try the same look with a micro-skirt. Maybe for Devereaux's appointment. Llewellyn's had chided her and told her that it would be wasted on him, but Charity had faith, and never gave up hope.

"And here," she said, holding out a bare, slender arm towards Gwendolyn's studio, "is where each construct was sculpted."

"Mmmhmm," Ivana agreed with a look of cultivated boredom. Rather than being offended, Charity took note of the expression, deciding to practice it herself.

Ivana looked to be a woman of late middle age with an artificially slim figure, upswept hair that was at one time naturally blonde, and eyes that were blue – but a much lighter shade than Charity and Llewellyn had. Ivana was not only human, but an Earthling as well. And her wealth was even greater than the mighty snowcapped mountains that dominated the country from which she had been bred and born.

"Each one of the First Seven we made is unique, so you

would be owning a one of a kind. It is possible that the next run will be handmade as well, though we expect duplicates, and the third run will be cast from molds."

"Mmmhmm." Each of Ivana's breaths sounded like a scarcely controlled sigh. Charity smiled and tried to memorize the sound, thinking about her conversation with her grandfather the night before.

Charity, though she already considered herself a shark when it came to everything from business to sex, did not feel above any advice and had taken Cronus to dinner the night before Ivana's arrival at one of his favorite restaurants. Llewellyn, who accompanied Charity just about everywhere, was uncharacteristically quiet. She had decided for once to merely watch and listen. She knew when Charity was after a good time, which was often, and when she was after a good lesson, which was often needed.

"Ivana is old money," Cronus had told the girls at dinner.

"As opposed to new money, I assume?" Charity asked, glancing at the dessert menu. "And what is the difference?"

"You can't spend old money."

Charity laughed, but the sound had a nervous edge to it. "Any money can be spent," she said.

Cronus smiled and shook his head. "Let me explain it better," he advised. The graying elf leaned back in his chair and steepled his fingers. "I am new money. I was successful from the beginning as a scientist, but I come from a long family of Dyer Makers and not much was passed down besides the craft itself. Dolls did not sell for much, at least not back then. I made my money in cybernectics, I invested the money I made, and continue to do so. If I did not do so, I could spend it all in my lifetime."

"And Ivana?"

"Ivana Uri-Van Zandt does not work nor invest, and

yet she could never spend all of her money no matter how extravagantly she chooses to live. If she had a dozen children, and they all had a dozen children, they could never spend the money."

"If that were the case," Charity mused, "then the money isn't stagnant, it is still multiplying. At an unbelievable rate. How is that?"

Her grandfather's gray brows went up and down like a shrug. "Diversified investments by her great-grandfather. Compound interest."

"Diversified investments," Charity whispered. "Compound interest." She looked over and met Llewellyn's eyes. Llewellyn gave her twin a slight nod, showing that she was thinking the same thing, repeating the same words.

"If you have what she wants," Cronus told them, "she'll get it. The cost is inconsequential."

Charity had lifted her chin, envisioning the future and branding those words into her brain.

Diversified investments. Compound interest.

"Here we are!" Charity announced to the woman with the supposedly inexhaustible amount of money, extending a hand towards the door that Thomas was holding open for them.

Ivana gave her a patient smile and walked a few steps through the door and stopped short, her spiked heels clattering and her breath catching in her throat. Charity could not keep the shark-like grin from her face as Ivana regained her composure and entered the room completely, gazing up at the flawless face and imposing form of B28. Charity followed.

"Ms. Van Zandt," Llewellyn was saying, "please come in."

"My Gode in 'eaven," Ivana exclaimed quietly, staring at B-28 as he took her hand and kissed the back of it in the manner that Charity had shown him.

"This is Ivana Van Zandt," Charity said, introducing the woman to the perfectly manufactured being in front of her.

"And dis is?" Ivana asked in a whisper, indicating the construct she could not tear her eyes from.

"Well," Charity said, "that depends on you. What would you call him, if he were yours?"

Ivana's chest swelled as she considered. She let out a breathy sigh and her chest swelled again. "Bjorn," she said in a rush. "I vould call heem Bjorn!"

B-28 smiled at her pronunciation. "I would like that," he said.

Ivana gasped at the sound of his voice. "Vhat does he do?" she asked, still unable to tear her gaze from his piercing green eyes to look back at the saleswoman/hostess that had brought her there.

Charity paused for the briefest of moments, almost unwilling to say what she must say next. Something clutched in her chest and suddenly everything felt wrong.

"What does he do?" Charity repeated, feeling lame.

Visions of time she had spent with him flashed through her mind, along with all the meetings with her sisters – all their plans and what they really meant now crushed her with a gravity she had never felt before. Fingers of panic crept up the back of her neck and she looked at 28, feeling like a cornered animal.

His green eyes flicked to her blue-eyed stare for less than a second, but it was all it took. That quick glance told her to get on with it, and not to worry. Charity smiled, reclaiming her composure.

"Why, anything you want him to do," she told Ivana, the tone of her voice carrying a deeper meaning than her actual words. There was a sharp intake of air from Ivana as she processed the implications of Charity's words.

"He can pilot any plane or jet," Llewellyn informed the woman. "And drive any class of ground or air car."

"Oh mai," Ivana said. She breathed a sigh, examining his gimlet eyes and the sharply chiseled line of his jaw. "And he is completely manufactured?" she asked, her sharp accent tinged with amazement.

"Yes."

"And he vill do....?"

"Anything you ask him to."

Ivana contemplated the perfectly constructed being in front of her and gave another one of her breathy sighs. Then suddenly she drew herself up and faced Charity, chin lifted and pale blue eyes full of sauce.

"Ze price is five billion?" she asked.

"It is."

Ivana nodded. "Very vell," she said. "I vill give you five billion for heem."

Charity began to give her a respectful nod in acceptance but Ivana continued.

"And eenother five billion to sign a contract saying that you will not make eenother one like eem. Not ever."

Charity bowed deeply from the waist. "But of course," she said. "I will have the contract drawn along with your bill of sale. If you would like to accompany me to our conference room, we can have everything signed there."

"And eem?"

Llewellyn smiled. "Will be ready to take you anywhere you desire once you are done. And do everything you ask of him."

Ivana's smile was as depraved and ravenous as ever as she sauntered from the room in what to her was almost a hurry. She could not help but throw a look back over her shoulder at her latest prize, and she could barely control the shudder of pleasure she felt as his green eyes met hers with the same lascivious smile on his perfectly carved face.

*

Cronus coached Charity on the sale to Mr. Harasuka as well. Though he was even more difficult to communicate with than Ivana (not because of the language barrier – simply because he and Ivana shared a similar disinterest in life in general that could almost be classified as a language of its own), his sale as well turned out to be more than she could have hoped for.

"Never make eye contact with him," Cronus had instructed the girls. "Bow to him, often. He considers women far beneath men."

Charity had made a face and looked at her twin. "Maybe you should take this one," she suggested.

"No way," Llewellyn assured her. "You have more control than I do. I might laugh in his face. Or worse."

Charity knew this to be true, which was why she was now bowing for what must have been the hundredth time in half an hour. She gave the man, who looked continuously either at his watch or over his shoulder, a short tour of the compound. He was as bored as Ivana had been, perhaps more.

The compact Mr. Harasuka, with his pale sallow skin and jet-black hair, was accompanied by two bodyguards. No one had to be told that they were Yakuza. Their fame, usually as a dire warning or threat, always preceded them.

"I am sure you will be pleased," Charity told him as they reached the room used for the meet and greet.

The man's eyes, black and almond-shaped, darted to his guards as he muttered something that was no doubt his skepticism at being pleased.

"We have made her in the old style," Charity continued as she touched the door and it slid open, "in the fashion of your ancestors."

More skeptical mutters ensued but were cut off as soon as he stepped inside the room. But it was not G1, the construct that had been made especially for him, that caught his eye. Next to the perfectly sculpted and immaculately groomed geisha bedecked in pearls and a rich, pink silk kimono, sat N7-PA2.

The two female constructs often kept company with one another these days, though N7 certainly should have known that this was a day for them to keep to themselves. Charity couldn't be certain. N7, however, rose to her feet to hurry away as soon as the door had opened but Mr. Harasuka blocked her path.

N7 bowed her blonde head, waiting.

"Please," Mr. Harasuka implored, in a sudden bout of interest and an attempt at Anglicus, "sit back down."

N7's brilliant blue eyes darted to Charity, who nervously motioned for her to retake her seat.

"Of course," Charity acquiesced. "N7 here can tell you all about the Geisha."

"N7?" Mr. Harasuka asked, stunned. "This too, is a construct?" He held a hand out in N7's direction as his men entered the room.

"Well, yes."

Mr. Harasuka tugged down on his black jacket, seemingly satisfied for the first time since his arrival, as he looked the petite female construct up and down. "I take her."

"Oh, Mr. Harasuka," Charity stammered. "It is the geisha that we had made for you."

Mr. Harasuka gave the geisha, who sat with her dark head

bowed so low that he could not see her features, a black look. He remembered speaking to one of the de Rossi's about acquiring a geisha from the old world and the thought of one that had been perfectly manufactured had intrigued him. What he could not remember was if he had given a verbal agreement to purchase such an item. If he had, he would have to fulfill it. His honor would be lost if he did not.

Then his eyes sought out the PA with deep blue eyes and pale blonde hair. She reminded him of the drawn movies he had watched as a child. Perfect nose, perfect lips...perfectly made. More than any doll or drawing that he had ever seen.

"You trained them both to be subservient, is that correct?"

"Well," Charity said, "it is already their nature to be that way. But they have been trained in two entirely different things. N7 is..."

"Fine!" Mr. Harasuka exclaimed as if he had run out of patience. "I take both!" He spoke lowly to his consorts and there was a single word that Llewellyn understood. *Concubine.*

She opened her mouth to speak but Charity cut her off with a scathing glare.

"Put them on my craft," Mr. Harasuka instructed. "I will sign for money. But must be now. I have meeting."

Charity bowed low and then hurried from the room, already speaking into her comset and leading Llewellyn away by her elbow.

N7 and G1 were hustled into the wing of the compound that served as the dormitory for the constructs. I watched as they were packaged up, though a better term (and one my mother would have used) was "dolled up." It was fairly humane as it went, then they were escorted onto Mr. Harasuka's craft even as he was signing the bills of sale.

The sight of it brought home the reality to me, that these machines made human were to be sold and used as machines

- and there was nothing human about it. My gut clenched painfully with the knowledge that Mr. Deveraeux would be arriving within the next few weeks to select an assistant. And now there was only one to choose from, though it had already been assumed that M9 was the obvious choice – hence her specified training.

Being packaged up like dolls, like real toys! I felt a pang for N7 – she had tried a class with me and said she would return when she needed help. I heard her speak the French she had learned from a program and figured she'd be okay as long as she never had to go to France. It was doubtful, since she had learned Mandarin and Japonesa along with Elfin and Anglicus. She would probably be sent to Indasia.

The Geisha I never knew. They had brought in a specialist for her all the way from Earth. She had been taught Japonesa, Anglicus and Mandarin as far as human languages went, which was the reason why she probably developed a kinship with N7. But she was the only one schooled especially in ancient ceremonies – from serving tea and opening fans to folding blankets and pouring wine.

Confronted now with the cold reality that was coming for M9, my stomach lurched. I could not act as if she was some machine, which meant I could not just walk away – I loved her. I knew that as much as I knew my own soul. I had to do something. Considering who and what M9 was, it meant any action I took would have serious consequences. But I knew that the consequences would be worse for us both if I did nothing. I went to the one person I knew that was as serious as the grave, and would take me just as seriously. I went to Faith.

TWO TWO

The compound, at the time, was disguised as complete serenity – mostly due to Thomas. Only the core people knew what was being done, what had to be done, and what hung precariously in the balance.

Charity and Llewellyn were dissecting the galactic elite. Faith and Gwendolyn were already planning the second run of constructs. Hope was training what could possibly be the most effective and efficient universal killing machine. On top of it all, the company was under the scrutiny of the IGC, from almost every branch of military, medicine, and politics that the government had at the time.

Cloning was strictly prohibited throughout every galaxy under the penalty of death and there were doctors and scientists about at every moment – going through compute files, vids, or holding conferences with Faith.

Faith herself was also overwhelmed by meetings with people that I could only describe as humanitarian organizations.

And so it was to my surprise that she agreed to see me immediately. Though she had addressed me as Fletcher since our meeting about J7, she was about as warm and friendly as a moonstone. And, needless to say, she was always busier than a mosquito at a nudist colony.

As nervous as I was, I came right out and told her of my feelings for M9, and the way I was sure that M9 felt about me in return. Moreover, that we wanted to continue the relationship that was still only budding between us. Faith watched me for a long while after I had confessed, her silence enveloping the entire room.

I figured she was trying to decide whether to believe me, fire me, or have me shot publicly.

"I knew you two were fooling around," she said sourly. "I had no idea that it was serious."

"You knew?" I asked, swallowing.

Her expression, if possible, became even more sour. "Of course. But, like I said, I did not know it had become serious – serious enough to involve feelings. I would say feelings that might compromise the end to our means, but nothing in this universe is going to compromise that."

"I don't intend to try to compromise anything, Dr. de Rossi. But I know that you are the sole being that always has a solution to everything." Faith snorted to show she might not be of the same mind, but she let me continue. "Is there any way I can stay with M9? Follow her on a job, get employment on Mr. Devereaux's staff, anything?"

"No," Faith answered. "One complication will arise after another if you seek to be at her side." The line between her brows disappeared as she shifted into her normal, problem-solving state of mind. "The best thing is for you to stay here, where she can always find you... and where we will require that she be returned to for check-ups as often as plausible. Luckily, Mr. Devereaux will be in this system for some time. He will be returning to MW-1 in a few years, but I think we might be migrating out there as well."

I felt a load lighten from my shoulders, a giant that had been riding my back these past few months. It was more than I had even dared to hope for. I refused to believe that I would never see her again, but the where and the how were questions I had no idea on how to answer.

Now, I was being told that once, maybe twice a year, I could actually hold her in my arms and feel her whispers against my cheek. We could be alone. Really alone.

"Dr. de Rossi," I assured her, "if there is anything I can do to make that happen, I would be in debt to you for forever."

And I meant it. I felt as if my time with M9 was ticking away and I was trying ineffectively to diffuse a bomb.

Faith waved a dismissive hand. "I know what you are willing to do for M9. What are you willing to do for yourself? To yourself....?" She trailed off, leaving me to try and decipher her meaning. When I was too dense to understand, she sighed and continued. "I can see that you are a handsome man, Fletcher. You could be out at any time of the night with any girl and yet you stay here, even more so than at your own place. I see you make exceptions for her, but not for yourself."

"I...don't think I quite follow you," I stammered.

Faith smiled. "You have been here for almost five years now, is that right?"

"Yes."

Faith nodded. "Five years seems long at the time but, in the great scheme of things, it is actually quite short. It is less than nothing. Five short years and yet it shows on your human face. Not a lot – you're still so very young, but it shows. The lines around your mouth, the lines around your eyes. They are faint, for now." Faith leaned back in her chair and uncrossed and then recrossed her legs. "What you don't see is what is happening inside you. In a few more years, as your growth hormone diminishes, the cells in every part of your body will become slower at repairing and replacing themselves. Not long after, they will stop altogether."

I swallowed, starting to see what she was getting at, and it filled me with a sickening chill.

"You and M could carry on a perfect affair for decades, at

most. One day you will realize that you are well over fifty while she is still frozen physically at twenty-five. Your devotion may continue, but you will not."

I slumped in my seat, knowing she was right. M9 had been made to last forever. I had been made to last a century, at most. Even then, she would be the beauty that she was now. I would be an old man.

I had never, not once in my life, considered taking medications that promised an unnaturally extended life – it was considered the Devil's work by my grandmother's scripture. The scripture by which I had been raised. I believed that God had already determined my life, and it would be taken when my time was done.

This kind of talk, what Faith was beginning to get at, encouraged me to be God himself.

I knew that millions of people across the galaxies did it, especially humans, but not me. I was proud of my ideals and who I was to have them. Those ideals had always felt very strong, until that moment.

My love for M9 was stronger.

"Is there something you can do?" I asked, my voice barely above a whisper.

"Of course there is," Faith answered promptly. "But I need to know what you are willing to do. What do you want out of all this?"

I lifted my head up and looked into her brown and gold eyes. I felt like a worm being offered to a hawk, but I kept my face up and my back straight. "I want to take care of her," I said. "I know that I can't buy her, ten years of my salary wouldn't even buy me a week. Nor would I, if I could. I don't think it is right to own another person. But I will be there for her in any way I can. I simply care for her so deeply that I will do anything for her, from any distance."

Faith smiled. "Good enough." There was a look that came into her tawny eyes that was a bit feral. "I will do whatever I can with logistics to get her here as often as possible, though most times it will be six months or even a year. The storm seasons on the edge of the system make for hard traveling. Mad seasons. You will be given as much time together as possible."

I sighed. It was a far cry from seeing her every day, but something was better than nothing. Nothing would render me a ghost again. "Thank you," I said, and I meant it. I wanted to push my chair back and get the hell out of there, but those eyes had me pinned and I knew we were not done. "And the subject of my age?" I finally queried softly, hoping she had somehow forgotten that part. Not so lucky there.

Faith opened a drawer in her desk and pulled out a hypodermic needle. It was as if she had been waiting all night to use it. She probably had been. She motioned for me to come over to her.

I circled the desk and rolled up the sleeve over my left arm. I offered it to her, feeling every bit that I was offering a sacrifice to a heathen god.

"I might have time to pull some strings and get you two out of the compound for more than just one night," she said as she glanced around her surroundings and snatched a bottle off the table closest to the desk along with a cotton pad. The tang of alcohol stung my nose as she swabbed the crook of my elbow, making the skin cold before she plunged the needle into a blue vein under my skin.

I never had much time to reconsider, but it didn't matter. Nothing would have changed my mind.

I expected something shocking or painful, but the injection was no different from any other shot I had ever been given. It might as well have been immunizations for an inter-planetary voyage for all I knew.

Faith removed the hypo, swabbed the area again, and wiped a thin glob of gel over the puncture wound to seal it.

"What was it?" I asked.

"A cosmetic strain of elfin DNA. It will keep you from aging for a hundred years or more - depending on your lifestyle, time spent in cryo, etc."

I fought the urge to rub the spot. A hundred years at my current age. I didn't know if that was a blessing or a curse. I supposed it could be both. I was torn between feeling elated and terrified.

"Thank you, Faith."

She afforded me a rare smile. "You're welcome, Fletcher."

*

Dr. de Rossi, as heartless as she often seemed, gave us the most heartfelt gift ever - time. The sale of M9-PA1 was put off for another week and Faith miraculously arranged for us to spend a week together at Deluge, a resort for tourists just outside of the city. I was told that it was a beautiful place, and packed with attractions, excursions, restaurants, you name it. I wouldn't know.

M9 and I spent the whole time in the room – in the bed or wrapped in a blanket on the playpen sofa or in the oversized tub. We ordered food to the room and I don't think there was more than a minute here and there when our bodies weren't touching. We talked endlessly for hours, watched movies, snoozed, listened to music, and made love dozens of times.

It was the best week of my life.

The week after was the hardest.

The hardest I had so far, anyway.

I returned her to her room on the day before she was

scheduled to leave. I hated calling it the day of sale, like others in the compound did. We clung to each other as we said our goodbyes and it felt like a storm was beginning to coil in around us. The gentle caress of the winds of change before the maelstrom tore us apart.

"There's nothing we can do?" she asked, her face buried in my shoulder. It wasn't the first time she had asked me. Every time I wished I had a better answer for her.

"I will see you as soon as I can," I whispered into her dark hair. "If you stay busy with work, time goes by faster." It was something my grandmother had always told me (in French of course) but something I had always found to be true.

"What if I don't do a good job?"

"You are going to do a great job," I assured her, touching her chin and turning her dark eyes up into mine. "But you have to save all your stories for me, so we can laugh about them the next time we see each other. I'll do the same. You'll always know where to find me."

"I love you," she said.

"I know," I replied, kissing her curls and then her cheek and then her mouth. "I love you, too. I always will."

Though I didn't want to come to the sale the next day, Faith insisted. I didn't think I could bear to watch another man pay money for the woman I loved and then just walk off with her while I just stood there. I had no idea what Faith had in mind, but the idea seemed worse and worse, and as I neared the meet and greet room my blood was boiling so hot I almost turned away. I stood in front of the door an entire minute, then two.

"God hates a coward," I finally whispered, and pushed open the door.

I was late.

Or Devereaux was early.

He was a human man, possibly in his late fifties. I wondered out of the blue if he was naturally that way or if he had been frozen like I had been. He had brown hair with a few strands of gray. His suit was sharply tailored and expensive. My first thought was that he needed a haircut.

M9 stood before him in a prim brown skirt suit and low heels that she made look beautiful but did nothing for the body I knew was underneath, and for that I was glad. She stood subservient yet poised before her new owner.

Faith was the only de Rossi present, which surprised me. She had not yet attended a sale, not in person anyway. And Charity and Llewellyn were strangely absent. The only other company person was Thomas, also for the first time.

"And this is?" Mr. Devereaux asked as I entered - obviously perturbed at the interruption.

"This is our head tech," Faith lied. "He will be doing regular assessments on M9-PA1. Since these constructs are the first run, it is crucial that we run checks every few months. We will inconvenience you as little as possible. If she can't be sent here I will send him to a rendezvous point."

If I wasn't already head over heels for M9, I might have fallen in love with the cold-blooded Dr. de Rossi at that moment. She was damned smart.

"Fine," Devereaux agreed. I will be in this system for the better part of the next decade before I return to my home galaxy. My business is primarily done on Earth. She speaks all the languages that I requested?"

"She does," Faith affirmed. "Should you require any others, I can have our tech here run the necessary programs."

"How is her French? It is important that it is perfect."

"Flawless," Faith assured him. "Native accent, as you requested. You won't find better off-planet."

Devereaux grunted in response. "Well," he said appraising

his latest acquisition. “She looks well enough. Professional, proper, servile.”

I wanted to clench my fists but instead found myself smiling with half of my face the way I often saw Faith do.

“Her accounting skills?” he asked.

“Better than anyone you have ever employed.”

“Management skills? I have an exceedingly full schedule.”

“Mr. Devereaux, if she is not everything I promised and more, I will gladly give you a full refund.”

Again the grunt. “Very well, we should get going. I have a meeting this afternoon. My current PA will take her under her wing so to speak. She is leaving in a month to get married, so…” he stopped abruptly and looked at M9. “What is her name?”

Faith smiled. “That is entirely up to you.”

His expression was priceless. It was the only thing that had caught him off guard so far. “What do you call her?”

“M9-PA1.”

Again the blank look. It was like when I told Faith my name. He looked from Faith to M9-PA1 to me. The level of imagination with these people was horrible.

“How about Mira?” I suggested, since his blank eyes still rested on me in a hopeless manner. From over his shoulder I could see Thomas and the trace of approval that briefly crossed his countenance.

The blank look on Devereaux’s face brightened and he nodded. “Mira…yes…I like that.” He turned his gaze to her. “Does that suit you…Mira?”

For the first time I took heart that the guy wasn’t a complete asshole. He wanted her opinion on an important subject.

M9’s smile was beatific and huge. “It does, sir.” Her eyes darted to me. “Thank you,” she said, staring into my eyes before she looked back at him. "If that pleases you, it suits me just fine."

Mr. Devereaux smiled to show that it did indeed suit him and he gave a quick nod of satisfaction. "Very well. Let's get going."

M9, now Mira, gave me a parting smile and it was more than I could ever hope for – because it was one not forlorn or full of sadness or dread. It was full of love and assurance. She knew she would be coming back, and that she could handle anything in between. It was all I needed to return the same smile. I held two fingers to my lips. Most would surmise it was the sign of a man deep in thought. She knew that I was thinking of her two lips against mine.

Her face twitched in a strange way, just short of a convulsion and for a second – just a second – I was terrified. Then I realized that she was trying to wink at me. Maybe it was something singular to humans, or something she had only seen on a holo and was trying to emulate and could not. All I knew was that, to me, it filled my heart with unadulterated joy.

TWO THREE

I was in the reception room fixing a chair the next day when Ynestra Malin came. It was a ridiculous job for someone of my station and one that I could have had any of the men working for me take care of, but I was determined to keep busy.

Though Mira was foremost in my mind, I knew that if I kept my hands active it would distract me enough to get through the day. Not an easy task since the compound had been complete for some time and there was no more French to be taught. Faith had me drawing plans for the next place, an actual manufacturing plant, but I had that set aside at my place to keep my mind occupied for the next month of lonely nights I was facing.

I looked out the window to see a small elfin woman with white hair that fell past her waist and eyes so large they seemed to take up half her face, like an Aridian. My first thought was that it was an unusually windy day outside, watching the way her hair and clothes swirled about, but as she entered I realized that she had some field on her person that was generating the moving air.

I rose to my feet and backed away from the door, knowing that it would be unseemly for work to be going on while a client was present.

The Malin woman was accompanied by five male elves, sharply dressed with upturned collars and gray hair like Cronus, but they were all smaller – like the woman. I knew enough about elves to know that it meant they were from a different planet than Cronus and the girls. One opened the door for her and she entered, her skirts and the voluminous sleeves of her long, thin coat billowing about her tightly laced boots.

Unlike Mr. Harasuka or Ivana Uri-Van Zandt, who had looked at everything and everyone with disinterest and thinly veiled repugnance, Ynestra Malin was gentle and carried an air of reverence, as if she had just entered a chapel rather than a corporate reception room. She looked around with a child-like awe, though I knew she was hundreds of years old. Thomas bowed to the group as Charity entered the room, already alerted of their arrival. She bowed as well and led them away in hushed tones.

I changed the setting on the hand tool I carried, watching the device flip attachments and rearrange itself into a quarter inch socket wrench. I finished with the broken chair and then tightened the legs on the other four chairs just for good measure. I straightened and looked around.

"Is there anything else I can do?" I asked Thomas.

His dark eyes regarded me with surprise. "Such as?"

I shrugged. "Anything else that needs mending?" I asked. "Blazes, I'll file your nails if you need me to."

Thomas eyed me suspiciously, not knowing if he should be amused or offended.

"I've got nothing but time, right now," I explained.

He picked up his own tool, a fancy new device called an acrylic. It looked like a thick piece of glass filled with words and light. He moved his finger along its surface and a blue glow shone on his brown skin. I knew he was going over the needs of the girls – from oldest to youngest.

He looked up at me. "Anything?" he asked, dubious.

"Anything."

His head dipped and he looked back at his contraption. "The light pad in Dr. de Rossi's office has a loose screw...are you sure you don't want me to ask Henley?" he asked, looking up at me again. Henley was one of my guys, just a kid really, and the lowest guy on the totem pole.

"No, I got it. Loose screw. What else?"

Again the dubious look, but he continued. "The countertop in Miss Gwendolyn's studio is horribly chipped and dented, it should be replaced. The lavatory near Miss Llewellyn's office has a faucet that drips. The rack in the training room where the droids are kept has a loose shelf."

He rattled off another half dozen repairs that needed to be done at the compound and I made a mental note of each one.

"Do you want me to send you a list?"

I shook my head. "I got it, but I'll check with you tomorrow just to make sure."

My assurance seemed to satisfy him and he gave me a smile as he tucked the heavy piece of glass under his arm. "Thank you, Fletcher," he said. "I think you are the only employee here that works almost as much as I do."

That's because we both love someone here, I almost said. But Mira was my secret and no longer here. Also, I realized that his secret was more sacred than mine. It was one that could never be spoken to anyone, and his love would never be returned. At that moment I felt a stab of agony for Thomas, yet I wondered who had it worse. At least he got to see Faith every day. I wouldn't see Mira for a year. Or more. Or longer.

My thoughts clung to me desperately, raising horrible voices in a wail of anguish till I slammed a door upon them.

"I'll start with the light pad in Dr. de Rossi's office," I said, tucking my universal-t into my belt.

Thomas smiled at me, pleased. "Thank you, Fletcher," he repeated.

"Don't think about it," I said. Luckily, he thought I was talking to him.

Before I could leave, the doors between us and the hallway to the compound swung open to admit Ynestra Malin. She entered the reception area, her hand tucked into the elbow of the GwenSeven elfin construct. I thought he looked like a miniature version of Cronus but the one time I ventured to say so Llewellyn had laughed heartily and called me a racist. I suppose there were plenty of differences besides the height, but they were lost on me.

I stepped back to give them plenty of room, mesmerized by their soft speech. Her entourage followed and I could tell by the carefully controlled stares of her bodyguards that Gwendolyn had pulled off another flawless specimen. They must have known the original as well. If so, his face and form must have been just as shocking as his personae.

From arguments I had gleaned between Faith and Charity, the younger de Rossi had acquired enough info, vids, and holos on the elf that they could have produced a military-quality beta simulation of the man himself. Faith, however, had argued for originally produced and copy-writable DNA. She won the argument reminding Charity that the new father would be different by reciprocating interest, offering encouragement, and giving his daughter the attention and validation she so acutely desired. The irony was not lost on Charity, nor was the fact that Ynestra would be head over heels in a hurry to pay for what her heart desired most – the approval of the only man she had ever loved.

TWO FOUR

Last to go was BG-Syn, but it wasn't until a month later. Hope was obsessed with perfecting his prototype, as much as he was obsessed with Hope. They spent a lot of time together those four weeks. Hope constantly watched him train and toyed with his genetic make-up. In turn, it seemed that he doubled his efforts in an attempt to please her.

Faith began taking trips with Cronus and helping him with the project he had lined up when she wasn't working on the second run of constructs. I saw Gwen in her studio, working on the next run as well. Occasionally I saw her with J7, or Evan as they called him, the one of the First Seven they had taken offline. I wondered if they were trying to fix him.

Charity and Llewellyn became the face of the company that was now getting a blinding amount of press coverage across every galaxy.

Hope started working what Gwen called "Faith hours," which pretty much meant around the clock. She spent all the day hours with BG-Syn, asking him questions, watching him train, keeping him company in the recovery room. Thomas had me turn one of the classrooms into an office for Hope, where she spent most of the dark hours in front of her compute screen, pouring over thousands of lines of words and numbers that I could not have made sense of if I had ten lifetimes to learn.

Thomas kept everything running like a well-oiled machine.

Madeline might as well have been a ghost, which was how I

felt once again without Mira.

I kept as busy as any of them. Mira was always on my mind and even more so on my heart, which was fine by me and I hoped it always stayed that way. But if left to myself, I worried constantly.

Faith had implanted a small device in each construct, just under the skin on the backs of their skulls. When pressed, it would open an emergency communication line to the center. I could feel Mira's every time I pulled her close for a kiss (it felt like a small coin, hidden under her dark curls) and I was always careful not to press on it. Now I cursed myself for never having tested the damn thing out. Until I saw it work, or saw Mira again, I fretted by the minute with an imagination much larger than I ever suspected could be lodged within my own brain.

On the day before the buyer for BG-Syn was to arrive, Hope cancelled the training session he was to have and instead had Thomas prepare a picnic lunch for them to share on the grass behind the compound.

My hands idle and my heart heavy for the moment, I watched though a window while Thomas shook out a large blanket and laid it out for them. He was careful to choose a shady spot under a large tree to protect their pale skin.

To me they looked like children, dressed in adult's clothes. The construct wore mechanic's coveralls, though they (along with his perfectly manicured hands) were much cleaner than any mech I had ever seen. Hope, with her long copper curls, looked like she should have been wearing a flowing gown at a medieval ball. Instead, she wore slacks and a lab coat that she shucked off onto the edge of the blanket to reveal a plain white shirt underneath.

What buried itself in my memory the most, however, was the way he looked at her. I noticed it first that day I had hung the flat screen in the Recovery Room. It was the way Mira and I looked at each other, though the ardor in those eyes of his burned with the power of twin blue suns. It was more like the way Evan always looked at Gwen – with an intensity that could be frightening. More frightening was the way that the look went unnoticed and unreturned by Hope. The poor girl had the dreamy distance of Madeline coupled with the laser-focused drive of Faith. I had become fond of her, as I had become for all the girls, and I worried for her.

"How are you feeling?" Hope asked the construct, shooing Thomas away so she could unpack the basket he had provided. The ever-vigilant assistant drew away long enough for Hope to retrieve a pair of sandwiches, then he reached in the basket to pull out plates and napkins.

BG-Syn considered her question thoughtfully before he answered. "Good," he replied. "Whole and healthy, but a bit fluttery inside."

"Thomas, please!" Hope scolded, taking chilled bottles of sparkling water from his hands. "Doesn't Faith need you for something?"

"Dr. de Rossi is away on business. And I am happy to help."

"Well, thank you. But go help Charity or Llewellyn. I'm sure they need a drink."

Thomas straightened and looked at his watch. "Not for another five minutes," he informed her. "But if you truly insist..."

"I do!" Hope insisted with good nature as his tall, dark form leaned back down to open the bottles in her hands.

"Very well," he agreed with a short bow. "Call me if you need anything."

Hope's only reply was a wry smile as he made his departure back to the compound. "A bit fluttery inside?" she asked the construct, picking their line of conversation back up as she handed him a bottle of effervescent water.

BG-Syn nodded as he took a sip. "Nervousness, I suppose

would be the term."

Hope laid a hand over his and his face lit up. "You are going to do fine," she assured him. He laughed lightly.

"Oh, I am sure I will," he answered. "You have made sure of that. The flutter is because I don't know what it will be like not to see you everyday."

This time the light laugh belonged to Hope. "I'm sure you will be too busy to miss me," she told him. "You will always be on guard, always on watch. You must be ever mindful of your duties."

"Ever mindful of my duties," he repeated carefully as Hope handed him a sandwich and a napkin. "What about when I am alone?" he asked suddenly. "Will it be alright to miss you then?" In truth he already did not think about Hope when he was busy training. But at night, before he went to sleep, she was all he thought about.

Hope smiled, wiping her mouth with a napkin as she nodded. "Of course you can miss me. I'll miss you."

"You will?" BG-Syn asked, his food raised halfway to his mouth.

"Of course!" Hope said with a shrug as she dug back into her sandwich. "And we will see each other once a year, when you come in for your check-ups."

"That's right," he whispered as if realizing it for the first time, which he was. "You will be here, every year for that?"

"Absolutely," Hope assured him with a grin. "I don't trust you to Faith!" She laughed aloud at the irony, considering who was to be purchasing him, but he did not seem to get the joke.

"Then I will have something to look forward to, every year!" he exclaimed. He nodded to himself as he finally began eating his lunch. BG-Syn decided it was the best day of his life. Talking to Hope, watching the sunlight shine through her magnificent curls, and now with the knowledge that he would be back to see her every year.

When they were through with their picnic, they found Charity and Llewellyn waiting for them in BG-Syn's room. They were quick to embrace Hope and exchange kisses before Llewellyn presented BG-Syn with his clothes for the next day.

"Is it a dress?" he asked, not offended but simply curious at the long robes pressed between thin sheets of plastic.

"No," Llewellyn replied, stifling a laugh.

"It might as well be!" Charity chirped and then Llewellyn did laugh.

"They are church robes," Llewellyn explained. "We thought that the buyers might want to see you in their own...ahem... uniform."

BG-Syn nodded and hung the robes in his small closet. "That makes sense," he agreed. "And the large sleeves will be the perfect camouflage for my machetes."

"Indeed," Charity murmured, her blue eyes on BG-Syn. "We will see you in the morning."

She called me an hour later with a request that was doable but no more crazy than anything that she had me do in the past.

*

The next morning seemed an auspicious occasion. The last of the first constructs was (hopefully) to be sold, and Christa de Rossi was there for the event. The girls made sure that their mother, a devout follower of The One Church, would be able to meet the Bauam. The man was considered by many (and by all those of the religion he led) the holiest man in the universe. He was the supreme leader and head of the Church of The One True Faith. It was an opportunity rarely afforded, since The One religion spanned the width of three galaxies.

The man was the youngest ever to be the head of the order

and, though his creed prohibited the use of age-extending drugs, he was quite robust for a human of seventy-five years. It was no secret that the man was ambitious and had great plans for the church. Had I known of the plans, I would have killed him myself on that day. And I was never the killing type.

He arrived at the compound in a military-grade transport and was preceded by a troop of droids that streamed out and encircled the carrier. Another squad of droids followed and formed a pair of columns between the vehicle and the reception doors of the center. Two gargantuan humans with thick necks emerged from the transport as if being birthed from the portals. After them came a gaggle of church cronies in different colored soutane robes followed by two more enormous human bodyguards.

The odd-looking entourage walked with chins held high into the building where Christa de Rossi greeted them warmly before she knelt and kissed the hem of the Bauam's dark blue cassock. The man blessed her in Lannish, his words a mixture of Latin and old Elvish as he inscribed the air over her head with a pair of circles.

Christa rose to her feet and the black-robed Sauam – the priest from her own church introduced her to the other robed men. The Hauam, a thin elf of middling height cloaked in forest-green vestments, was the head of the One True Church for the entire planet. The portly human in purple robes was the Thauam, one of only three. He was the head of the entire Flower Galaxy and the only one of his order that traveled with the Bauam.

Christa bowed deeply to the men and turned, extending a slim hand towards Charity and Llewellyn. "Honored gentlemen, let me introduce my daughters." Introductions were given and the two girls bowed to the priests, already having been instructed not to touch them.

"If you gentlemen will follow me?" Llewellyn chimed, as

Thomas opened the door from reception to the hallway. The four priests and four bodyguards followed the girls down the corridor with Christa bringing up the rear.

She led them to the room that Jake and I had spent half of the night setting up. We had taken everything from the conference room, save for the holo screens I had bolted to the walls (thank God she didn't need those) and set everything back up in the largest carpeted room at the center. It was twice the size of the conference room but Charity had me set it up to the original dimensions, so that the conference area was on one side of the room and the other half was completely clear.

"Tell us of this droid," the Hauam asked Llewellyn as they walked along. The dyer shook her blonde hair emphatically.

"He is not a droid," she corrected. "He is human, only manufactured, not born. And specialized for the skill in which you are in need."

The Thauam leaned towards the Bauam, repeating every word in Lannish.

"But if he is manufactured, then he must be a droid," the Hauam argued gently. "This is so. No?"

Llewellyn gave him a brilliant smile as she placed her palm on the pad outside of the double door. "No," she said. The doors swung open and she ushered the men inside, and waited while they took their seats. The bodyguards stationed themselves around the room with equal distance to the Bauam.

"Droids," Charity explained after she had taken her seat, "are linear thinkers, if thinking is even an appropriate term. They are d-class computers attached to limbs. They approach, as I am sure you are familiar with, the defense of a human the same way they would approach assembling an aircar. Methodical. Mechanical."

"So," interjected the Thauam, stroking his jowls, "you are speaking of skin covered robotics but with higher relays?

Predictable...ahh...thinking?"

The Thauam mumbled at the Bauam and the man nodded, following the translated conversation.

Charity and Llewellyn laughed gently in unison, looking at one another.

"Skin covered robotics," Llewellyn repeated.

"Sounds so crude," Charity said, wrinkling her nose in distaste. She turned her face to the priests at the table. "Gentlemen," she said, intending to explain more on the construct when the doors swung open.

The bodyguards stiffened, their massive bodies tense and braced to move.

BG-Syn came through the doors, accompanied by Hope. The youngest de Rossi had shed her usual lab garb for one of Madeline's flowing floral dresses and her copper curls were loose and riotous. But her beauty paled in comparison to the young man standing next to her.

Straight and tall he stood in the stiffly starched blue robes of the cassock he wore. His skin was like pale milk, emphasized by the spattering of freckles across the nose and cheeks of a perfectly sculpted face. Only the azure eyes that blazed within his gentle countenance like blue flames outmatched his shining auburn hair.

Charity forced herself to keep her smile cool and professional, especially when she could hear every man seated draw in a sharp breath.

The Bauam asked a question in Lannish and the Thauam translated. "Is this a follower come to see His Holiness? From some far off planet? He wears a Zealot's robe but not the scar."

Both Charity and Llewellyn fought to keep a straight face as their mother spoke, delighted to contribute. "This is the bodyguard my daughters wish to present to the Bauam," she explained.

"Gentlemen," Llewellyn announced. "I would like you to meet BG-Syn."

There was another collective intake of breath from the men at the table as their suspicions, as unbelievable as they may seem, were confirmed. The beautiful young man that had come into the room was indeed the bodyguard construct they had all come to see.

The priests at the table stared at each other with wide eyes before they all began talking at once to each other. They fell silent quickly as the Hauam turned to Charity.

"This...man," he began, indicating BG-Syn, "is not human?"

Charity gave him a dazzling smile. "Yes, though not what you are used to. He is manufactured."

"A constructed human!" the Sauam exclaimed. "Blasphemy!"

Again the priestly men began their cacophony but the Bauam raised a hand, silencing them. He began to speak and the Thauam translated, looking at Charity. "To attempt to create life, human life, is indeed an act of blasphemy against The One, the True Creator. If, however, this creation is truly a thinking droid as you claim – then no crime against The One has been committed."

The other priests ahhed and cooed and nodded their assent.

Charity wanted to tell them that she had never claimed that he was a droid, and in fact had told them repeatedly that he was not, but she knew that the blessing of The One Church was crucial – as much as it irked the ever-living shit out of her. So she made an effort to be politic.

"BG-Syn, along with very few others, was manufactured to perform duties for humans and elves. Each of his kind was made for specific labors, yet especially pleasing to the eye. But don't let his looks fool you. He is quite deadly, and better than any droid or human you have now."

There were snorts and murmurs from the men at the table. Even the bodyguards exchanged looks of humorous scorn. Save for the Bauam who kept his shrewd gaze fixed upon BG-Syn.

"Tell us again what you are asking in price?" the Hauam inquired.

"Five billion," Charity replied.

This time the men laughed aloud and their protestations were riotous.

"How can you possibly ask so much?" the Sauam asked.

"We don't even know if he is worth anything!" the Thauam exclaimed.

"If he truly can protect the His Excellency, then you should give him freely," the Hauam said earnestly – to which Llewellyn laughed aloud.

"Gentlemen," she chortled, "if you are looking for charity, this is the wrong one!"

"Llewellyn!" Christa exclaimed as Charity bit her own lip in amusement and the men bristled.

"I understand your hesitancy," Charity consoled. "But he truly is one of a kind – nearly priceless. If we may demonstrate?"

The priests tugged down on their robes, collected their dignity, and looked at the Bauam who nodded.

"If I might employ the help of your guards?" Charity asked.

Again, the men seated at the table looked at the Bauam who, again, nodded – first at Charity and then at his guards.

Llewellyn looked up, her blue eyes flicking across the faces of the muscled men who stood strategically around the room. "One million IG credits to the man that can hit the girl," she announced, motioning to where Hope stood.

All eyes in the room looked at Hope, except for the eyes of

the Bauam. Since his eyes were still fixed upon the perfect face of the construct, he was the only one to see the slight line that creased his porcelain brow.

He did not know of this beforehand, the Bauam surmised. *This is news to him, and not welcome news at that. Still, he is otherwise unmoved.* The Bauam saw that his guards were watching him, awaiting instruction or permission. He gave them another nod.

Though the men were large and powerfully built, they were shockingly fast due to artificially jacked reflexes. Still, they converged on the girl slowly, cautiously. Like wolves they surrounded the young woman and the construct and one of them paused to look questioningly at Llewellyn.

"Do we attack one at a time," he asked, "or all at once?"

Llewellyn's lips were tight with amusement. She raised her chin. "I suggest you do it all at once. It's the only chance you have."

Not a second more passed before they all lunged forward, intent upon striking the woman with the wild, copper-colored mane.

Though their speed might have been shocking for their size, the speed of the construct was wickedly faster.

BG-Syn moved with blinding velocity, too fast for the eyes to follow. He was an apparition of light and motion, punctuated by the sounds of breaking bones and snapping limbs. The guards fell one by one, but with a synchronicity that was seamless.

Most stayed where they fell, clutching elbows and knees or curled into fetal positions. The first to go down, however, felt more rage than pain. He spun away with furious speed, snatching one of the chairs against the wall and spinning back intent upon smashing it down over the girl's head or the head of his adversary. His jacked reflexes, however, preserved him by arresting his eminent action as he found a half-meter-long piece of sharpened steel against his throat.

The final guard was not the only man in the room that was holding perfectly still. The blade had been drawn but not used, every guard debilitated without a drop of blood being spilled. They crouched on the carpet, clutching their injuries, but the men at the table were frozen in place.

The air was still save for their panting until the Bauam broke the silence. Charity knew enough of the ancient languages that she did not need a translation.

"Pay them anything they want."

BG-Syn looked at Hope and she answered the question that was blazing behind his blue eyes. "You did fabulous!" she assured him, giving him a hug that made a blush creep his ruddy cheeks. He made his blade disappear into a sleeve before she put a slender arm around his waist and guided him to the table.

Once there, he left her embrace and circled the table to where the Bauam was extending his arms out to him. He let the man take his smooth hands into his own gnarled fingers as he started speaking to him but BG-Syn did not understand. He looked at the man sitting closest.

The Thauam smiled at him. "He says your name is to be John Pierre."

EPILOGUE

Faith looked around the conference table at her sisters, her dyer sisters, and a lonely mason. The girls, of course, were the only ones that sat with her. I leaned against a wall like the proverbial fly – watching and waiting and listening.

It had been five years since the first of the constructs had been sold and they had each returned every year for a physical and diagnostics test. Mira had been in a month ago for an entire week. Though Faith's tests usually only took a few hours and she kept watch for another twenty-four, she always tried to stretch out Mira's time so we could be together. We also got to see each other every Sunday via a com-cam and a flatscreen. It was always the best hour of my week. I'd be lying if I said the five years flew by, but it would also be untrue if I said they were unbearable. I was busy with a job I loved and a woman I loved even more.

The others had been in more recently. BG-Syn, the bodyguard to the Bauam that they now called John Pierre, had left just yesterday. With five yearly check-ups done, the constructs were finally free to leave the orbit of the Riverlen System. Their next set of checks would not be for another five years. After that it would be every ten, then every twenty,

As for the company, we were packing up shop and blowing town. I had been busy as hell. The new compound would make our first one look like a child's dollhouse. I had spent the past years in constant meetings with architects and subcontractors, overseeing the work that had already commenced in another galaxy.

Thomas filled water glasses for everyone at the table except for Charity and Llewellyn, who were already having cocktails though it wasn't even lunchtime. He looked at me with his dark brows raised on his brown face and I shook my head. Thomas and I were not close, but I felt a strange kinship with him, more every year.

I always saw the way he looked at Faith and wondered if he really thought he was disguising the adoration he felt for her. I knew it was the same way that John Pierre's eyes always shone when he looked at Hope. It was a look that proudly claimed that he would step in front of a bullet for her without a second thought. John Pierre, however, could dodge or deflect a bullet with his blades. Thomas, not so much. It still wouldn't stop him, though. I admired him for that.

Thomas left the room and the door closed behind him.

"Well," Faith said, her tawny eyes flashing. "It is obvious that the first run was an incredible success."

The girls looked at each other around the table in a way that I can only describe as companionable smugness.

"Mostly in the fact that Grandfather got his due," Charity quipped. Madeline gave her a languid smile.

"And you didn't siphon off a bit of...his due?" she asked.

Charity looked at Hope's dyer, her blue eyes wide. "Why, Madeline! I had no idea that you were so astute to...to..."

"My surroundings?" Madeline asked. She laughed softly. "Just because I am quiet does not mean I am blind," she remarked good-naturedly. The sound of gentle laughter followed from those that were seated. Madeline left the conversation to stare dreamily at a blank wall panel. Though astute at times, Hope's dyer tuned in and out in a way that reminded me of an old radio my grandmother used to have.

"Be everything as it may," Llewellyn continued with a grin as she shook her white-blonde hair, "it is time for us to move on.

The Six have hit the press and we are the only thing the media is covering round the clock, save for the tour of the Bauam, which also includes us thanks to his infallible bodyguard. The hoi polloi are clamoring at our door. We need to move, and move fast. Start making deals and collecting deposits while the iron of our forge still billows smoke."

All eyes, including my own, went to Faith.

Her tiger-like eyes went to me.

"Are we still on schedule?" she asked me.

"Ayuh," I answered.

"And?"

I modestly dipped my head to hide my smile. "Construction has started and is progressing well. I will be there to oversee the final stages."

The final stages would begin in just over a standard year. The manufacturing compound was being built in the human galaxy of MW-1 and it would take us almost the whole year to get there.

Faith traced her bottom lip with the nail of her left thumb. "Who is your Super?" she asked.

"Jake Merstadt. You might remember him from the work he did here."

She nodded quickly. "I do. How is he doing?"

"Almost as good as me."

"Have you needed to change anything?"

I shrugged. "There's always changes. What is on the plans and what is actually built is never exactly the same. Nothing big enough for me to bother you about so far. Mostly changes to the building materials, window sizes, changes to the wiring."

"As long as all the wires come out where I want them," she advised with a wry smile.

"Of course," I assured her, taking a breath so deep that it seemed to go down to my toes. The location of the new compound would take me back to my home galaxy and I was even thinking about visiting my family. But the best part, was that it was where Mira would be. Devereaux was in constant movement between Earth and Jupiter. It was highly probable that I would be seeing more of her, possibly on a regular basis.

"Outstanding," Faith commended, making me swell even as she glossed over from me to Gwen. "Ironically, if I am using that term correctly, if we want to keep the price high, we need to keep production low – lucky for you."

"But you cannot replicate in their entirety the First Seven," Llewellyn reminded her.

"I know," Gwendolyn said. "Though we were paid handsomely not to reproduce Bjorn," she said, using the given name for B28, "I won't reproduce any of them. They should all remain universally unique for the infinite length of their existence."

"So..." Hope prodded.

Gwen smiled. "I have made molds. Seven of them, since that seems to be our lucky number. Any objections?"

The only response she received was a series of encouraging smiles.

"That will be fine," Faith said. "The final number to be cast from the molds will be determined by Charity and Llewellyn. Be it a single cast or a hundred."

"I think ten runs for a total of seventy would be good," Llewellyn said. "We can keep price high and production low with a control like that," she explained.

Charity put down her cocktail, the rings on her right hand clinking against the glass. "And it will give Gwen time to make the mass molds – the ones that will follow. The ones to fill the needs of the general populace."

All the girls around the table nodded solemnly as if having adhered to that fate long ago. A silence fell over the room and I'm not sure why. Maybe the enormity of what lay before them, or the exhaustion of what lay behind them.

"Well!" Hope announced with false cheer, driving a crack of apprehension into the previously positive mood. "I can only hope that *we* are still of some use," she chirped.

All eyes looked back to Faith, whose eyes did not waver as they looked at her youngest sister.

"Your talents are needed as well," Faith said, "if you are willing."

Hope's smile converged into a leer. "You need a spy again," she said.

Faith shook her head. "Not a spy really, more of a liaison. But I would like the opinion of someone who has worked in the field. And I trust you."

"What is it?" Hope asked. She made no attempt to disguise her disgust. Faith, in turn, made no attempt to show hesitation. The past five years had not been kind to their relationship.

"Grandfather is intent as ever upon pursuing the Zero Point Energy field. If we can bring in the ones who are first to harness such power, he has agreed to finance the new compound as compensation. Everything we make monetarily from here on out would be profit."

Charity and Llewellyn's blue eyes glittered as they looked at Hope.

"And?" Hope prodded.

"We have discovered the ones who have not just harnessed the ZPE, but are using it productively. They are already on their way to convene with us but we need to meet with them as soon as possible."

"Before someone else does?" Hope asked in a dry tone.

Faith nodded. "I should be the one to go..."

"So what is stopping you?"

"I am," Faith told her, losing her patience. "I can only be in so many places at once. Someone needs to meet with these men in person. But I have to oversee the finishing of the plant as well as generating the second run."

Hope gave her a cold stare and then nodded. "Fine. I'll do it."

"We'll do it," Madeline amended.

Hope glanced at her dyer and smiled. "We'll do it, " she agreed. "Where are they?"

Faith's lips disappeared for a second into a white line before she spoke a single word. "Andromeda."

Hope shrugged as if it made no difference. "Fine."

"It will take at least two years to get there," Faith said, her voice so low that it seemed she was baiting Hope to change her mind. "Possibly five."

Hope nodded, realizing where her sister was headed. "So I won't be around for BG...John Pierre's next check."

Faith nodded.

"Then maybe you *should* be the one to go," Hope agreed.

"I could run the checks on BG-Syn," Faith suggested.

"And you could meet with whoever these people are!"

Though Faith was outwardly calm, I could sense that she was boiling like a pressure cooker. I wasn't the only one. Gwen laid a hand over the wrist of her twin and looked at their youngest sister.

"Why is it so important that you be the one to run his tests?" she asked Hope. "It would seem a simple thing for Faith to do."

"First, because I promised John Pierre that I would. Also,

since I had so much involvement with his programming, I should be the one to run his checks. Frankly, I don't think Faith would know what to adjust in his DNA, should it be necessary."

Gwen looked back at Faith, unsure of how she would respond or how to proceed, but her twin was nodding as her mind raced along.

"If that is your concern, there might be a better solution," Faith said. "The Bauam is traveling to the same system, though he will be making many stops along the way. Still, what if you were to meet up with him for the checks on BG-Syn?" she asked Hope, forgoing the construct's new name.

"It would please The One Clergy, that's for certain," Charity said. "They were upset about returning for the checks because of how it would change their travel plans."

Hope was silent for a few seconds as she considered. "That truly may be better." As exhausted as she felt, Hope was eager to be gone from everything and everyone for a while. The sooner she could put distance between herself and Faith, the better. "Can we get passage on a cryo-ship?"

That brought a look of surprise to every face at the table.

"Cryo?" Charity asked.

"What in the world..." Gwen started, her hand coming up to cover her mouth.

"Why?" Llewellyn asked.

"I could use a nap," Hope told them. *A long, dreamless nap.* Her dreams of late had been haunting and frantic. She had recently looked back over the entries in her Dream Journal and thought that they looked like the ravings of a woman on the verge of lunacy.

"That would certainly make the trip five years, at least," Faith advised. "Possibly ten. Cryo ships are never in a hurry."

Hope shrugged her narrow shoulders to show that it made

no difference to her.

"I can arrange it," Faith told her. "And I can arrange the rendezvous, though it might be early. You might have to do a five and five, or a four and six, depending on the time it takes for your trip and the closest coordinates of the Bauam."

"That will be fine," Hope agreed with a sigh.

"Afterwards," Faith continued, "you can decide if you want to return to cryo or stay awake for the return trip. It will be longer, since you will be joining us in MW-1, rather than here. Optimistically, with the monks."

"Monks?" Madeline asked.

Faith nodded. "The men who have harnessed the field are monks," she informed them. "Zenarchists."

"They're not scientists?" Hope asked, leaning forward over the table, her green eyes wide with astonishment.

"It appears that they are not," Faith said, leaning back in her chair and looking amused for the first time since the meeting started. "At least, not in the conventional way you and I are."

"Well," Hope mused, sitting back in her chair. "This is something I just have to see."

*

It took three weeks for us to pack. Well, it took me three days, including all of my tools at the compound. The rest of the time I spent helping Faith (helping Thomas actually) pack up lab equipment, computers, and machines that did only God knows what.

It was the day before we were supposed to leave. We were scheduled to depart on a very nice ship, much nicer than the one I had come in, to begin overseeing the completion of the first GwenSeven manufacturing plant. I would be returning to my home galaxy. The good old Milky Way.

"Don't they have enough money," I complained to Thomas, "to hire a company to do this?"

I was sweating heavily, tilting back a machine that weighed a figurative ton if not a literal one, waiting for Thomas to toss a bubble-spec underneath. It was the tenth such machine I had been needed to move.

"Not more than forty-five degrees," Thomas reminded me for the tenth time as he squatted down in his gray suit and flicked the lighted packet underneath. "Go ahead and lower," he said, stretching out his long, brown fingers and grasping the metal edges to steady the thing as I lowered it as gently as I could. "And no, they don't have the money," he reproached, though not unkindly. "Dr. de Rossi's grandfather was given all the monies from the sales. We are fortunate that he is covering all of the costs for our travel."

"Right," I said as we held the machine as stable as possible while the spec spread out under its metal bulk. We watched the plastic ooze out from the bottom and wrap around the metal sides, stretching for the apex.

Cronus had gotten all the profits, as agreed by Faith before they had even begun. I had borne witness to that deal.

Thomas and I both pulled our hands away before the melting plastic could touch us and we watched as it reached the top. Once the entire machine was engulfed, the plastic expanded outwards, filling layer after layer with air.

When it was done I sighed and looked round. There was only one thing left in the lab – Faith's enormous desk.

"Can't we leave it?" I asked.

Thomas smiled at me from behind a brand new pair of black, round-framed spectacles. Supposedly, they had a chip that – by glancing up and to his left - let him access everything that he normally could from his own compute screen. I had already teased him that with those, and the earpiece that he had implanted, he was halfway to becoming a droid.

"I'm surprised at you, Fletcher," he said in his odd yet beguiling accent. "You are the last one to shirk hard work around here."

"I'm just tired," I lied. In truth, I was more than anxious to be off. Devereaux, and Mira with him, had left seven weeks ago, almost immediately after the constructs had been given their five-year leave. Each day put more distance between us. I would never say this to Thomas, though, who could never breach the distance between himself and the woman he revered. "Besides, that old thing..."

I was interrupted by the same piece of furniture flashing red as a klaxon horn deafened us as if to violently refute my testimony. Our eyes looked up and met. It was the emergency line for the First Seven.

Thomas pushed on the side of his ear, apparently trying to control whatever emotion was threatening. "Dr. de Rossi?" he asked as calmly as he could.

"I'm right here!" Faith announced as she pushed open the door to her lab and half-ran for her desk. She touched a button on the edge of the frame. The light disappeared and the horn went blissfully silent. "Hello?"

My stomach sank as I heard Mira's voice. "Hello. Faith? Is that you?"

"Yes, Mira. What is it?"

"Are...are you alone?"

"No. Thomas and Fletcher are here with me."

In the pause that followed I knew that not only was she surprised at my presence, but that she did not want me to be there.

"Mira, honey?" I asked. "What is it?"

The next pause that followed seemed to last minutes to me,

though I'm sure it was only a second or two.

"I'm sick."

"You're *what*?" Faith asked, incredulous. The constructs had been made not to get sick. There wasn't a known pathogen that they were not immune to, as far as Faith knew.

"I'm sick," Mira repeated. "I just vomited."

"Honey, I'm so sorry," I said, commiserating. "Do you know what it could be from? Travel? Something you ate?"

"No," Faith answered for her. "She is immune to such things." Faith glanced about, obviously looking for something on her desk, but everything was packed away. "Mira?" she asked, "are you having any other symptoms? Anything else out of the ordinary?"

Again the short pause that drew out for an eternity.

"Yes, in fact, I thought it might be the food – like Fletcher said. Lunch smelled, I don't know, off? And dinner was worse. But I was with Mr. Devereaux so I made myself eat as much as I could."

"Anything else?"

"I'm dead tired. Fatigued, I guess – though my workload is the same as it has been for years. I never get tired."

"She gets tired!" I whispered before I could help myself. Mira heard me.

"Fletcher!" she scolded. "It's certainly not from that!"

Faith flashed me a look of dangerous exasperation and I shrank back. "Mira?" she asked again. "Is Devereaux there?"

"Yes. He is in his office, on the other side of the ship." Devereaux lived aboard his ship, something that resembled a space-faring mansion. "I'm in my personal quarters."

Faith looked up and locked eyes with Thomas. He gave her a curt nod, letting her know that he was ready for anything.

"Call Mr. Devereaux," she instructed him. "I need to speak with him immediately. On a vid-line."

"Yes, ma'am." He turned away from us and touched the button on his ear, giving it commands.

Rather than asking Mira where they were, Faith typed something onto the sole remaining ghostpad on the surface of her desk. A hologram popped up over its metal surface, showing our planetary moon, and the next one closest. A red blip hovered in the air between them.

"You're not far," Faith said. "It looks like you have another twelve to fifteen hours before you can make your first jump. I'm..."

Thomas spun around at that moment. "Dr. de Rossi? I have Mr. Devereaux on the line for you."

"Thank you, Thomas."

She touched another light on her desk and the holographic map was exchanged for an image of a room that resembled something between a library and a store for leather goods and hides and horns of wild animals. Mr. Devereaux sat front and center behind a great desk of stained walnut topped with glass.

"Mr. Devereaux?" Faith opened. "Thank you for taking my call."

"Of course, Dr. de Rossi. What can I do for you?"

"I'm afraid I'm going to need Mira to come in."

I was in a position where I was out of sight from Devereaux. But I could see Faith's hand, fisted so tight that her knuckles were white, as well as the crease that formed between Devereaux's brows.

"But she was just there two months ago! I was told that she would not need another appointment for five years," he said firmly. "I was planning on taking an extended trip."

"My apologies, Mr. Devereaux. I was called away unexpectedly during her testing and I am just now looking over her results."

"Is something wrong?"

"I'm not sure. That is why I would like to have her back for more tests, I'm afraid it could take some time."

Devereaux looked away as he considered, the thumb of his left hand pushing at the cuticles of his fingers. I glanced up as I heard a strange echoeyness from the line Mira was on and realized she must have started for Devereaux's office and, by the sound of it, was almost there. Then she closed the line.

Devereaux gave his head a quick shake. "I cannot change my trip, nor can I spare Mira. Both are too important."

Faith's thoughts were so quick I could have sworn I caught a whiff of ozone in the air. "Can she work remotely?" she asked.

That seemed to catch him off guard. "She will be able to work while these tests are being run?" he asked.

"Absolutely. I can see that she is supplied with everything you require, and when we are done I will have her transported to any location you desire."

Devereaux cocked an eyebrow. "I was headed all the way back home."

"That will not be a problem," Faith assured him.

This time both his eyebrows went up and he nodded appreciatively. He leaned back in his chair, making the leather creak, and steepled his fingers as he thought.

"I am about to embark on a year-long pleasure cruise with a gentleman friend, finishing with a tour of the Satellites of Saturn. Mira would have been running things on her own anyway, my calendars, calls, appointments and the like. I suppose it is no consequence whether that be from here or there." He turned his face towards what I assumed was his office door. "Mira?" he called.

The door opened and Mira strode in, her acrylic in hand, and I knew why Faith had requested a vid-line. She was hoping to catch a glimpse of Mira. My lady wore a sharp-looking suit with a pencil skirt in the same dove-gray that Devereaux wore, her long dark curls standing out in beautiful contrast. Though her expression said she was ready for anything, I could read through it.

Her face was pale and drawn. The top of her forehead had a barely perceptible sheen, showing that it was dewed by a fine sweat. I looked at Faith and saw that she was seeing the same.

"Mira," Devereaux intoned, "if I sent you back to Esodire, would you be able to work from there?"

"Of course, Mr. Devereaux."

"Can you see to it that she is given personal quarters?" Devereaux asked, looking at Faith. "Where she can work and live comfortably?"

"Certainly," Faith agreed.

A few more seconds of eternity ticked by.

"Very well," Devereaux finally acquiesced. "I can't make an actual stop, but I can put her aboard a shuttle at the Esodire Satellite when I pass by – should be ten hours from now, maybe a little longer."

"That will be more than sufficient. Thank you for your understanding. I will be in touch with you to arrange for her return."

Devereaux clicked off without saying goodbye. I knew Faith hated being dismissed in such a manner but she was too preoccupied with Mira to care. She looked around to where Thomas and I waited in the wings, but it was half a minute before she spoke. I could see her eyes glaze as she calculated and thought, trying to decide on something. The suspense was excruciating but I held my tongue.

"We can't wait," she finally announced. "And I certainly don't want to unpack," she said, glancing around. She fixed her eyes on Thomas. "Wrap it up here, get help if you need it, and contact the ship and tell the captain I want to leave tonight. We can pick up Mira at the Esodire Satellite."

"Yes, ma'am." Thomas turned on his heel and was out the door, already talking on his implanted com-chip.

A panic rose up, threatening to engulf me.

"What it is?" I asked. "Do you know what it is?" My throat felt like it was coated with wool. "Is she alright? Is she going to be okay?"

Faith looked at me, her lips pressed together in either amusement or disgust, I couldn't tell. Then I realized it was neither. It was a look of accusation.

"She'll be fine," Faith assured me. "Eventually."

"Eventually?" My heart rate skyrocketed. I suddenly felt as ill as Mira had looked. "What's wrong?"

"Though I considered it highly improbable, it is entirely possible. The only possibility that I can think of, but of course I will have to run some tests. Well, just one test to start with really."

I could have choked her at that point. I certainly wanted to.

"Dammit, Faith! What's wrong with Mira?"

She looked at me with that same accusatory expression of amusement and disgust. "Nothing is wrong with her, but a congratulations might be in order. Fletcher, I think you are going to be a father."

AUTHOR'S NOTE

Well, crap. Is it possible that I bit off more than I could chew with this book? Possibly. Did I realize how much I had to cover in a prequel? Not really. Do I overextend myself in just about everything? Most likely. It's okay. I've learned to be gentle with myself, even if some of my readers are not. I'll tell you one thing, though – I learned a lot this past year.

First, I learned that so much happens in just one year of a person's life, not to mention five. Think of yourself and what you have done in five years. If you need help remembering, look back on your social media, credit card receipts, or browser history. If those don't help, just take a look into your recycling bin for the past week. That might bring a quick and total recall. Now multiply that mere half a decade by thirty. Now take those one hundred and fifty years (you should be so lucky) and think of what has gone on in the lives of ten of your friends (or people you know) over that span. Yeah, it's a lot.

The next thing I learned was that some years are busier than others. That may seem like a no-brainer but let me give you a small glimpse at my writing schedule. I try to finish the rough draft of a book in six months (February to August). That gives me six months to rewrite and edit while my friends read it and pooh pooh about whatever. Everyone's a critic. This time August rolled around and I was still a long ways away. Then September. Then December. The next thing I knew it was February, when I usually have a completed project, and I knew I wasn't even halfway through the *draft*. Panic is the normal reaction for most, myself included.

Before I go on, I'm going to digress on what took up such a large amount of my time. One, was homeschooling my sixteen-year-old daughter. If you are one of those people with a motivated teenager then you were probably Gandhi in your last life. I must have been Attila the Hun. It was like pulling a donkey up a ladder; a donkey that also likes to bite. Still, I don't regret it. The donkey and I had a lot of laughs. The second thing that took my time, and I don't regret, was spending time with my grandmother. She took care of me when I was little, and when she fell ill in 2015 at the age of eighty-nine, I took care of her. We had a lot of laughs, too. So, come February, I was sitting in my chair next to her hospital bed with my computer on my lap and wondering. Wondering where the time went. Wondering what to get her for lunch. Wondering how I was going to wrap up the story. I knew how I wanted it to end. I just had too much to tell before I got there. Then I looked at my grandma who was peering into a little mirror, fixing the make-up I had helped her put on so she could flirt with the EMTs when they came by. Then I had the crushing realization that *we don't get to choose when the story ends,* our own or anyone else's. There may be a lot more we want to say, but most often our tales are ended before we can do so. I looked at the last chapter I had written and knew that the story, for now, was done. I spent the next few weeks doing a hasty rewrite, helping my mother with funeral arrangements, doing edits, and saying goodbye.

James Cameron said that in science fiction people never really die and I think the same is true in real life. People who impact us are with us forever. Maybe they don't simply pop up in the next novel, but who knows? Maybe they do.

Now, back to *our* story. Yes, there is still a lot to tell. So much happens that shape the characters and the story before we even get to what happens next in the saga of our Jordans, the Chimera, and the IGC. But first there is another tale that must be told. Hate me if you must, but I gotta keep it real.

Real. Real was where we started.

Does anyone remember what that means?

CPSIA information can be obtained at www.ICGtesting.com
Printed in the USA
BVOW01s2134290916

463762BV00012B/96/P